HOPE

The Daughters of Allamont Hall
Book 6

A Regency Romance

by Mary Kingswood

D1089537

Hope: The Daughters of Allamont Hall Book 6

Published by Sutors Publishing

ISBN: 978-1-912167-17-3 (revised paperback)

Cover design by: Shayne Rutherford of Darkmoon Graphics

A traditional Regency romance, drawing room rather than bedroom.

Hope has no wish to marry, but it's almost five years since her father died, and the final peculiar clause of his will is about to come into effect: if Hope's brothers can't be found, then the whole estate will be bequeathed to the church, and Hope must move to the Dower House with her mother. There's just one way out: her cousin Hugo can inherit Allamont Hall, but only if he marries Hope. Can she bear to give up the chance of finding a man who loves her, even if it means saving her home?

Hugo was a wild, troubled young man until his father suggested he help out his fatherless cousins and look after the finances at Allamont Hall. He discovered an unexpected passion for the house and the land, and there's a chance he can own it all, if he can just persuade his cousin Hope to marry him. And even if he manages that, there's still the risk that her long-lost brothers will turn up and snatch everything away from him.

About *The Daughters of Allamont Hall*: a series of six traditional Regency romances, featuring the unmarried daughters of Mr William and Lady Sara Allamont. When their father dies unexpectedly, his will includes generous dowries for the sisters, but only on condition that they marry in the proper order, the eldest first.

Book 1: Amy
Book 2: Belle
Book 3: Connie
Book 4: Dulcie
Book 4.5: Mary (a novella, free for mailing list signups)
Book 5: Grace
Book 6: Hope

Table of contents

1: A Marriage Of Convenience

Hope Allamont watched dejectedly as the agents made their farewells to her mother. They were very respectful, almost obsequious to Lady Sara, bowing as low as they could without falling over, every sentence milady this and your ladyship that. Nevertheless, the task they were charged with could not but be deeply unpleasant to everyone. To have people crawling all over Allamont Hall, measuring, inspecting, looking under carpets and behind paintings, and silently assessing the value of the property was unspeakable.

The pleasure in their eyes as they moved from room to room was clear to see. Allamont House was a splendid property, built in the grand style common in the last century, with well-proportioned formal rooms and all the facilities required for living in the country. It was perhaps a little old-fashioned now, but nothing that some slight refurbishment could not ameliorate, and with fine pleasure grounds and woodlands. Yes, no doubt the agents could not believe their good fortune in having such an admirable property fall into their laps like a ripe plum.

As soon as they had left, Lady Sara whisked upstairs to her sitting room. She was presently in one of her cold, withdrawn moods, and who could blame her? She must be as downhearted as Hope this summer. In just three months from now, they would be thrown out of their home, and mother and daughter would be obliged to move to the Dower House, and what comfort would be theirs then?

Hope saw her cousin Hugo watching her, his face as dark with gloom as hers must be.

"Come," he said, with a flick of his head. "Have a glass of ratafia, or something stronger, if you prefer. Nothing else to do but drink and be sorrowful together."

She followed him into the book room, once a cheerless place devoid of ornament or picture, where she and her sisters had recited their lessons or read from the Scriptures or translated a passage of Greek under her father's hawk-like eyes, trembling with fear of his disapprobation. He was long gone to his grave, and since Hugo had taken over the management of the Hall, the book room had become a warm, friendly place, books and papers and rolled-up maps scattered on every surface, and his three dogs lolling in front of the fire. Hugo was no more than a distant cousin, but he and his family were their only relatives who lived nearby.

"I still do not understand why they need to measure everything so soon," she said for perhaps the fiftieth time. "Why could they not wait until October? For the church cannot have the Hall before then, can they? They must wait the full five years for the terms of Papa's will to take effect, surely?"

"They cannot have possession, that is true," he said, pouring ratafia for her and Madeira for himself. "They have to wait until the very last day, because there is always a small possibility that one or other of your brothers will turn up to claim his inheritance. But October is a difficult time of year. Houses are much easier to sell in the summer, when people may travel more easily to inspect a property. The bishop wants to set a day for prospective buyers to look around before the weather turns bad, and to do that the occasion must be advertised widely, and to do *that* they must know the exact numbers of rooms of each type, and their proportions, and the size of the linen cupboard and so forth. And then there is the value of the estate. Someone is to come next week to inspect the accounts, to determine the exact income from the tenants and holdings."

"You can tell them that to the penny."

He smiled then. At twenty-two, the same age as Hope herself, he was an odd looking man, far too thin, dark of hair and eye. She supposed he was handsome enough, in a melancholy, brooding sort of way, but his strange little lopsided smile gave his face a quirky charm.

"They will not take my word for it," he said, with a lift of one shoulder.

"But you are so good with the accounts."

"Oh, but I have always loved numbers. It was the only subject where I excelled at school, so working through the accounts is the greatest pleasure to me. To the bishop's agents, however, I am not to be trusted, since I have a personal interest."

"I suppose that is understandable." Her voice trembled slightly, her tears not far away. "Oh Hugo, this is so horrid! I do so wish we could stay in the Hall."

She could have bitten her tongue for her foolishness, for his face lit up eagerly.

"You do not have to leave it, Hope, you *know* that. Marry me, and we can keep the Hall. You would not even have to change your name. Should you not like to be Mrs Hugo Allamont, the mistress of Allamont Hall? For I tell you honestly, I should very much like to be Mr Hugo Allamont, the master of Allamont Hall."

How many times had he made the same speech, or some variation of it? And all because of a casual line in her father's will — if the long-lost sons could not be found, then any of the three cousins could inherit if they married one of the daughters. Hope was the last of the daughters now, for all her sisters were married. And Hugo was the last of the cousins, since James was married and Mark had gone off to Scotland to become a teacher.

"I should not mind being mistress of Allamont Hall," she said, as she had told him so many times. "I already am, in many ways, for Mama takes no interest in the household. And you have already taken the role of master here, and we are most grateful to you for that. But I am not sure whether I want to marry anyone at all. Although," she added punctiliously, "it is most obliging in you to offer, Hugo, and if I were minded to marry at all, you would be my first choice."

He raised an eyebrow. "So it is not my person in particular that repels you but the very notion of marriage? Your sisters are all happily wedded."

"Oh yes, and no one could be more delighted for them than I. But they were lucky — they each met a man who adored them and looked at them with fire blazing in his eyes. I was so fortunate as to experience that once, long ago, and I cannot settle for less, Hugo. I cannot marry a man who does not look at me in that way. And then — there is your mama," she added in a low voice. "I do *not* want to die because of a baby growing wrong."

"I can understand that," he said seriously. "Poor Mama! How she suffered at the end, when even the laudanum began to fail her. And many women die during the birthing of a baby. It is a terrible, dangerous business."

"Oh yes! I have not forgot poor Mrs Wills! Such a tragedy, and Mr Wills so grief-stricken."

They were both silent for a while, Hope sipping her ratafia and nibbling a bonbon, and Hugo rubbing the ears of one of his dogs.

"You know, Hope," he said suddenly, leaning forward in excitement, "there is a way around this. We could marry but not... erm, not be husband and wife, if you see what I mean."

"How could we be married but *not* be husband and wife... oh!" She blushed crimson. "You mean, no bedroom... erm, *happenings*."

"Exactly! A marriage of convenience. So long as we marry before mid-October, and there is no sign of Ernest and Frank, we would inherit the Hall. What do you say?"

"But then there would *never* be a man who would look at me with fire in his eyes," she said, her voice quivering.

He sat back in his chair, defeated. "Will you at least think about it?"

"I cannot see that my feelings will be any different tomorrow or next week or next month."

He sprang to his feet, to the alarm of the dogs, and paced restlessly back and forth. "Then our only hope is to find Ernest and Frank. We still have time, and there must be a way. I cannot believe they are dead!"

She looked up at him warily, knowing his fidgety moods of old. "Aunt Lucy from Liverpool is trying to find them. That is where they were last seen, so surely that is the best place to search."

He spun round, his face alive with enthusiasm. "You are absolutely right! Liverpool! But she is merely asking here and there. We need to broadcast our situation more widely. An advertisement, that is what we must put out. There must be newspapers in Liverpool."

"When Papa died, Mr Plumphett posted notices in all the newspapers, I believe," she said.

"Oh, Plumphett! He is such a pompous old fool. I am sure he is a good enough sort of solicitor for common matters, but he drew up this will of your father's in the first place. I hold him entirely responsible for the extraordinary nature of parts of it."

"I daresay he only wrote what Papa told him to," Hope said. "No one could change Papa's mind when he was set on a certain path."

Hugo laughed then, and stepped over the dog to take his seat again. "Of course you are right. Perhaps I should talk to Plumphett before I do anything, to understand what was attempted to discover Ernest and Frank. Still, another try at advertising can do no harm."

~~~~~

"Hope, I should like you to come down to the Dower House with me tomorrow," her mama said one evening as they drank their tea after dinner. "The refurbishment is almost complete now, so it will be the perfect opportunity for you to choose your bedroom."

"Must I? The very thought of moving there is so lowering. The weather is so fine, I had hoped to begin my sketch of the northern aspect."

Hope hated these evenings when the two of them were alone. They seldom entertained, but often Hugo stayed for a night or two when he was busy on estate business, and then he would play cribbage with her, or sing while she played the pianoforte. Occasionally he read poetry to her, for he had a fine voice for such recitations. But when he was not there, and she and her mother were alone together, Hope had the darkest vision of their lonely future in the Dower House.

Lady Sara set down her cup. "You are very sentimental about this house, Hope. All the drawing of this and that angle is well and good in its own way, and a perfectly acceptable accomplishment for a young lady to pursue, but it does not do to become too attached to any place. Few people are so fortunate as to reside in one house from cradle to death bed.

October will see us settled in the Dower House, whether you will or no, and it is as well that you become accustomed to the idea."

"Indeed, I am accustomed, Mama, but I need not like the change. Having lived all my life in the Hall, every room, every chair, every picture has memories for me."

"They cannot all be good memories, surely? Your father was a harsh and intolerant man, with few redeeming qualities."

"Mama!"

Her mother sighed. "There is little point in pretence. He was an evil man in many ways, and we all suffered at his hands. I was glad when he died, I will not lie about it, and Allamont Hall has few happy memories for me. Perhaps you were luckier, although I cannot say. Your father had the raising of you and your sisters, and I knew little of what went on in the nursery. He refused to let me see you, did you know that? Each one of you was lifted from my arms when you were but three days old, and taken away from me. I was permitted an hour with you on Sundays, that was all, until you were old enough to eat family dinners with us." She picked up her cup again. "But this will not do. Your melancholia is afflicting me also, Hope. Ugh, this tea is cold."

"May I fetch you another cup, Mama?"

"Thank you, Hope. You are a kind girl, even if I deplore your sentimentality."

"To regret leaving one's home of many years is surely something more than sentimentality, Mama. I shall not complain when we are in the Dower House, but I cannot but feel the loss keenly."

"I wonder you do not marry Hugo, then, if you feel so strongly about it," her mother said.

Hope shuddered. "That would be to give up all possibility of a marriage for love."

"Sometimes I despair of you, and your sisters were just the same. Love — that is all you young people think about these days. You read too many novels, I think. That circulating library in Brinchester has a great deal to answer for, and your sisters *will* keep sending you silly books and filling your head with romantic notions. Love does not answer, Hope. It never has. Such a flimsy, insubstantial emotion, liable to blow away at the first puff of wind. Men are wicked creatures, every one of them, and not worth giving one's heart to. Take their money and position in society, if you must, but do not look for happiness in marriage."

Hope was too depressed to answer.

~~~~~

The Dower House was a pretty enough little place, Hope had to concede. Built at the same time as the main house, which it greatly resembled in style, the outer appearance was reassuringly familiar, even if it felt tiny by comparison. Outside, piles of detritus from the renovations still littered the drive and buried overgrown bushes where once were flowerbeds. Inside, the bare wooden floors echoed hollowly in every empty room, and the air smelt overpoweringly of freshly cut wood and distemper.

"This is the dining room," Lady Sara said. "The ceiling still needs work, but the size is adequate. We shall be able to seat fourteen, or sixteen at a pinch. And this will be the drawing room. The aspect is not what one would wish, but we must make do. And through here is the morning room."

"It is very dark," Hope said.

"It is. I fear that massive tree on the lawn will have to go. It must have been pretty enough once, but now it is too monstrous for words. Now, upstairs we have four bedrooms.

This one is mine, but you may choose any of the others that you wish. Then the other two will be for a guest and your companion."

"Companion?" Hope said in a faint voice.

"Of course. You will need a companion for those times when I am away."

"Might I not stay with one or other of my sisters, or with Cousin Mary?"

"You cannot constantly be packed up and dispatched to this house or that like a piece of luggage! Far better to stay quietly at home. I will advertise for a companion for you, or perhaps I might ask Miss Endercott to recommend someone. She knows everything that goes on in the neighbourhood, and will be sure to know just the person. Such a pity Miss Bellows left. I must say, it was most inconsiderate of her to go off and marry like that. At her age too! What can be more ridiculous than a middle-aged bride?"

"It was an excellent match, Mama, and she could not keep Mr Graham waiting indefinitely, just so that she might chaperon me about when you are not here. But perhaps if you were from home less, or... or if you were to take me with you..."

Her mother turned her gaze full on her daughter, her still-beautiful face alight with merriment. "I do not think *that* would answer! If you find your situation difficult, Hope, you have brought it upon yourself by refusing some very eligible offers for your hand. Your father gave you an excellent dowry, your accomplishments are adequate, you dance well and you have enough beauty to appear to advantage in company. You would be nothing special in London, but here you may have had your pick of young men any time these last three or four years. Yet here you are, two and twenty and still unwed. If you dislike the prospect of living in the Dower House, then the solution is in your own hands. You may marry tomorrow if you please. I could

14

name half a dozen young men who would be delighted to win you."

"To win my dowry, you mean," she said. "That is all that interests them. They court me with glib words and promises, but they care nothing for *me*."

Her mother shrugged. "I am tired of this fruitless discussion. You may return to the house while I talk to the builder."

Hope needed no further prompting. She could barely wait to be outside again, out in the clean air, untainted by paint or plaster or the sound of hammering. As she walked up the drive, she came upon Hugo, supervising one of the gardeners who was pulling weeds out of the gravel. He stood up at once, and, waving the man to continue, fell into step beside her.

"Hope? Are you all right?"

"Could anyone be all right who is expected to leave all this behind?" She waved an arm to encompass the western face of Allamont Hall, mellow in the summer sunshine. "The Dower House is so tiny, Hugo! I shall suffocate there! And Mama is not planning to stay at home any more than she does now, so I must have a companion, she says. A stranger to spend my days with — what could be more dreadful."

"Well, if you have to spend your life with a stranger, you would do better to marry one, for then you would at least have your own establishment."

Hope was much struck by this thought. "That is true! A husband, even if one knows him well, is still a stranger in many ways. I recall Connie saying something of the sort — how Lord Carrbridge liked things to be done in a certain way, and she felt quite lost at times, just at first."

"I daresay marquesses are trickier to deal with than plain old misters," Hugo said. "But I am no stranger — you could marry me and know exactly what you are in for."

"I am not so sure," she said seriously. "I know that you enjoy kippers for breakfast, and prefer claret to Madeira, and that you like your dogs and your horse better than most people, but I do not think one can ever know what sort of husband a man will be until it is too late."

He stopped then, turning towards her, his face eager. "But if one has known him for years and years, has seen him grow from boy to man, and at his worst as well as his best — surely that is enough of a guide? You could say then with a great deal of confidence that this man would be a good husband. You cannot deny it, Hope. You *know* I would make you a good husband, none better."

She was taken aback by his intensity, and tried to laugh it off. "Well, you do not beat your dogs, so that is a promising sign that you would not beat me."

He grabbed her arm, and would have said more, but abruptly he released her and spun away. "Ah, Hope, if you only knew how alike we are! We both despair to leave Allamont Hall. Yet you will not take the obvious step."

"Do not tease me about it, Hugo. We have time still, and something may yet happen to change our situation."

They walked on in uncomfortable silence, Hugo with his head lowered. She could not tell whether he was offended, but she had no wish to cause another outburst so she made no attempt to find out.

In the entrance hall, the butler, housekeeper and footman were huddled together, whispering. They sprang apart as Hope and Hugo walked in.

"Miss Allamont! Mr Allamont!" the butler began, then stopped, flustered. In his hands, he held a newspaper.

This was so unlike him that Hope said, "Whatever is wrong, Young?"

"It is the newspaper, Miss. There is a notice…"

He folded the newspaper and placed it on a silver salver, presenting it to Hope with a bow. Hugo snatched it and vanished into the drawing room.

"Really, Hugo!" she cried, following him. Then she saw his face. "What is it? Tell me the worst! Has something terrible occurred?"

"It is the church's notice about Allamont Hall. There is to be an auction in October, and day for viewing is set for next month. We will have people trampling all over the house, and poking about in the bedrooms, and disrupting the kitchens."

"Oh no!" She took the newspaper from him, but her tears fell so fast that the words blurred together. "Oh Hugo, what are we to do?"

He wrapped his arms around her and rocked her gently. "If you hate this as much as I do, then marry me, Hope. Marry me and we can put a stop to this once and for all."

Her head shot up. "Yes!" she said fiercely. "I cannot bear it, so yes, I will marry you, Hugo."

2: Meetings In Brinchester

Hugo was so exultant that a great shriek burst from him, and then he started laughing. "Oh, Hope, what a tease you are, to keep me in suspense for so long! But this will be so good, you will see. At last I will be able to extend the stables, and repair the glass houses, and put a more modern range in the kitchen. I shall be master here, in my rightful place at last. I cannot wait! When shall we be married? Let it be soon!"

Hope laughed, too, as much from surprise as anything else. How had she found herself in this position? After all her careful reasoning of why it would never do, she had agreed to it on a childish impulse. And yet, it felt right. One, at least, of the daughters of Allamont Hall would stay on, and the name would live on… Here her heart misgave her, for had they not agreed that the marriage would not be a real one? So there would never be another generation of Allamonts living in the Hall, and that was a terribly sad thought.

It brought her down to earth, however. "We must talk to Mr Plumphett about the exact terms of the will," she said crisply. "There is no point in us marrying immediately if there is still time for Ernest or Frank to be found."

He deflated at once. "True. I have posted advertisements everywhere I can think of to try to uncover their whereabouts, so it is still possible we may be beaten at the final furlong. What a pity we did not settle things between us sooner! However, it cannot be helped now. As to the date, I daresay all we need to do is to be married before five years have elapsed since your father's death, but it would be as well to ensure we have the details exactly right. Imagine what a disaster it would be if we went to all the bother of getting married and then found we had misjudged it by a day and the church got everything after all! We would be stuck with each other, with only your dowry to live on."

"Twenty thousand pounds is a substantial sum."

"It is, but it would only give us a few hundred a year to live on, and I have nothing at all, whereas the Allamont estate is worth two thousand eight hundred."

"Is it? Papa's income was above three thousand, I have been told."

"So it was, but he had the interest from Lady Sara's portion. She retains that for her lifetime. Two thousand eight hundred, although that could be greatly increased by some improvements to the land which I have in mind." His mind flew at once to the next problem. "I suppose I had better present myself to your mama as her future son-in-law. Not that this will come as any surprise to her, and she has never expressed any dislike for the idea, but it is as well to obtain her blessing. We must do everything in the proper form, as is fitting for the Allamonts of Allamont Hall. I shall go at once."

So saying, he swept out of the room, across the entrance hall and took the steps down to the drive two at a time. He had not gone many paces before he encountered Lady Sara herself, making her way briskly back up the drive.

"Just the person I had hoped to meet," he said. "I have been so fortunate as to obtain Hope's acceptance of my offer of marriage. May I also have the happiness of your blessing?" They were not the most elegantly formed words of his career, but he was too excited to consider better phrasing, and he could not suppress his broad smile.

Lady Sara's expression showed neither pleasure nor vexation. She carried on walking at the same steady pace, so that he was obliged to turn and walk alongside her. "So you managed to talk her into it at last?"

"It was the notice in the newspaper which persuaded her, Lady Sara." He had never quite had the courage to address her as Cousin Sara, as his sister Mary did sometimes. Lady Sara was too aristocratic and haughty by far for him to take liberties. As often as not, he found himself saying *'my lady'* to her, as if he were a servant. No longer, for he was now an Allamont of Allamont Hall himself, and could hold up his head in any society.

"Notice?"

"Of the day for prospective purchasers to view the Hall, and of the auction to follow."

"Ah."

She said nothing else, so he rushed on, "It cannot be a long engagement, of course. We must talk to Plumphett, to establish the exact dates and so forth. Then we can settle on a date for the wedding."

Still she said nothing. Rather daunted, he lapsed into silence himself. She mounted the steps to the entrance, where the butler had thrown the doors wide for their arrival, as Hugo followed two paces behind.

Hope, lurking near the foot of the stairs, looked up hopefully as her mother collected several letters from the butler's salver, then stopped with an exclamation of dismay to break the seal on one of them.

Quickly, she scanned the single sheet. "Oh, what a bore. Young, I shall need the carriage tomorrow to go to Brinchester. Eleven o'clock."

"Yes, milady."

"To Brinchester, Mama? May we come with you?" Hope said.

"I shall not be going anywhere of interest to you. This is a matter of business, and very dull."

"We need to see Plumphett," Hugo put in eagerly. "If it would be no inconvenience to you."

She looked from one to the other, considering. "If you are *both* going to visit Plumphett, then you may accompany me. Eleven o'clock. Do not keep me waiting." She looked at Hugo, lifting one eyebrow. "I daresay we shall have you about the place even more than before, now. You have the disposition of the rooms quite settled in your mind, I am sure."

"Of course not," he said, smiling.

But he had, naturally. He had planned everything long ago.

~~~~~

Lady Sara was at her most silent and regal on the drive to Brinchester. She was accompanied by her maid, a sour faced woman who never spoke at the best of times. How Mama could put up with her, and why she had replaced the very pleasant maid she had had for years, Hope could not understand.

Hugo chattered away, but he never seemed to require an answer, so Hope sat glumly beside her mother, wondering for the hundredth time whether she were doing the right thing. If she married Hugo, she would keep her home and would not have to watch as strangers tramped all over it, and perhaps a new family moved in and changed everything about. They might chop down the old apple tree where Grace used to climb, or dig up Amy's shrubbery, or pave over the sweet-smelling rose garden. Perhaps they would knock down the old glass houses altogether, and Hugo would never see grapes grown there. It was too horrid to contemplate. But if she did *not* marry him, there was still a chance that she would meet a man who would make her feel warm inside, the way Mr Burford once had, when he had been so much in love that he could not even speak, but stammered and blushed and was everything enchanting. It was so difficult.

Brinchester was dusty and crowded, for the wool exchange was in progress and the streets were full of men in smocks or rough woollen jackets and oddly shaped hats, and barely a lady or a gentleman to be seen. Queen Anne Square, where the finest buildings were located, was a little less crowded. The carriage disgorged its passengers here, and rattled away over the cobbles to the White Rose Hotel, where they were to meet after conducting their business.

"May I see you safely to your destination, Lady Sara?" Hugo said politely. "There are some boisterous types on the streets today, and I should not wish you to be harassed."

She laughed, but said, "You are all consideration, Hugo, but I do not think I need your protection." With that she turned and set off at a rapid pace, the maid trailing two paces behind.

Hugo offered Hope his arm, and they made their way down the fashionable street that led to Mr Plumphett's offices. With the death of one of his uncles, the legal firm of Plumphett, Pratt and Plumphett had recently become Pratt, Plumphett and Farringer, and the fresh paint and gleaming brass plate on the front door proclaimed the success of the venture. While their cards were sent in, Hope and Hugo were admitted to the waiting room, where several men stiff in their Sunday clothes eyed them curiously. They had not long to wait, for Mr Plumphett himself emerged from an inner fastness to greet them.

"Miss Allamont! Mr Allamont! Such a pleasure indeed. Do come inside."

He creaked as he bowed, his corsets straining, for Mr Plumphett had not got any less stout over the years since Hope had first seen him. That had been just after Papa had died, and the solicitor had come to the Hall to explain the will to them.

The terms had seemed so impossible then — that all six of the sisters must marry in order of age, or they would lose their dowries. And such dowries! One hundred thousand pounds between them, and the amount had grown over the years, so that each of her sisters had received more than twenty thousand pounds. Or so she supposed, for she had not heard the details of Dulcie's or Grace's dowries, but they could not have received any less, she was sure.

In Mr Plumphett's well-appointed office, chairs were brought forward for them, offers of Madeira or tea made and refused, and then, finally, Mr Plumphett eased himself into the large carved chair behind his desk and the business could commence. Hugo explained their situation, and the solicitor nodded thoughtfully, steepling his pudgy hands.

"How delightful! Another wedding in the family — quite splendid! My felicitations to both of you. May you be as wonderfully contented as I am with my dear Mrs Plumphett, and, I venture to say — I feel I am not making too bold an assertion — as my dear wife is with me. It is a great comfort, marriage, I have always said so, although finding just the right person with whom to share one's life is..."

He went on in this vein for quite some time, and Hope tried not to let her mind wander. Instead, she focused her gaze on the portrait on the wall behind Mr Plumphett's head, of a man in a tightly curled wig, sporting a richly decorated coat and a frilled neckcloth. One of the deceased Plumphetts, she guessed, or possibly a Pratt. How odd it must be to have one's father or grandfather always looking over one's shoulder. She was glad there was no portrait of Papa at home. Not that she needed one, for his features were burned into her memory. Occasionally she would catch a glimpse of a stranger on the street or at the assembly who reminded her for a moment of her father. A jolt of fear always ran through her, until she remembered that he was dead and she had nothing to fear any longer.

Hugo's voice, sharp with irritation, cut across her reminiscences. "The will, Plumphett?"

"The will! Ah, indeed, the will, Mr Allamont." He tapped his fingers together thoughtfully. "It is a complicated matter, but my colleagues and I went into the precise details of the stipulations when Mrs Langdon was here last year. Your aunt, Miss Allamont."

"Aunt Lucy from Liverpool, yes, yes," Hugo said impatiently "Do get on with it, Plumphett."

The solicitor looked offended and harrumphed twice, but said, "We are agreed that the *'five years'* specified in the will shall have expired on the day of the fifth anniversary of the late Mr William Allamont's death. That is, the sixteenth day of October in this present year of our Lord. So any claim must be made *before* that date to qualify to inherit Allamont Hall, and for the convenience of all, we have settled it that any such claim must be made here in this office by the close of business."

"So we shall marry on the fourteenth," Hugo said. "Then we present our claim to you on the fifteenth before close of business. But how do we prove that we have indeed married? Must we bring the parson with us?"

"If you would be so kind as to advise me of the exact time and place of the happy occasion," Mr Plumphett said, "I should be most honoured to attend your wedding in person. Then there need not be the least doubt of the veracity of your claim."

He beamed paternally at them.

~~~~~

"It was unkind in you to be so rude to him, Hugo," Hope said, as they made their way to the White Rose Hotel to meet Lady Sara. "He is very stuffy, I know, but he means no harm."

"I have no patience for such prosy fools," Hugo said moodily. "He never uses one word when ten would do, or better yet, twenty or fifty. It is not to be borne. Anyone would think we paid him by the word. If he would merely answer the question at once, we could be about our business all the quicker."

"And then we would have an age to wait for Mama," Hope said with a smile. "I wonder how long she will be. If we knew what she is about, we might be able to guess. Did she tell you anything of her plans for today?"

"Nothing at all, but then she never does. She was always secretive. Do you think she has something to hide? A lover, perhaps? Just imagine it, the high-flown Lady Sara Allamont concealing a secret passion."

"You do talk nonsense, Hugo. As if Mama would ever do such a thing."

"Well, what does she get up to in Shropshire, eh? All those visits she undertakes. And London, too."

"In London I believe she goes to visit Aunt Tilly, although she has not been there recently. Just lately she never stays away more than a night or two."

"Oh? I wonder if they have had a falling out. But a night or two — definitely a lover, then."

Hope was spared from a retort against this ridiculous notion by the appearance of Mama herself, waiting calmly at the entrance to the hotel, parasol raised against the sun. There was no sign of the maid.

As they approached, a man walked past Mama, then stopped, turned and made a little bow. He seemed to be speaking to Lady Sara, but she stepped back, shaking her head. The man followed her. She stepped back again, and again he matched her, so that she was pressed against the wall of the inn.

Hugo lengthened his stride, and Hope had to half run to keep up with his long legs. They came up against the two in a rush. The man was dressed in a flamboyant provincial style, and Hope was reminded of her mother's friend at one time, Mr Eddington.

"...it *is* you, Maud, I swear!" the man said with some heat. "Why do you deny it? I cannot be mistaken on this point."

"Is this person causing you distress, my lady?" Hugo said. "Shall I see him off for you? Or call the constables?"

The man turned to stare at them, but Lady Sara answered composedly, "He has mistaken me for someone else. I have tried to explain that I have never seen him before in my life, but he refuses to believe me."

"But I recognise you," the man said, although with a puzzled air.

"You are addressing the Lady Sara Allamont of Allamont Hall, sir," Hugo said indignantly. "If she says she has never met you before, then she has never met you. Be on your way at once."

He raised his hat. "Beg pardon, milady. No offence intended, I'm sure. I must have got you confused with someone else."

Lady Sara gave him a curt nod and swept away into the hotel, leaving Hope and Hugo standing.

The man, hat in hand, gazed after her. "I could have sworn..." he said under his breath, shaking his head in bemusement.

Hope felt sorry for him, but a possible solution to the mystery suggested itself. "My mother has an identical twin sister. Perhaps you have met her instead? She lives in London."

His expression grew even more forlorn. "That will not answer, for I have never been there in my life. I have barely left my home town until I moved here a few days ago. Besides, she will be a lady, too, I suppose, and the one I met was no lady, that's for certain." He looked at Hope then, and straightened. "Beg pardon, miss. Just my mistake, I dare say. Best go after your mother now."

With a small bow, he moved on, and Hope and Hugo took his advice and ran after Lady Sara.

But it was very puzzling, all the same, and Hope pondered the problem all the way home.

3: *Visitors*

When they arrived back at the Hall, Hope's mother said, "Hope, dear, do come to my room. We should have a little talk."

Hope followed her up the stairs and towards her mother's bedroom, but the maid said something to her mistress in a low voice, and Lady Sara stopped abruptly.

"Quite right, Rushton. Hope, wait for me in my sitting room."

Hope curtsied silently and did as she was bid, but she was disappointed. She had never yet been invited into her mother's bedroom, but Grace had, once, and had told her about the picture of Mama with her twin sister, Aunt Tilly, their arms round each other's waists. Hope had always wanted to see it, but her mama was a very private person, she understood that.

The sitting room was elegantly appointed, with modern furnishings and yellow Chinese wallpaper that made it sunny and warm. Every other room in the house was old-fashioned, full of the heavy furniture so admired by previous generations, but this room had been redecorated only five years ago.

Her mother appeared very soon, divested of her pelisse, bonnet and gloves. "You may remove your bonnet now, dear," she said with a smile. "There! Now come and sit beside me, and tell me about this business with Hugo. You have resisted him for so long, I should like to be assured that this is entirely your own decision and he has not put you under excessive pressure."

"Oh no, nothing of the sort! It is my own choice."

"And you are happy with the prospect of marrying Hugo? He was very wild when he was a boy, was he not?"

"Oh yes, but he had such a difficult time at school, for James was the best in his house at all kinds of sports, and Mark won prizes for Greek and Latin and oratory, and Hugo was no good at anything very much, except mathematics. He had to be a little wild so that the other boys would respect him, he said. It is so difficult being the youngest in the family," she added sadly.

"Yes, I can appreciate the problem," her mother said, patting her hand. "And then I daresay he was bored at home, with no sensible occupation and no money for amusements."

"Exactly!" Hope said. "He has been much more settled since he began to look into the accounts here, and take on the management of the estate."

"I can see that he enjoys the work and does it well, but one does not choose a husband because he is good at keeping records and collecting rents. Nor are his reasons for offering disinterested, for I fear that he does rather see you as his key to obtaining the house."

"Oh yes, but so is he mine," Hope said. "I do not want to leave here, and I have discovered that I care more about that than the unlikely possibility that I might fall in love again."

"You are still comparing every man you meet to Mr Burford? Most young ladies would have said he was nothing special. I have nothing against red hair myself, but Hugo is by far the better looking."

Hope twisted her hands in her lap, lowering her head. "Appearances are not the only measure of a man," she said quietly. "There was a steadfastness about Mr Burford that appealed to me."

"Until he fell in love with your sister," her mother said, but her tone was unwontedly gentle.

Hope looked up at her. "True, but I do not blame him for that. I do not blame either of them. But for a while, he *adored* me, and no one has adored me since, not in the way that the marquess adores Connie. And when Mr Drummond looked at Dulcie, there was such an *ardour* in his eyes, a great hunger that only she could satisfy. Until a man looks at me in just that way, I cannot fall in love with him. And so I might as well marry Hugo."

"Ardour..." her mother said softly. "Yes, I see the problem. If one cannot have a great, all-encompassing love, then one might as well marry for purely practical reasons, and such matches can work out very comfortably, with a little care on both sides. Hugo will not be the easiest man to deal with, perhaps, for he does tend to swing rather swiftly from the dismals to the heights and back down again, but you will learn how to manage him. Very well, I shall say no more about it, but you must beware, Hope."

"Beware? Of what?"

"Sometimes a great, all-encompassing love sweeps you away just when you least expect it."

"I do not think I will ever fall in love again," Hope said sadly.

~~~~~

Hugo had written to his father to tell him of his successful suit, and this brought forth such an outpouring of delight and goodwill as could not be contained in a mere letter or even a common call. So it came about that Mr Henry Allamont was to make a stay of several days at Allamont Hall. This was not an unusual event, for ever since the death of his second wife a year ago, he had felt the need of more company than could be found at home. He stayed sometimes with his married daughter, Mary, and he had his eldest son, James, and his wife, and the

Burfords as neighbours, but when Hugo stayed at Allamont Hall, his father often stayed there too.

This time, he also brought James and Alice with him. James was a personable young man of five and twenty, who had once courted Amy with the same intent as Hugo — to inherit the Allamont estate if the sons of the family could not be found. He greeted his younger brother with the greatest delight in his good fortune.

"Well, Hugo, so you succeeded where I failed," he said, slapping his brother heartily on the shoulder. "A good catch on your part, for Hope is quite the prettiest of the lot, and she will not be the kind of wife who will give you any trouble."

"Trouble?"

"Harass you when you do not do just as she wishes. Women can be the very devil, if they set their minds to it. The last thing any man wants is a shrewish sort of wife like mine." He roared with laughter, and his wife laughed just as much.

"Take no notice of him, Hugo," Alice said. "As if I could stop him doing whatever he likes."

Alice was a farmer's daughter, pretty and plump, a good-humoured girl who had innocently fallen for James's well-practised seduction. He had been obliged to marry her rather hastily, putting an end to his hopes of restoring the family fortunes by marrying an heiress.

Hugo's father couched his congratulations more formally. "Well done, Hugo! I wish you both joy! Such wonderful news — I cannot express my delight in this happy outcome. Now we can all be comfortable knowing that the Hall is in safe hands. Three thousand a year — or more, I daresay."

"A little less, in fact, but I have some plans—"

"Naturally you do. Some refurbishment, of course, and perhaps a new saloon, or a ballroom, even. You might consider a new lodge and entrance on the northern side to connect to High Brafton."

"No, I meant—"

"And you will want to set up your London house. Hope will like that, and you already have an entrée into the highest society through Lord and Lady Carrbridge."

"That possibility has not been a matter for discussion," Hugo said. "It is a little early for such decisions. We must wait until we have the Hall secure first."

"Quite right, quite right. No rush at all. We must get you safely wed before we consider the rest."

All this took place on the drive before any of them had managed to make the short distance from the carriage to the front door, while Alice was embracing Hope as if she had not seen her for a year, instead of a mere week earlier. Only when Lady Sara emerged and urged them into the house did they begin to move, leaving the servants to unfasten the vast number of boxes they considered necessary for a stay of less than a week.

Because of the celebratory nature of the occasion, Lady Sara had invited to dinner as many of her married daughters as lived near enough to attend. Belle and Mr Burford arrived from Willowbye later in the afternoon, to stay for two nights because of the Sabbath the following day. Amy and Mr Ambleside and Grace and George Graham lived so close that they could return home before midnight. Hugo's sister Mary was also invited, but her husband Sir Osborne Hardy was often unwell, and in the event she came alone. She, too, was to stay for two nights.

Dinner that evening was a jollier affair than usual, with Hugo the subject of much teasing about his soon-to-be-acquired right to sit at the head of the table. He took it in good part. Such thoughts filled his own mind, too, and although he considered it improper for him to express them himself, he was not averse to having others express them on his behalf.

Hugo found himself sitting next to his sister Mary. "I am sorry Sir Osborne is not well enough to be here. I hope he has not suffered a relapse?"

"Oh no, nothing of the sort, but the exertion of the journey might overset him. His constitution is not strong, and the least effort may cause a setback. He is better to stay quietly at home."

"But he does not mind you leaving him?"

"A little," she said, smiling. "Nor do I like leaving him, even for so short a time, for he always frets when I am away. But he has Mr Merton to attend him, and he never prevents me from any activity for his own convenience."

"You are fortunate to have so considerate a husband," Hugo said.

"Indeed I am. Sir Osborne is the kindest and most generous of men. I hope you will be just such a husband, Hugo, for it will be an awkward situation for Hope."

"How so? She will be mistress of Allamont Hall, and I cannot see any awkwardness in that."

"No, that part of it will not trouble her at all. But marriage is a difficult adjustment for a woman. We are taught from infancy to keep men at arm's length, to speak only of the commonplace, to eschew any degree of closeness, and then abruptly one is thrust into intimacy. Such a change is easier when one is in love."

"Oh, if you mean what I think you mean, you need not worry, for we have agreed not to bother with such things."

Mary raised an eyebrow. "You should not speak of your private compacts, Hugo, for it is of concern to no one but the two of you, but I will tell you this — that arrangement, too, has its difficulties. If you have left any of the spiced mushrooms, I believe Papa would like some."

Thus chastised, Hugo turned to his father on his other side, offering the dish.

His father smiled at him. "Much obliged, Hugo. You must get used to playing the host, you know. Shall you entertain a great deal when you are master here?"

"Certainly! Or at least—" He threw a quick glance at Hope, busy chattering to her sisters. "I should very much like to. It is so quiet here now, with just Lady Sara and Hope. I like to see the place filled with people, as it should be."

"Ah, that is your mama's blood in you! She was ever at her best in company. But that reminds me — I have finally had a response from the *avocat* in Paris who is dealing with your mother's affairs."

"After all this time? I had thought they must have forgotten it, or lost the papers, or some such."

"It took me a long time to deliver all the documents they needed, for I could not just send them, I had to find a man to take them for me, and travel is still uncertain over there. It was a great expense and I cannot think it will be worth it."

"I never knew that Mama had any money of her own," Hugo said. "She always said she had not *deux sous à son nom.*"

"Indeed, and she took enough from me to prove it," his father said with a wry expression. "I understood that she gave whatever money she once had to a sister — or a half-sister, perhaps. But her family was supposed to be wealthy, so perhaps she left some jewellery behind in France, who knows? She certainly left a will, so it is to be presumed that there is something to be distributed. My French is not perfect, but the *avocat* uses the expression *'beaucoup de félicitations'* several times, so it is to be presumed there is something to felicitate about. Although there was also *'une petite somme d'argent',* which does not sound so very much, does it? I would have noticed the words *'petite fortune'*, I believe."

"I believe *'argent'* is money generally, not just silver," Hugo said. "Even so, *'une petite somme d'or'* would be more enticing."

His father laughed. "True. I shall not get my hopes up, then. Still, even a little would be useful."

"You are comfortably situated now, I think?" Hugo said. "Money is not the worry it once was."

"My income is more than sufficient for my reduced needs. No, it is not of myself that I speak now, but I should have liked something for the three of you."

"It is of no consequence," Hugo said with a shrug. "James is a farmer now, and Mark is earning his bread honestly for once."

"And you will have the Hall, true," Henry said. "But a little extra never hurts."

When the ladies withdrew, the men gathered around Hugo with the decanters, and then the ribbing became more masculine in nature, putting him to the blush. His brother James was the worst offender, aided by George Graham, and although Ambleside looked rather disapproving, the others enjoyed the joke.

They had just begun to consider re-joining the ladies when Young came in, and coughed rather self-consciously.

"What is it, Young?" Hugo said. "Are we wanted by the ladies?"

"As to that, sir, I could not answer, but a difficulty has arisen."

"A domestic difficulty?"

"No, sir. A family matter, but I do not wish to alarm the ladies."

"You are alarming *me*, Young," Henry said brusquely. "Out with it, man. What has happened?"

"There is a gentleman come, sir."

"Yes?"

"It is... it is Master Ernest, sir."

4: *Refusal And Acceptance*

Hope was uncomfortable. How should it be so, surrounded by three of her sisters, and James's wife, too, who was an inoffensive soul, she could not say, yet they made her restless. All they could talk about was babies and teething and difficulties with nurses and the best arrangements for night and day nurseries. Even Grace, who had always been Hope's special friend and devoted supporter, seemed like a stranger now. Hope had seen Grace's new baby not long after it had emerged into the world, a red-faced, squalling bundle of protest, and decided at the time that babies were not worth all the trouble they caused. Yet Grace seemed delighted with hers, and all of them were capable of talking endlessly about their little heirs and their odd habits that needed to be interpreted with such difficulty.

Amy, oddly, was the expert now, Amy, who had never before expressed an opinion of her own and who could barely be in company without Mr Ambleside alongside to sustain her spirits. Yet on the matter of babies, she exuded confidence. How calmly she reassured Grace that a slight fever was not a matter for concern unless there was a rash also. How rationally she explained the methods for maintaining the optimum temperature for the nursery, and the best feeding regime. Even Belle bowed to her superior expertise.

To Hope, it was dispiriting. For her, there would be no babies, and she was not sure how she felt about that. She could not forget Cousin Vivienne, Hugo's mother, who had died because a baby had grown wrongly inside her, and Mrs Wills, who had died just three days after her only baby was born dead, and she shivered and hoped she never had to face that terrible prospect. On the other hand, how lovely it would be to produce another generation of young Allamonts to fill the Hall with their laughter and drive away the echoing emptiness that was its customary state now.

After a while, she crept away from her sisters and Alice, and made her way across the room to where her mother and Mary were talking composedly. Mary had no babies either, and although the subject under discussion, Sir Osborne's continuing illness, was not a cheerful one, still it was less dispiriting than the baby chatter.

Young slunk into the room with the most horribly guilty look upon his face. Hope wondered what crisis had overcome the servants' quarters to cause him to look so. But she wondered even more when Young crept behind her mother and hemmed discreetly.

"Yes, Young?" Lady Sara said, not in the least discomposed.

"Beg pardon, my lady, but the gentlemen would like you to step into the dining room for a moment."

She turned to look at him fully, silently considering. "Very well." She rose in a rustle of silk, and without haste made her way out of the room.

"What do you suppose that is about?" Hope whispered to Mary.

But she shrugged, looking as puzzled as Hope felt.

~~~~~

Lady Sara entered the dining room in her usual serene manner, the gentlemen all rising. Young shut the door softly behind her, and Ambleside brought forward a chair for her. She sat, waving them back to their seats. Hugo was relieved when his father took it upon himself to explain the situation. He was still too stunned to think, never mind string together a coherent sentence.

Ernest! After all this time of utter silence, all the fruitless searching by his father, then Plumphett and latterly the aunt in Liverpool, yet it must surely have been his own advertisement which had brought forth this result. It was, of course, gratifying to consider that he had succeeded where every other effort had failed, yet his success must entirely crush his own hopes. No longer could he anticipate his future role as lord of his modest domain, sitting at the head of the table, carving the meat and giving orders to his servants. Now they would not be his servants at all, but Ernest's.

"Sara, you must prepare for a shock, for there is someone come who was not expected."

"Do I need to have my smelling salts to hand?" She smiled, fumbling in her reticule, before laying a vial upon the table. "There. Now shock me as much as you will, for I am quite prepared."

Henry swallowed hard. "Ernest is here."

There was a long silence. Hugo had never seen Lady Sara discomfited, but he could swear that her usual calmness had fled. Her cheeks grew red, and she breathed harder than usual. "Ernest? He is here?"

"He is. He presented himself at the front door, but, not unnaturally, he does not wish to distress you by a sudden appearance without warning. Young thought it best to ask us what to do. Ernest waits in the book room."

"You have not seen him, then?"

"Not yet. It is for you to determine how we respond to this approach."

She rose, and all the men rose too. "Respond?" She said crisply. "We do not respond. Those boys left this house without a word eleven years ago, and in all that time, I have not known whether they were alive or dead. If they suppose that they can walk back in as though nothing has happened, they are much mistaken. If this person wishes to make a claim on the estate, then he must apply to Plumphett."

With that she would have left the room, except that Henry reached the door before her.

"Sara! Are you so hard-hearted? This is your son! Surely there is some maternal feeling still residing in you? At least see him and —"

"No! A thousand times no. They made their choice all those years ago. I *never* want to see either of them, not ever."

And with that she swept regally out of the room, head high.

There was a long, stunned silence in the room.

Eventually Henry said, "I suppose I had better see Ernest, and tell him Sara's wishes in the matter."

"Might we *all* see him?" Hugo said. "I feel we owe him that much courtesy, at least. Besides, I confess to an interest in seeing what sort of man he has become."

"I should like to know where he has been all these years," James said.

"And why he made no attempt to communicate with his family," Burford said. "His poor mother! How distraught she must be at the prospect of a reunion. She must feel it beyond anything. No wonder she cannot bring herself to see him immediately. She will need time to accustom herself to the idea of the return of her son."

Hugo had never thought Lady Sara capable of that depth of feeling, but he said nothing. Her anger, though, had taken him aback. Surely any mother would be thrilled to have her child restored to her, even so wayward a child as Ernest?

"Are we agreed?" Henry said. "Shall I have Young bring him in?"

Ambleside raised a hand. "You are of the family, Allamont, and perhaps you have the right to see this man. For myself, I barely remember him as a child, and I do not feel comfortable disregarding Lady Sara's express wishes in the matter. If she does not wish to receive him, I do not feel that I can do so either."

This view of the matter had not occurred to Hugo, but he had to admit the justice of it.

His father grunted and nodded. "That is an excellent point, Ambleside. It would be disrespectful to Sara to see this man here when she has refused to do so. She is still mistress of this house, after all, albeit for a short time only."

So it was agreed, and Young was summoned to convey Lady Sara's message, that Ernest must submit his claim formally to Plumphett.

"It is an odd time to be calling," Hugo said. "I wonder why he came so late, and where he will go now."

"Perhaps he is used to town hours," Burford said. "He may have expected to find us not yet sat down to dinner. As to where he will go, he must be staying in the village at one of the inns, unless he has acquaintance nearby."

"It is hardly likely that he still has any friends hereabouts," Ambleside said. "He broke all connections when he left. He has a great deal to answer for, to cause his parents so much distress, and then to turn up on the doorstep like this, quite unannounced. It is reprehensible. It is not difficult to pen a line or two to give fair warning of his intended arrival."

"I daresay he wanted to surprise everyone," Burford said.

"Then we may all agree that he has achieved his objective," Henry said with a smile. "I must confess to feeling a great deal of curiosity about Mr Ernest Allamont. It is a thousand pities that we could not have talked to him, and satisfied ourselves on some of the most pressing questions of the years of his absence."

"You will also want to assure yourself of his suitability for the position he must now undertake, Allamont," Ambleside said. "It is a great responsibility, managing an estate of this size and assuming the appropriate role in society. We could have deduced a great deal by a look at the man himself, and the sort of carriage or horse he keeps."

Hugo had been sunk in his own thoughts, but this roused him. "He came on foot. We heard no horse or carriage, so he must have walked down from the village."

"Interesting," Burford said. "As to his person, we shall have an excellent chance to observe him on Sunday in church."

"This is a blow to you and Hope, Hugo," Henry said. "You must have felt yourselves to be secure after five years with no word. But you must go to her at once. It will be the greatest shock to her — she will be distraught."

"Go to her?" Hugo said, struggling to grasp his father's meaning.

Henry's lips twitched. "You are betrothed, are you not? It is your duty to offer her comfort on such occasions."

"Oh — of course, sir."

They made their way to the drawing room, where the tea things were just being brought in. Lady Sara was not there, and it was obvious from the relaxed chatter around the room that no word of the evening's events had been conveyed to the ladies.

"Take Hope outside — somewhere private — and tell her everything," Henry murmured in Hugo's ear.

Hugo crossed the room to where Hope sat with Mary, laughing at some shared joke. As Hope saw him approach, she looked up with such merriment in her face, that his heart constricted at the thought of the news he bore. It was not so bad for him — he might, perhaps, gain employment somewhere as an estate manager. But what was Hope's future now? Nothing but the continuing dreary wait for a suitable husband to come along and the slow decline into the role of village old maid.

"Hope, I... I need to talk to you. Alone."

At once her face changed sharply to apprehension. "Now?"

"If you would be so good."

He offered her his arm and led her away into the south gallery, where a pair of lamps on low tables cast a dim glow.

"Will you sit?" he said.

But she was too agitated. "No! Tell me the worst! What is it — Connie? Or Dulcie? One of the children?"

"No, no, nothing of the sort, I assure you. No one is ill or dead."

"But it is bad news, I can tell by your face."

"I am not sure whether it is good or bad. You must make up your own mind on that, for I cannot at all decide. The strangest thing has happened — Ernest is come back."

She was so silent that he thought that she must not have heard him aright.

"Do you understand me? Ernest came here tonight, and where he has been all this time and why he stayed away and why he left in the first place I cannot tell, but he was here, in this house, only your mama sent him away again."

"Ernest? Not Frank, just Ernest? But why did Mama send him away?"

"You must ask her the reason for it, for that is as much a mystery to me as anything else."

"And he is well? Did he look well?"

"I cannot tell you that either, for none of us saw him except Young."

"Oh." She was silent for a long time, her head held low, and in the dim light he did not at first notice the tears coursing their way down her soft cheeks.

"Oh, Hope, you must not cry," he said, wiping away one tear only to have another follow it at once. She was so sorrowful and so fragile that he was filled with a fierce desire to protect her from the cold winds of the unfriendly world.

She gave a little sob. "That is the end of it, then. It was always too good to be true. I knew something would happen to spoil everything, and now I shall be stuffed into that horrid little Dower House with some bird-witted companion and Mama, who will be away half the time anyway, and everything will be so dreary."

"Hush, now," he said. "Hush, hush." And somehow, he could not quite tell how it came about, his arms were round her and she fluttered in his embrace like a bird, emitting little sobs of distress. "It will all work out for the best in the end, never fear. I shall take care of you. I promise you will never have to live in the Dower House."

"Truly, Hugo?"

She lifted her tear-streaked face to him with a hopeful expression. Only a monster could have denied her the comfort she needed so badly, and Hugo was not a monster. He pulled her closer and patted little kisses all over her face — her forehead, her wet cheeks, her nose, her chin and finally, encountering no protest, her lips. He pulled away once, but she made no move to disengage, so he bent down to kiss her again, a long, lingering kiss that filled him with warmth and made him a thousand times more optimistic than he had been just five minutes ago.

"That was very nice," she whispered shyly. "But did you mean what you said? About taking care of me?"

"Truly I did," he whispered, stroking her hair. "I suspect Ernest will need an agent to run this place for him until he finds his feet, so with your dowry we shall live very comfortably."

"Thank you, Hugo," she said, still sniffing slightly. "I think I am glad that Ernest is come back, on the whole, even though it is not so good for us. But I am very glad that I have you, and that you are not casting me off at once, for that would be very lowering, do you not agree? I thought you would — cast me off, I mean. It makes me so happy that you are not."

And only then did he see the shackles he had walked into with his eyes wide open. Somehow the betrothal that was based solely on the inheritance of Allamont Hall had become a different arrangement altogether, and he was irrevocably committed.

5: *Sunday*

Sundays were never a favourite of Hugo's and this particular Sunday was worse than most. He slept well — he always slept well, to be truthful — but the instant he woke, he was assailed with a jumble of thoughts about the previous day. Ernest, principally, but also Hope.

Ah, Hope! What was he to do about her? So pretty, so delightfully trusting, so responsive to his kisses — yet did he really want to marry her? When she came with the house and an estate worth two thousand eight hundred a year, plus a dowry of twenty thousand, then the question resolved itself rather easily. But remove the house and estate, and what was left? Not enough money for them to live independently, that was what was left. He would have to find some kind of employment, and even then they would be living in much reduced circumstances.

Then there was his glib suggestion of a marriage of convenience. With a substantial income he would not have minded that, for he could have made other arrangements, but with only a modest income his options would necessarily be limited. And there was the awkward fact that he was not even sure whether that aspect was a part of their agreement or not. He had suggested it, Hope had refused for the twentieth time, and nothing more had been said even when she had accepted him. How foolish of him to find himself mired in a binding contract without even knowing the full extent of the terms. He could foresee a very tricky conversation at some point in the future.

Too restless to lie abed, he longed to call for his horse and gallop off his ill-humours in the fields and lanes, his dogs running alongside, tongues lolling out. That was too frivolous a pursuit for a Sunday, so he rose and dressed quickly, and then briskly walked the two miles through Brinmorton Woods to the village of Lower Brinford, there to sit in pious silence through Matins. Outside the church, he would have set off at once back to the Hall, for his stomach was anxious for breakfast, but Miss Endercott stopped to speak to him. The vicar's sister was close to sixty, but as hale and sharp-minded as many a younger woman.

"Ah, Mr Allamont! How splendid to see you in attendance so early in the day. Shall we have the pleasure of seeing Lady Sara and Miss Allamont later?"

"I cannot speak for Lady Sara, but Hope will certainly be here, with quite a large party." He hesitated, but if he did not give her the names, she would pester him until he did. "My father is staying at the Hall just now, with James and Alice. Also the Burfords and Lady Hardy."

"Quite a family gathering of the two branches of the Allamont family," she said. "I heard also that the Ambleside carriage passed through the village last night, and that of Mr and Mrs George Graham. One might almost think there was a celebration under way."

He laughed. "It does rather look that way, does it not?" He was not about to tell her of his engagement. Let her work it out, which she was quite astute enough to do without any help from him. But it occurred to him that she might have knowledge of Ernest. "I wonder, Miss Endercott, since you are so friendly with Mrs Camelford, whether there are any unusual guests at the Haddington Arms just now."

Her eyes sparkled with interest. "Do you have any particular kind of unusual guest in mind, Mr Allamont?"

"A gentleman of about my age, or a little older."

"Ah. There is no one of that description at the Haddington. However, there is a Mr White staying at the George and Dragon. He is rather reticent about himself and his business here, but he just might have taken a walk in the direction of Allamont Hall last night. Or so I have heard."

She did not ask any questions, for which he was grateful, since it was not his secret to tell. But perhaps she already knew it, for Ernest must have been known to many in the village. Surely someone would recognise him, even after all these years? Hugo had a burning desire to see Ernest for himself. Really, it had been a mistake to send him away last night.

"Is he here?" he said, looking about him at the small congregation clustered in chattering groups outside the church.

"I have never seen him myself, but I can tell you that there was no one at this service who was unknown to me. He might attend the Eucharist, however, so you could take a look at him then. There will be several from the inn who can point him out to you."

Hugo strode back through the woods, head down, heedless of the summer beauty around him. If there had been streams overrunning the path, he would have walked straight through them. If a wild boar had run across in front of him chased by a wolf, he would have seen nothing. His mind was turned inward to his own problems, and the odd matter of Mr Ernest Allamont, who gave himself a false name, kept himself to himself and stayed at the cheap inn. That might be a very proper desire not to set the neighbourhood by the ears, but it might also hide something less high-minded.

He arrived late to breakfast, finding everyone already seated around the table, even Lady Sara, who usually kept to her chamber until noon. Today she was smiling and sharing a joke with his father, a circumstance even more shockingly unusual than her presence so early in the day.

"They are in high spirits," Hugo said, sliding into a seat beside James.

James grinned. "Indeed. Interesting, is it not? Lady Sara is astonishingly lively these days, and Papa seems to have mastered his grief rather well since he came out of mourning. Alice thinks they will make a match of it."

Hugo's slice of buttered toast stayed its motion towards his mouth. "Really?" He looked again at the two people in question, still chortling, heads close together. "Oh."

It was a thought that had not previously crossed his mind. Lady Sara had always been a cool, distant figure, but when his mother had become ill the previous year, it was Lady Sara who had rushed to her side and stayed with her for many weeks until all hope had been lost. Since then, she had visited many times to console the widower, or he had been invited to stay at Allamont Hall. Now Hugo wondered if the consolation had gone deeper than mere family affection.

James leaned closer, and whispered, "Mary told me once that Papa nearly married Lady Sara once, long ago, but they quarrelled and went their separate ways. He married Mary's mother and Lady Sara married Cousin William, and that was an end to it. But now that they are both free..."

Hugo said nothing, but he wondered greatly at it. Lady Sara had never seemed to hold Papa in higher regard than any other man. He could see his father's affection for her shining down the years, even when they had both been married to other people, but Lady Sara had never shown him anything other than icy disdain. If she had harboured a secret passion, she had concealed it very well. He shook his head at the incomprehensible ways of older people.

After breakfast, the ladies waited for the carriage to be brought round to convey them to church, while the gentlemen walked with the servants through the woods.

Henry stopped to admire the vista afforded by a break in the trees, and called it to Hugo's attention. By the time they moved on, the rest of the procession was some distance ahead.

"Hope seems to have taken the news well," Henry said, keeping his voice low, although no one was near enough to overhear. "I had expected her to be distraught, for she's a sensitive little thing."

"There were a few tears," Hugo admitted. "However, she recognises that it must be a good thing to have Ernest restored to the family."

"As to that, who can say? But you are still betrothed?" Hugo acknowledged it. "That is no bad thing, for either of you. She has harboured her *tendre* for Burford quite long enough. Most unnatural in a girl of that age. Given all the admirers she has had, it astonishes me that she never fell for any of them. But it is a good match for you, for you have not two farthings to call your own, apart from the allowance I make you. Hope will make you a good wife, and give you a fine set of Master and Miss Allamonts, I make no doubt."

Hugo was on the brink of confessing that such an occurrence was unlikely when he remembered Mary's advice not to tell people about his arrangement with Hope. Besides, his own uncertainty as to the exact situation existing between them made the subject excessively awkward.

Instead he said slyly, "But perhaps I may soon be wishing *you* happy?"

Henry laughed and demurred, but although he did not admit to the possibility, neither did he deny it.

As they entered the church, Hugo looked at the pews where strangers without acquaintance in the village might sit, but could see no one of Ernest's age. Miss Endercott confirmed it as soon as he emerged into the churchyard.

"He is not here," she said without preamble. "All I can find out about him is that he is pleasant enough, seldom talks about himself except to say that he comes from Liverpool, but likes to sit in the taproom of an evening with his valet, chatting to the locals."

"That is very singular!" Hugo said. "Why would any gentleman do that?"

"That I cannot answer, but he has been overheard to ask questions about Allamont Hall. He has an interest there, perhaps?"

"Does he have his own carriage?" Hugo said, sidestepping the question.

"He arrived on the public coach, and has hired neither horse nor vehicle. When he goes out, he is always accompanied by his valet, and they walk everywhere."

Hugo frowned and fell silent.

Miss Endercott said gently, "It is not my concern, of course, Mr Allamont, but a man who has honest business at the Hall would present himself at once, and during daylight hours, not creeping about in the dark, as if he wished to hide his face. Nor would he lurk at an inn for a fortnight."

"A fortnight! He has been here so long?"

"It will be a fortnight this coming Tuesday. I should think he knows everything there is to know about the Hall and its family by now, after all those tankards of ale provided for the villagers and farmers."

Hugo lost no time in telling his father, James and Burford this interesting news as they ambled back to the Hall.

"That is most helpful," Henry said. "I must say, Miss Endercott is a positive mine of information. I do not know how she does it, but she is quite a treasure. Still, I am at a loss to account for this behaviour. Why delay making an approach for almost a fortnight? It is inexplicable."

"Perhaps he wishes to be sure of how matters stand at the Hall before he presents himself," Burford said, although in doubtful tones. "It would show a high degree of delicacy to ensure one was not encroaching at an inconvenient time."

"It is difficult to imagine a time which would *not* be inconvenient for such an appearance," Henry said.

Hugo thought back to Miss Endercott's opinion that an honest man would not lurk at an inn for a fortnight, and was obliged to agree with her.

"Such behaviour is not inexplicable if one is of a suspicious nature," he said ruefully. "One might say that the case is very understandable if a man wished to pass himself off as Ernest, but needed first to find out all he could about the family in order not to be caught out."

"I have wondered that, too," James said. "Who would even recognise Ernest after all these years? I am very sure I would not. His mother, perhaps, or his sisters, but even then, there might be some doubt. He has been gone such a long time! This fellow could be anybody."

"The thought has crossed my mind also," Henry said. "Yet the timing is against any falsity. The moment for such a deception was surely just after my cousin's death, and it would have been a man with local connections, knowing the family's circumstances, who attempted it, surely. Why would any outsider try to perpetuate a fraud now, so close to the end of the five years? How would anyone know of the situation?"

"That may be my fault," Hugo admitted sheepishly. "I posted notices in various newspapers asking for information about Ernest and Frank, and mentioning that the inheritance of the Hall was at issue. The date by which a claim must be made was also given."

"When were these notices posted?"

"Three weeks ago."

"Then we have grounds for suspicion in the timing alone," Burford said. "But if this man is truly Ernest, he will likely have papers to prove it, and failing that, he will know details from his childhood that only a true member of the family would know."

"So all we have to do is to ask him questions? Like the name of the scullery maid at the time, or the coachman?" Hugo said.

"Not that, no," Burford said. "Anybody might know such things. It must be something that only the children would have known. You must ask Mrs Burford and Miss Hope for ideas. They will be bound to recall something to the purpose."

~~~~~

It was not difficult for the sisters to devise a series of questions which would prove beyond all doubt whether the man at the George and Dragon was indeed Ernest Allamont. Hugo was not minded to delay putting him to the test.

"The sooner we settle this, the better," he said as the gentlemen sat over their port after dinner that night. "If he does not come again tonight, then I shall go to the George and Dragon tomorrow and question him."

"Allow me to come with you," James said. "Two against one."

"He has his valet, too," Burford said. "If you will take my advice, I strongly recommend a larger party. If this is indeed Ernest, you are at no risk, but if he is just an opportunist, he may choose to fight his way out of trouble. I have done a little boxing in my time, and I would be very happy to accompany you."

"Let us all go," Henry said. "Four of us will discourage any incipient belligerence. Besides, if this is indeed Ernest, I confess to a lively desire to see him for myself, and this way we shall not be transgressing against Sara's wishes. I suggest we leave early tomorrow, to catch him at his breakfast, but perhaps we need not trouble the ladies with our plans. It will be time enough to enlighten them after it is all over, and the identity of this man is settled."

6: *The George And Dragon*

Hugo leapt out of bed the following morning, filled with excitement. After a day of doubt and confusion, he would at last have an answer to the identity of the man who claimed to be Ernest Allamont. He tried not to hope for one answer or the other. Either would be good, he told himself firmly. If this was truly Ernest, then that would be wonderful for the family. But if it was not... a little ripple of excitement ran through him every time he thought of it. If it was not Ernest, then Hugo was exactly where he had hoped to be for so long — the inheritor of Allamont Hall.

He would not be human if he did not yearn for one outcome rather than the other. Two futures lay before him, one of wealth and a position in society and ownership of an estate he had grown to love, and the other one of scratching a living as best he could. He thought of Hope learning to manage on cheap cuts of meat and only two new gowns a year, stitched by her own hand, and his heart ached for her. He wanted nothing but the best for his betrothed, and scrimping and watching every farthing was very far from the best.

But there was still a chance, if this man was an impostor.

The four men met in the entrance hall, their faces serious. They strode through the woods in silence, with just the rustle of a few fallen leaves underfoot to mark their passage. Even the birds had abandoned their morning chatter in observance of the solemnity of the occasion.

"Let me take the lead," Henry said to his sons as they approached the inn. "I want to see if he recognises me at all, for I do not suppose I have changed as much as you two have, and Burford he will not know at all. When we need to ask him the questions about his childhood, you may do that, Hugo, for you have the highest stake in this venture."

They marched into the George and Dragon, and Brodie, the keeper, was there at once to greet them, almost as if he expected to see them. And perhaps he did, Hugo thought, for if Miss Endercott knew of the connection between the supposed Mr White and Allamont Hall, others must do so too. In any event, Brodie displayed no surprise when they asked to be directed to Mr White.

"In the best parlour, Mr Allamont, sir. This way, if you please. Good day to you, Mr James, Mr Hugo, Mr Burford. Take care on the stairs, Polly has been mopping the treads. Just along here, gentlemen."

"Do not give our names, if you please," Henry said to him in an undertone.

He nodded, knocked briskly, then threw open the door and stood aside to let them past.

Henry was the first into the room, then James and Hugo. Bringing up the rear, Burford closed the door firmly behind him, then stood in front of it, arms folded. Burford wasn't a tall man, but there was a solidity to him that was immensely reassuring.

Two men jumped up in alarm from a small table laden with cold meat and breads, tossing their napkins aside. One was a thickset man of perhaps forty, with a nose that looked as if it might have walked into a fist once or twice. The other was younger, perhaps the right age to be Ernest.

"What is the meaning of this?" the older man said, moving round the table to stand protectively in front of the younger man.

"Good morning, Ernest," Henry said in his blandest tones, leaning his head to look around the obstacle of the older man to the younger man hidden behind. "How splendid of you to return home after all these years. You remember me, I am sure."

"Of course he does," the older man said at once, relaxing his stance, and moving aside. "Ernest, come and talk to your cousin." There was the slightest emphasis on the word *'cousin'*.

The younger man licked his lips, throwing the other an anxious look, but he moved forward willingly enough. "Good morning, Cousin Henry." His gaze turned to the rest of the party, but he made no attempt to name them.

Hugo stared at him, unsmiling. Was this indeed Ernest? There was nothing about him that looked familiar, but then a boy changed a great deal between the ages of fourteen and twenty five. The hair was a little fairer than he recalled, the face too rounded, the eyes — no, that was wrong. All the Allamont Hall children had their father's dark eyes, but now Hugo gazed into a pair of soft blue eyes. He smirked.

"You remember my eldest boy, James, of course," Henry was saying now. "And my youngest, Hugo."

"Of course. We played together as boys, many times, when you visited from Willowbye."

Now he was smiling, sure of himself. He was well versed, Hugo had to give him that. All that hanging about in the taproom and plying the locals with ale had certainly paid off.

"You were so good at battledore and shuttlecock," Hugo said. "And we used to play with that mangy old dog of the head groom's — what was the creature's name?"

The young man smiled and shook his head. "I cannot remember. It was a long time ago."

"But you were very bad sometimes," Hugo went on. "Do you remember the incident on the stairs? I never thought you would get away with it, it was so outrageous."

"I know nothing about that," Henry said, taking his cue from Hugo. "What happened, Ernest?"

He smiled and shook his head. "No, no! I cannot! Let it be forgot."

"What harm can there be after all these years?" Hugo said, his smile widening. "Tell everyone what you did."

There was a silence, the young man still smiling although his eyes flicked from one to another. "No, no," he said, subdued now. "It is too bad to bring up all my childish misdeeds when my character is quite different now."

"So it is," Hugo said quietly. "Your character is very different now. So different that I do not even recognise you as my childhood playfellow."

There was a long silence. The older man's face hardened and again he moved to protect his young friend.

"There is a public coach passes through the village a little after ten o'clock," Henry said. "If you hurry, you can be on it before the constables get here."

"Now just a moment—" the older man began, quite willing to make a fight of it judging by the bunched fists. But the solid form of Burford shifted just a little, and the younger man drew back.

"The game is up, Dick," he said. "Let's just get away from this place. I never liked the rig above half anyway."

"Remember to pay your shot to the innkeeper," Burford said pleasantly, holding the door open for them.

The younger man whipped through like a rabbit released from a snare, but the older man stuffed as much of the food into his pockets as could be held there and sauntered out with his head high.

~~~~~

Hope discovered that the gentlemen had gone out as soon as she woke the next morning, for her maid was full of the news.

"Mr Henry, Mr James, Mr Hugo and Mr Burford, all on foot and heading towards the village, miss, and Mrs Cooper all agitated, not knowing whether they intend to be back for breakfast or not, for they left no word."

"I do not know either, Janet, so we will just have to hope they will be back in time. I daresay they would have mentioned it to Young if they had no plan to return."

She guessed their intent, for why else would they all go to the village so early in the day? There could be no other reason but to talk to Ernest — or whoever it was.

She was dressed and downstairs in time to see the first of their visitors departing, for Mary wished to return to Sir Osborne as soon as may be. Belle was also up and about, and when Mary's carriage had disappeared down the drive, the two ladies withdrew to the morning room, where they set to work on their stitchery with industry.

"Is he *very* ill, Sir Osborne?" Hope asked her sister, as she cut a piece of ribbon for a reticule. "For he has always fussed a great deal about his health, and it is difficult to know which part of his concern may be real and which is mere nervousness."

"He is truly ill, I believe," Belle said. "Mary is concerned about him, you know, and she is not at all prone to unnecessary anxiety."

"He coughs a great deal," Hope said. "I do hope it is not... what I think it may be. For that would be very bad."

"Consumption." Belle's voice was almost a whisper. "That is what Mary fears also, but the physicians she has engaged will not use the word, not unless there is no other possibility. A weak chest, or a prolonged cough, or summer fever — so they term it, even when the summer fever becomes a winter fever without remission. But he has the very best of care, and he may yet defeat it. We must pray that he does."

"Of course. But how miserable for Mary to be tied to a sick husband, so that she can barely leave her own house for fear of what may happen."

Belle smiled. "That is a part of marriage — *'for better or for worse'*, is that not how it goes? And Mary is fortunate that her husband is considerate and generous, and does not keep a mistress as Papa did, or gamble away his fortune as poor Mr Wills almost did. All men have their odd little quirks that their wives must learn to live with, as you will discover soon enough."

"Oh. What are Mr Burford's quirks? Oh, I beg your pardon, sister, is it impolite in me to enquire?"

Shaking her head with a smile, Belle said, "Nothing outrageous, I assure you. He frets so over the children. He spends more time in the nursery than I do, I swear, and when he and Nanny get together to discuss an incipient rash, there is no dragging them apart. He will want to be on our way home directly after breakfast, if I know him."

Hope listened, wide-eyed, to this description and could not reconcile it with her memory of the Mr Burford who had once adored her so much that he could not speak a word, and blushed to the roots of his hair whenever he looked at her. He had been a god-like being who had loved her to the exclusion of all reason. Then he had turned to Belle instead, who had reduced him to the state of a mere man in the mortal realm, a man who found spots and crying babies fascinating. Hope was glad they were happy together, but seeing her hero brought so low was dispiriting.

It was Hope who heard the first distant sound of masculine voices, and then the crunch of gravel. She flew to the window.

"They are coming, and... they are in high spirits."

What did that mean? It must be good news, but what sort? Had they talked to Ernest?

"It went well, then," Belle said, in her calm way.

Hope raced out into the entrance hall just as the gentlemen gained the front door. Hugo was the first through, his face alight with joy.

"All is well, Hope!" he cried as soon as he saw her. "We have seen the scoundrel off and we are safe! The Hall is ours!"

He strode across the floor, scooped her into his arms and swung her round.

"Hugo! Put me down!" she squealed.

But he was irrepressible. "You should have seen Papa. He was tremendously clever, for he pretended that he believed it all, and then I followed on with the questions that you and Belle came up with, and of course the fellow had not the least idea. So he is gone, and will trouble us no more."

"So he was an impostor?"

"Certainly he was. His eyes were quite the wrong colour. The audacity of it! He had seen my advertisement in one of the Liverpool papers, and decided to try to wheedle his way into the family, I daresay. As if we would fall for such nonsense. But we had the better of him, and now all is well."

"But there might be more," Hope said. "If one man thought it might be possible to deceive us, perhaps others may come."

"Then we shall deal with all of them," Hugo said grandly. "No one can fool *us*. The Hall is ours, Hope. No one can take it away from us."

Except the real Ernest, she thought, but did not quite like to dampen his enthusiasm by mentioning it.

All through breakfast, Hugo babbled away excitedly, with James and occasionally Cousin Henry helping to tell the story, although it was a long time before Hope could make sense of it, for Hugo told it so disjointedly. And at the far end of the table, heads bent together, Mr Burford and Belle were deep in earnest conversation. Talking about the babies, no doubt. He was so serious, Mr Burford, and she wondered that she had never noticed it before.

By contrast, Hugo was fired with enthusiasm for the future. He loved the Hall more than his betrothed, she understood that, but he was full of plans, full of joy, full of enthusiasm. He was handsome, too, in a dark, dishevelled way, and he dressed very well on his limited budget. How well he would look when he could call upon the best tailors in London to outfit him! It would be no hardship to be Mrs Hugo Allamont.

After breakfast, while the Willowbye visitors disappeared to supervise their packing, Hugo seized Hope's hand and kissed it.

"Go and fetch your bonnet, Hope," he said, grinning. "I need some fresh air."

"Should we not wait for Mama to emerge from her bedchamber?" Hope said. "I know we are betrothed but I am still supposed to be chaperoned."

"Oh, pooh to that," he said with an airy wave. "We need not go far from the house if it bothers you, but I cannot sit still, you know, and a walk is more fun with company."

Obediently she fetched her bonnet and a shawl, and let him lead her down the terrace steps and across the lawn. The dogs bounced enthusiastically around their feet, and Hugo bounced almost as much, still too full of the morning's adventure to be still. Walking sometimes alongside Hope and sometimes backwards in front of her, his hands windmilling constantly, he rattled away in excitement. She smiled, for his happiness wound itself around her like gentle wisps of cloud, lightening her heart. So when they reached the shrubbery and he spun round to wrap her in his arms, she made no protest and lifted her face for his kiss. His lips were so warm, so firmly pressed against hers, that when he broke away she wondered if her own lips were bruised, they tingled so.

"Ah, Hope!" he murmured into her ear. "This will be so good, you will see. What a fine husband and wife we shall be. Mr and Mrs Hugo Allamont of Allamont Hall. It will sound splendid in London, do you not agree?"

Before waiting for her answer, he pulled her tightly against him, his body solid and masculine, smelling faintly of horse and dog and something indefinably male. And while she was wrapped in his strong embrace, her worries about Ernest and Frank and the Hall and this strange marriage that she had agreed to slipped out of her mind for a time, as she let herself luxuriate in his passionate kisses.

7: Assembly

"Well, that is too bad, I declare!" Lady Sara said, setting down her teacup with a clatter that made Hope jump.

"Mama?"

Her mother waved the letter she was reading. "The bishop will not cancel this wretched viewing that he has ordered."

"But the estate will not be going to the church now, so what need is there for anyone to view the place?"

"Precisely the point I made when I wrote to advise him of your betrothal to Hugo. But listen to this. *'It behoves me to follow the counsel of prudence in this matter, for the marriage has not yet taken place. So far as I am aware, the banns have not thus far been called and no notice has been posted in the usual vehicles for such announcements. It is entirely possible that the marriage may not take place at all, for young ladies and gentlemen have not the constancy of purpose of their elders, and furthermore, all our earthly concerns are in the Hands of our Wise Father, such that none of us shall be permitted to see what will come to pass. Until the happy event of which we speak has indeed occurred and acceptable notification of the same has been received by me, we must proceed on the path previously agreed.'* Pompous old fool! He as good as calls you a flighty piece of baggage."

Hope was rather shocked to hear her mother speak so forcefully, but the image of the bishop saying anything of the sort made her giggle.

Her mother tutted at her. "And now you act as if he is right." But then, quite abruptly, her anger turned to laughter. "It seems to me that your approach is the better one after all. It is absurd, of course. We shall have people marching all over the house to see if they would like to buy it, when it is not going to be available for purchase at all."

"Perhaps that will deter those who might otherwise have wished to come," Hope said.

"You may be right. But we must make sure that the betrothal is well known, so that everyone will see the futility of looking around the house. Hugo must send the notice to the Gazette and the Chronicle, and we must make all our friends aware of your happy news. Go and put on one of your best gowns, dear, and drag Hugo out of the book room. I shall order the carriage at once. We are going to make some calls."

They spent the afternoon working their way around Lower Brinford, moving further afield the following day. It was rather pleasant to be congratulated by all of her acquaintance, Hope discovered. Everyone, it seemed, was happy for her, and delighted that Allamont Hall would not now be given to the church to be sold to strangers. Hope was kissed repeatedly, and hugged, and wept over. Hugo's hand was pumped, and his back slapped in jocular fashion. Many bottles of Madeira were broached to toast the happy couple. Miss Endercott smiled and seemed unsurprised. Lady Humbleforth showed them a spectacularly ugly epergne and promised to make them a present of it for their dining table. Grace squealed and clapped her hands excitedly. Only Mr Wills, still in deep mourning, shook his head sadly and said he hoped they would be more fortunate than his dear departed wife.

"You must wear your best gown for the next assembly," her mother said as they returned to Allamont Hall in the carriage. "What do you have?"

"The green with the net overskirt is very pretty," Hope said. "Or the gold..."

"I will have a look through your wardrobe, and help you choose, and I am sure I can find a suitable piece from my jewellery box. Or perhaps we will go into Brinchester a little early for the assembly, and Hugo can buy you a nice necklace or earrings or some such to celebrate the occasion. Have you much money to hand, Hugo?"

"Fifty or so, no more than that. That will not be enough, I daresay."

"Not for something appropriately impressive, no. But there will be estate cash lying about, so we can use that."

"The tenants' rent money?" Hugo said, his eyebrows rising.

"It will be *your* money soon enough," Lady Sara said crisply. "You may dance the first set with Hope, and the one before supper, but no more than that, for it would not do for you to be seen to be trailing about after your betrothed, you know. A proper degree of observance, but otherwise you may go off and do whatever men do at assemblies."

"They dance, mostly," Hugo said, eyes twinkling. "Or should I retreat to the card rooms and drink a gallon of Madeira like the old married men?"

She laughed, and tapped his hand playfully. "If you wish to amuse yourself at the tables, that would be acceptable. Or you may dance if you wish, but not more than once with any lady. In case Hope should become jealous, you understand. And Hope must not stand up with any gentleman more than once, in case *you* should become jealous." She laughed again, a melodious tinkling sound. "I hope the baron will be there, for his wife is a dreadful gossip and will be sure to spread the news everywhere. And I must see if I can spot Lady Corning..."

Hope listened in amazement, hardly daring to say a word in case she drew her mother's censorious eye. When had she ever taken an interest in what any of her daughters wore, or offered jewellery, or talked in that teasing way? It was the strangest sensation to feel that there were depths to her mother that she had barely suspected.

When Lady Sara paused for breath, Hope tucked her hand around her mother's arm and said, "Thank you, Mama."

"Whatever for? Offering a little motherly advice? Is that not my role in life? Besides, you are the last to be entering the state of matrimony, and naturally I want to fire you off creditably."

So that explained it, Hope decided. Her mother had always said that she wanted nothing more than to see her daughters married off as soon as may be, accepting the first man who offered. Grace and Hope must have tried her patience to its limits by refusing so many eligible offers. No doubt Mama's life would be easier once Hope was gone, and she could do as she pleased, travelling to Shropshire or London or wherever she wished, without a worry about chaperons or instilling proper behaviour into the six of them. Her work would be done, and she would be free.

Hope sighed. If Mama was regaining her freedom, Hope was just about to lose hers.

~~~~~

At the assembly, Hugo had done his duty by Hope, and a couple of other young ladies besides, and felt justified in retreating from the dance floor, and out of the reach of those with calculating eyes who saw him now as the future owner of Allamont hall and a man of consequence in the county. He made his way to the upper floor where the card and supper rooms were situated, and secured a glass of Madeira from a servant passing by with a tray. There was a gallery here from which those not dancing could look down on the couples below, giving a fine vista of the movements of the dance. Hugo turned his gaze to the whirlpool of colour below, and there she was, her face glowing with delight in the dance, her skirts swirling around her, and her arms exquisitely positioned. Lord, could she dance, his Hope. *His* Hope, totally, utterly his. He smiled as he watched her move this way and that, the picture of an elegant young lady, and could not deny that he was a lucky man.

A slight cough at his elbow alerted him to his surroundings once again. A man of perhaps fifty years, soberly if correctly dressed, his face suffused with embarrassment.

"My deepest apologies for disturbing your perusal of the charming scene below, sir, but might I enquire where you obtained your refreshment? For a glass of something would be most welcome just now."

"Of course. The supper room will have something, but the card rooms have the best selection."

The man looked blankly about him. Hugo could have snapped his fingers and summoned a servant, for several hovered within sight, but he was mellow with the pleasure of watching his betrothed and minded to be helpful. Besides, there was something familiar about the man, and he did not want to begin his stewardship of the Allamont estate by offending some visiting dignitary or minor nobleman.

"Allow me to show you the way," he said genially, and then, as the man began to protest, he added, "Please, it will be my pleasure. You must be new to Brinchester, I think."

"Oh yes," the man said, puffing alongside. "We have been here not yet a month, and this is our first assembly."

"Here we are," Hugo said, pushing open a door. "This is the large card room. Most of the games may be found in here, if you are minded for cards or dice, but no one plays high. The serious play takes place in the smaller card rooms. Now, here is the decent claret, or brandy, or perhaps you would prefer Madeira. What will you have?"

"Oh, claret would be most acceptable, sir, but please, there is no need for you to—"

But Hugo merely smiled, poured a generous measure and handed it to him. "There, sir. Now you are officially a resident of Brinchester. Your good health, and may your time here be everything you hope for."

"Sir, your kindness to a stranger is beyond everything, and I have not the words to express my gratitude adequately."

"But I do not feel as if you are a stranger at all," Hugo said. "Have we met somewhere? I have usually a good memory for faces."

"I do not believe so," the man said, but he looked a little uncomfortable.

Instantly, Hugo remembered. "Of course! You are the gentleman who thought he recognised the Lady Sara Allamont."

Now he flushed deeply. "I am mortified to remember that day," he said. "Such a mistake to make! Now that I have been in the town a little while, I have been made aware of who Lady Sara is, and I cannot reflect on that day but with horror. I pray that I never meet her again, for then my humiliation would be complete."

"She would not remember it, I am sure. Shall you stay for the gaming? If so I must leave you, for my feet inevitably draw me to the dancing, where my betrothed is the shining star of all those on the floor. But if you will bear me company, you may tell me of yourself and your opinion of our fair town. I am Hugo Allamont of Allamont Hall," he added, and a thread of pure pleasure passed through him as he spoke the words.

"Leonard Carpenter," the man said. "I am quite delighted to make your acquaintance, Mr Allamont."

His delight lasted all the way back to the gallery. Hugo pointed out Hope and then, because he suspected that Carpenter would prefer to know so that he could avoid her, Lady Sara. She was surrounded by a great collection of family and well-wishers, all eager to know if the rumour that was circulating the room could be true, and offering their felicitations. Half the dowagers of Brinshire had gathered around to congratulate Lady Sara on arranging respectable marriages for all six of her daughters, and although they no doubt told themselves that substantial dowries accounted for much of the success, still they surely envied her the achievement.

"That is my family," Mr Carpenter said rather sadly. In a far corner, a little apart from everyone, sat a matron and a young lady, dressed in their finest, smiling determinedly. Beside them, a glum-faced young man. "My sister is a widow, and has been living in a quiet way under my roof for some years, but quite unexpectedly her boy — Simon Verdun — has become heir to his grandfather's title and estate, and now the viscount wants the lad and his sister brought into society. Once they are up to snuff, he will take them to London, but we are to live here in the meantime." He shrugged. "His lordship foots the bills, so we cannot object, but it has been an upheaval, that much is certain. We all miss the Shropshire countryside, and of course, as outsiders, we know no one."

Hugo knew all about being an outsider. Those first days and weeks at school had been the most terrifying of his life, so much so that he had never wanted to repeat the experience at university. And then they had lived so remote at Willowbye, and been so constrained for money for years, that he had never been able to move in society as he should. Having no money of his own and no expectations, many of the masculine pursuits, such as gambling or driving his own curricle, had been denied him, and mamas had steered their daughters away from him.

He was filled with a desire to help these outsiders find their place in society.

"You know *me*," Hugo said. "Does Miss Verdun dance? Will you introduce me, so that I may solicit her hand?"

The expression of delighted realisation that swept the man's face made Hugo smile. And the pure pleasure in Miss Verdun's eyes when he made his request was all the reward he needed. She was not a confident dancer, but with a little help she managed perfectly well. Her features were regular rather than beautiful, but her conversation was sensible and she showed an elegance of manner and dress that suggested she would not lack admirers. When he took her back to her mama, Hugo took Mr Carpenter aside.

"Does Miss Verdun have a dowry? It will help her take off if she does."

"Fifteen thousand," he whispered.

"And the boy?"

"He will have four or five thousand a year when he is Viscount Shillingham."

Hugo's eyebrows rose. "Shillingham, eh? I will spread the word, but if he dances at all, get him onto the floor. See the gentleman with the bright red waistcoat over there? He will introduce Mr Verdun to any young lady he wishes to partner."

And so Hugo spent much of the evening industriously informing everyone he could of the identity and wealth of the newcomers, and, Brinshire society being no less ambitious than any other, before long both the young people had as many partners as they could wish, and their mama was making friends with the other matrons.

Hugo reclaimed Hope for the dance before supper, and as he led her up the stairs his father appeared at his elbow.

"Your benevolence is unstinting tonight," Henry said with a smile. "Who are they, these provincials you have taken under your wing?"

"They are no more provincial than we are," Hugo said sharply. "They are from the depths of Shropshire, just as we are from the depths of Brinshire. They will not be provincial for long, however, for the boy is heir to Viscount Shillingham."

"Ah. And how did you meet them?"

"A chance meeting with Carpenter on the street. He approached Cousin Sara in the mistaken belief that she was an acquaintance of his."

Settling Hope with her sisters, the two men went in search of food for the ladies.

"Where did he meet Sara?" Henry asked, as they picked over what was left of a goose.

Hugo shrugged. "He never said. Why the interest in a provincial man?"

Henry grinned. "They come from Shropshire. Sara regularly goes to Shropshire. She has a liking for provincials, too — remember Eddington? Carpenter looks the same type, fresh from the warehouses, not entirely comfortable mingling with the gentry. It is entirely possible that they have met under circumstances which, perhaps, she would not wish to admit to. Have you no curiosity regarding her activities there? Even if you have not, I confess that I would love to know what she gets up to, and if this man has met her..."

"He was mistaken in that," Hugo said.

"Or so he says. Will you introduce me?"

Hugo hesitated. "Do you really want to know? If it is something unbecoming in Cousin Sara's past, would it not be better left there? Especially as you may become more than cousins before too long."

"All the more reason to ask questions," Henry said, with sudden force. "I am done with secretive wives, Hugo. I do not like to speak ill of your mama, but Vivienne tormented me for years, and if I am to marry Sara, then by God, I *will* know everything there is to know about her."

So when they had provisioned the ladies, Hugo led his father to where Carpenter and his family sat nibbling at ratafia cakes and sipping champagne, and made the introductions.

After the usual exchange of pleasantries, Henry said in genial tones, "I understand you met my cousin, Lady Sara Allamont, in Shropshire?"

Carpenter instantly looked uncomfortable, fiddling with his shirt collar as if it were too tight. "Oh, no, no, no, sir, not at all. I was quite mistaken on that point, as I have explained to your son. You know how it is when first one comes into a new neighbourhood, one imagines every face is familiar."

Henry smiled, not in the least deterred. "It is very warm in here, is it not? The supper room is always so abominably crowded. Let us step outside for a little air."

Carpenter looked anything but happy with this suggestion, but meekly he followed Henry into the passageway outside and then to a secluded spot hidden amongst potted shrubs on the gallery. Hugo, thoroughly intrigued now, brought up the rear.

"Now, Mr Carpenter," Henry said. "We are quite alone here, and we are all men of the world, are we not? So you need not fear to tell me exactly where you saw this lady who looks just like Lady Sara."

Carpenter licked his lips, and looked all around before speaking. "You will understand, I am sure, Mr Allamont, that I am not a married man — have never been married, you understand — so... there are occasions when..."

He grew puce with embarrassment, but Henry roared with laughter.

"Oh, Mr Carpenter, how splendid! How absolutely and thoroughly splendid! So you met her in a brothel!"

8: Inspecting The Hall

Hugo could not in the least understand his father's glee at the revelation that Lady Sara had been mistaken for a woman of low reputation.

"I see nothing amusing in the situation in the slightest," he hissed at his father, after Mr Carpenter had given them all the details of the establishment in question. "You will have all sorts of men claiming acquaintance with Cousin Sara, and think how tedious it will be."

"Oh Hugo, you can be so stuffy sometimes," Henry said. "Do you see nothing funny about it? If it were really her, then of course it would not be funny at all, but since it is not..."

"Hope thought Carpenter might have met Lady Matilda instead, for they are very alike, I am told—" He stopped, for his father's laughter had dropped away in an instant. "What is it? It could not be Lady Matilda either, you know, for she is every bit as much an earl's daughter as her sister, and just as unlikely to be found in such a place. Besides, she is in London, and Carpenter has never been to London."

Henry took a long breath. "London. Yes, of course. I cannot imagine what I was thinking, for of course it could not be Tilly either."

But Hugo looked at him oddly, all the same. Just for a moment, his father had considered the idea possible.

~~~~~

The notice of the betrothal was posted in all the appropriate places, Mr Endercott's services were engaged for the required day and Hope began to believe that the wedding was now a certain thing, and not some ephemeral event in the far-distant future. The only disruption to the steady progress towards matrimony was a succession of young men claiming to be Ernest, or occasionally Frank, but Hugo soon became adept at testing them and every one was found wanting.

The pleasant summer weather came to an abrupt end with unseasonable gales and drenching rain showers. Hope and her mother had three times to postpone an expedition to Brinchester to see about her wedding clothes, and even when a dry day finally appeared, their journey was so slowed by deep mud that they were forced to stay overnight in the town.

"At least all this dirt will make it impossible for anyone to come to this wretched viewing," Lady Sara said.

In this she was to be disappointed. The bishop's agents arrived two days before, armed with long lists of those with appointments to view the property, and Hugo was kept fully occupied determining which rooms were to be available for examination, and which were out of bounds. The prospective purchasers were to be shepherded about in small groups, to avoid unexpected encounters.

"All this upheaval is the outside of enough," Lady Sara said, as they sat at breakfast the morning before the day appointed for the viewing. "I cannot bear to see strangers tramping hither and thither as if they had any right to be here. Allamont Hall is *not* for sale, and why these people are coming here at all is more than I can understand."

"They are coming because you agreed to allow the Hall to be viewed, Mama," Hope said with a little smile.

"Oh. Well, that was very foolish of me," she said crossly. "I suppose I did not like to disoblige the bishop, but perhaps a little more firmness would have been preferable, in retrospect. I shall spend the day with Grace and the baby, I think. Shall you accompany me, Hope?"

"I believe I will stay here, Mama, if you do not object. It does not seem right to leave Hugo to bear the whole burden."

"It is no great burden to me," he said. "Go with your mama if you wish."

"I should like to stay with you," she said shyly. "I cannot be much help, but at least you will have someone to talk to from time to time."

"Well, that is very amiable of you," he said, with a pleased smile. "Thank you."

"There, that is settled," Lady Sara said, rising and smoothing down her skirts. "Hope, will you come with me to my sitting room?"

Surprised, Hope scurried after her mother, her heart sinking to her boots. A summons was usually bad news — some transgression or other, a task not completed to her mother's satisfaction, or notice of a tedious chore. But she consoled herself with the heartening thought that she would not be subject to her mother's whims for much longer. In just a few weeks she would herself be mistress of Allamont Hall, and no one could make her feel like a recalcitrant child any more.

The sitting room looked rather sad. Several of the heavier items of furniture had already been moved to the Dower House, and even though the rest had been shuffled around to hide the gaps, there were still indentations in the carpet to show where they had once stood.

Lady Sara said nothing about it, however, settling herself in a wing chair near the fire and indicating that Hope should sit in the other one.

"Now, dear, you will soon be a married woman, so we must talk a little about the ways of men."

Whatever Hope had expected, this was a surprise, and she found herself blushing crimson.

Her mother laughed. "You are not going to be missish, I hope, or scandalised by a little plain speaking. It is important that you know what to expect."

"Of course, Mama," Hope murmured. "Although... Hugo did say that perhaps we would not... we need not..."

Here words failed her, and she dared not look her mother in the eye. However, Lady Sara said in the calmest tones imaginable, "That is a sensible arrangement, perhaps, to begin with, but you may find in the end that it does not answer. You will want children, and Hugo... Hugo is too young and active a man not to want something more, in time, so unless you are content for him to take a mistress, you would be advised to oblige him."

Hope's embarrassment was so great that she could not say a word, but her mother's placid voice soothed her agitation.

"All you need to know about men, dear, is that they are easy to please. The intimacy of the marriage bed is the greatest delight to them. They desire it of all things, and so women have power over them. There are times in every man's life when the world seems to be a harsh and unforgiving place, and then his wife may offer him the comfort of her arms. Remember that, and your husband will be your devoted slave. Forget it, and he will look elsewhere. Now, pour us both a little ratafia, dear, and settle down comfortably, and I will explain everything to you."

~~~~~

Despite Hugo's claim that the day was no burden, it was, nevertheless, a long and dreary affair. For hour after hour, carriages drew up at the door, hats, gloves and canes were handed to the footman, cards were sent in to the empty room beside the winter parlour where the bishop's agents had established themselves, and small groups were led through the drawing room and saloons, up the stairs to the principal bedrooms and back down again to view the kitchens, pantries and outbuildings.

At first, Hugo was astonished at the number of potential purchasers. Where had they all come from, so many people who wished to buy the Hall? But then he began to recognise names and faces, and realised that his future home was become an attraction for all the idly curious of the county, people who had never been on social terms with the Allamonts and had come, as they would to a fair or a market day, to gaze at a spectacle and later describing it to their friends. He imagined them mentally noting every sideboard, every painting, every vase, every vista from window or door, and then whispering around the dinner table, *'Only two decent pictures in the whole place, and as for the drawing room furniture—! So shabby, my dear, that I should be ashamed to own it.'* And it was shabby, he acknowledged. The Hall had been fitted out in the first style and with little expense spared, but nothing had changed in more than twenty years. Every room was just as it had been when Hugo had visited as a boy. That would change when he was the owner, he was determined on that. Just a few more weeks and all this would be his.

So when one or two came to him in the book room with questions about the income from the tenant farmers or the acreage of land under the plough or the number of birds to be shot in season, he had no hesitation in refusing to divulge any such information. "Allamont Hall is not for sale," he said to one after another, and very few looked surprised at the news.

Hope stayed in the morning room for most of the day, so whenever there was a lull in the tramp of feet through the entrance hall, Hugo went through to see her. Each time she looked up with a pleased smile on her face, and the sight of her gave him a little thrill of happiness. His wife, or so she would very soon be, and what man would not be delighted at the prospect? Then he would fret over whether she was truly to be his wife or not, and wonder just how he could broach the subject. How very awkward it all was!

Late in the afternoon, the flood of visitors had slowed to a trickle, and Hugo ventured out to visit Hope again, and perhaps entice her back to the book room for a few kisses. The entrance hall was empty for once, except for one man gazing raptly at the large portrait of Lady Sara hanging on one wall.

Hearing Hugo's approach, the man said, "Beautiful, is she not? A most striking lady."

The man turned to face him, revealing a pleasant if undistinguished countenance. He was not much older than Hugo, much the same height although more solidly built. He was rather sombrely dressed, in the manner of a burgher of the town, his clothes well made but not in the first style of fashion.

Hugo grunted. "Have you become separated from your group, sir? Or are you awaiting your carriage?"

"Neither," he said, with a gentle smile. "How are you, Hugo?"

Hugo quirked an eyebrow. "You have the advantage of me, sir," he said stiffly.

"Do you not recognise me, cousin? I am Frank."

Hugo huffed impatiently. "Of course you are. That is to say, you are the third Frank so far — I daresay there will be more. There have been five Ernests to date. Why did you choose Frank, may I ask? For Ernest is a better bet for this game, being the elder of the brothers."

The stranger only laughed at this, not in the least discomfited. "I chose Frank because I *am* Frank — the real Frank."

"Then you will not mind answering some questions," Hugo said crossly.

"Oh, a test! What a splendid idea. Go ahead, cousin."

Hugo had been through the conversation so many times that he ploughed straight ahead. "What was the name of the head groom's dog?"

"Lord, that smelly beast? Sandy. It was just that colour, a washed out shade of pale brown. Nasty, vicious thing it was. It bit me more than once."

Hugo's other eyebrow rose, and a frisson of alarm passed through him. "Very well. What happened on the stairs?"

"The stairs?"

He frowned, and Hugo's spirits rose. The dog was perhaps a lucky guess, or he may have known someone local who had told him of it, but the staircase incident was known only to the Allamont children. Hugo himself had not known about it until Hope and Belle had spoken of it.

But then the man's face darkened. "You must be talking about that monstrous urn thing that stood just on the half-landing there. I broke it when we came down in the night for something to eat after Papa had sent us to bed with no supper. We picked up every piece and hid them all in the remaining urn, and then put that into the attic, and then we moved the other set from the gallery to take their place. They were quite the wrong colour, but no one ever spoke of it. Papa did not notice, thank God, and if anyone else realised, they were kind enough to say nothing. My God, but I was so scared! He would have beaten us bloody if he had known. I am sure the thing was worth a fortune, for all it was so ugly."

Hugo stared at him, his stomach knotted with disappointment. Surely the Hall could not be snatched away from him at the very last moment? It was too much to be borne. But there was yet one more question, and he had to ask all three. It would be remiss not to.

"What happened to the cockerel?"

The man's face twisted in some violent emotion. "Ernest killed it with his bare hands, tearing it apart. Lord, Hugo, must you bring up such evil memories?"

"It really is you," Hugo whispered. "There is one other for you to meet."

He strode across to the morning room, flinging open the door. Hope looked up eagerly, but then her face dropped.

"Hugo? What is wrong?"

"Come outside," he said, tucking her arm into his. "There is someone here."

Meekly she went with him, and when she saw the man standing there, a little smile playing about his lips, she smiled in response. "Good day to you, sir."

He bowed formally to her, but said nothing, waiting.

Hugo watched her face, open and unsuspecting, not recognising the visitor. Then her expression changed, puzzled. "I feel as if I should know you, sir."

"You do not recognise him?" Hugo said. "He answered all the questions correctly."

"Then it must be... Ernest? No, you are not Ernest. You must be Frank." But she sounded doubtful.

"No one recognises me," he said. "I have the world's most forgettable face."

Hope gasped. "But your voice — *that* I recognise! Frank? Is it really you?"

She burst into tears.

9: *Freedom*

Frank's smile vanished at once. "No, oh no! You must not cry! Everything will be fine, Hope, never fear."

"How can it be fine?" she sobbed. "Hugo has done *everything* for this place, he knows and loves every inch of it, he *deserves* it, and now you walk in and whisk it away from under his nose. It is so unfair!"

"I have no intention of whisking anything away from the two of you," Frank said firmly. "The last thing I wish for is to be stuck here for the rest of my life, I assure you. Good Lord, to be a country gentleman, caught in the web of propriety, moving in the same confined circles for ever? It would be suffocating, and I value my freedom too much." He spun round at the sound of voices on the landing above. "Someone is coming. Shall we discuss this in the book room?"

They followed him in, for he needed no guidance to find his way there, and Hugo closed the door behind them.

"Goodness, this room has changed," Frank said, gazing around him. "It was such a dark, dismal place in Papa's time. Or perhaps that was my fear of him that painted it in gloomy colours in my mind. But I like those landscapes on the wall, and you have a new rug in front of the fire. These chairs are different, but I see that you still have Papa's chair in that corner. I'd have burnt it, if I'd been here. And you fellows are new, too." He bent down to stroke the dogs, who were wagging their tails and sniffing him hopefully. "Oh, I beg your pardon, madam, for you are no fellow, I observe. No, I have nothing for you in that pocket, only some sugar for my horse."

Hugo could not help laughing, but now that he no longer doubted the visitor's identity, he needed the important question settled at once. "What did you mean by saying you will not take anything away from us? Does that mean we must expect Ernest to appear on the doorstep before long?"

Frank rose slowly, his face darkening again. "As to Ernest, I have no idea where he is. He may be dead, for all I know, and good riddance. But for myself, I have no intention of laying claim to the estate, so you need not fear to lose it, Hugo. It is yours and Hope's and I wish you joy of it, and a long and happy marriage here."

Hope gave a squeak, and hurled herself at her brother. "Thank you, thank you! Although — it is yours by right, you know. Papa left it to you in his will. Well, to Ernest or to you, and Hugo is —" She threw her betrothed an apologetic glance. "Hugo is the last resort. Otherwise, it goes to the church."

"So I understand," Frank said. "That was what first alerted me to the situation, for I saw the notice of sale in the newspaper. *'Under the terms of the last will and testament of the late William Allamont Esq of Lower Brinford in the county of Brinshire.'* Six weeks ago today I read those words, and until that moment I had not had the least notion that Papa was dead."

"Oh, Frank!" Hope said, kneeling at his feet amongst the dogs and taking his hand. "Were you hiding from him all this time? How dreadful! Papa never understood in the least why you ran away, but the rest of us did, and we never blamed you, never! How terrified you must have been!"

Frank tipped his head on one side. "Is that how it looked? Resentful, perhaps. Angry, definitely. Cowed, but not *afraid*, no. You see, Ernest and I were growing every day, both in height and in strength, and there were two of us... Sooner or later we would have turned on him, and Ernest—" He patted Hope's hand absently, almost as if she were one of the dogs. "We could easily have killed Papa. Not intentionally, you understand, but once a justified anger turns to violence, it cannot always be kept in proper check. So we left, and because Aunt Lucy had been kind to Amy and Belle when they went to London for their come-out, we knew she would be kind to us, too."

"But then you left again," Hope said.

With a heavy sigh, Frank said, "That was Ernest's fault. He was always desperate to go to sea, and so was I, at one time, but once I had grown accustomed to Liverpool and some of Aunt Lucy's family, I felt quite at home. But Ernest took no notice, and got me press-ganged onto a ship bound for the West Indies."

"Good God!" Hugo said involuntarily. "What a dreadful thing to do to a brother!" He had said little, leaving the sister and brother to exchange their news, as seemed only proper to him, but this was too astonishing.

"You might well exclaim in horror," Frank said. "Fortunately for me, I escaped and got ashore before the ship had left the river, but after that there was no question of returning to Aunt Lucy. The rift with my brother was too great to be bridged. I took shelter with Aunt Lucy's brother-in-law, who found me work in Shropshire, and I have not seen Ernest or Aunt Lucy from that day to this."

"You are better without them!" Hope said fiercely. "Ernest — I do not have words for what he has done, and to his own brother, too. As for Aunt Lucy, when she was here last year, she admitted that she was — well, not the most reputable of people."

Frank laughed. "She told you that? Not the most reputable of people... Lord, if you knew the half of it! When Great-grandfather changed his name from Albertson to Allamont and moved here, he left behind a whole snake pit of crooks. The Albertson side of the family is as disreputable as they come. It is a wonder they have none of them been hanged yet. They pay their taxes, I suppose. Anyway, Aunt Lucy and Uncle Roger are up to their necks in every form of vice."

"Oh, Frank! How dreadful for you to be associated, even briefly, with such people," Hope cried.

He smiled and shook his head. "You must not imagine me the innocent in that world, sister. Ernest and I were perfectly at home there. A little *too* at home, perhaps, for now I have not the least desire to be a gentleman and cut a dash in society, and the last thing I would wish for is to be Mr Allamont of Allamont Hall. This place holds nothing but bad memories for me. It pleases me greatly that the two of you are able to inherit it, and wash away the evil that lurks here still. I escaped from here, but my sisters could not, and it is only right that the estate should benefit one of them, at least. I remember all of you with great fondness. Timid Amy. Belle with her books. Connie and Dulcie always with their heads together, and Grace — poor Grace, always in trouble for a broken slate or a torn gown! And you, my sweet-natured little sister. I wish I could have taken you all away from this place."

"If I were in your position," Hugo said, "I am not certain that I could turn my back on two thousand eight hundred a year."

"Is that its worth? But I have all the money I need, and the greatest horror of being trapped here like a rabbit in a snare. Being a gentleman, marrying some fish-faced daughter of a viscount, filling my days with visits and dinner engagements and a season in London. What a hideous prospect."

"That all sounds splendid to me," Hugo said. "Well, not the fish-faced daughter, of course, but the rest of it."

"Then I wish you joy of it, both of you."

"A season in London sounds lovely," Hope sighed. "But how remiss of me, for I have forgotten to offer you any refreshment, Frank. Shall I send for tea? Some cake, perhaps?"

"Nothing that would bring the servants into the room," he said quickly. "I am not very recognisable, as you have discovered, but it is a risk I have no desire to take, and I certainly do not want my name known. Since I am about to vanish again, the fewer people who see me here, the better. But if you have a decent brandy, Hugo, that would be most acceptable. And then you can bring me up to date on all the Lower Brinford news."

~~~~~

Henry Allamont was not a man much given to introspection. It was just as well, because his life had been a series of, if he were honest, mistakes and impulsive actions for which he had paid dearly over the years.

His first, and by far the worst, mistake was to tangle with Lady Sara Heatherington and her sister Lady Matilda all those years ago. Identical twins were the very devil if they chose to be mischievous, and those two were mischief incarnate. Such a picture of innocence in the drawing room, the pair of them — heads demurely bowed, gowns modest and conversation everything that was proper. But that Christmas at Hepplestone was a revelation. Innocent — ha! That could not be further from the truth.

He had not realised the danger at first, drawn in by Sara's smiles, and confident he could distinguish one from the other by the ribbons on their wrists. And only Sara, with her red ribbon, smiled at him in just that way. Ah Sara, his beautiful Sara, who whispered her love as she seduced him — he would have married her in a heartbeat, and adored her for ever, but for those fatal words. So much misery had hinged upon those few words: *'Ah, but am I indeed Sara?'* she had said, laughing up at him, her glorious hair spread on the pillow, as he tried to find the words to express his love. And with that tiny doubt, his life had fallen apart. He had been taken for a fool, and that devilish pair were amusing themselves by playing games with him! How could he ever trust either of them again?

In blind anger, he had run away to France, first, to fall into Vivienne's orbit. But he was in no mood for her claws, so he moved on to Italy where he met his gentle Elizabeth, and she had soothed his spirits, persuading him to return home and make his peace with his father. But his father had died, and then Elizabeth too had died, and when, astonishingly, Vivienne had appeared on his doorstep, he had not the strength of mind to resist her. Another marriage, another impulsive mistake.

It was all so long ago, and now even Vivienne lay in the graveyard, her spite finally extinguished. Somehow, after so much turbulence, Henry had finally reached calmer waters. His daughter was safely married, his sons were settled and it was time to restore the joy to his own life.

He was not prone to vanity, but he looked long and hard at his reflection in the glass that morning. The coat was new, his breeches the finest Brinchester could offer, and his Hessians were polished to a high shine. His cravat was tied with exceptional care. In his pocket, the small box which held his offering — sapphires, to match her eyes.

He breakfasted early and then ordered the carriage. Normally he would ride to Allamont Hall, for it was far quicker across the fields than the long journey by road. But for such an occasion it was important not to arrive mud-bespattered and smelling of horse-sweat, so he was prepared to suffer the tedium of the road. Besides, it would allow him to polish his little speech. Not that there was much to say, for his circumstances were as well-known to Sara as her own, and she must surely see all the advantages of the match as well as he could. Indeed, she had been so encouraging that she must surely be expecting his addresses. Still, it was a long time since he had offered for a lady in form, so it was as well to rehearse a few key phrases.

The butler was impassive as always when Henry stepped down from the carriage and made his way up the steps to the entrance.

"Good morning, sir. Miss Allamont is in the drawing room with Mr and Mrs Ambleside. Should I announce you?"

"I wish to speak with her ladyship, Young. Alone."

"Very good, sir. Please wait here, and I shall ascertain whether her ladyship is at home."

It seemed an interminable time before the butler's ponderous steps made their stately way down the stairs again. "Her ladyship will receive you in her private sitting room, sir. Please follow me."

Was that disapproval in his voice, or did Henry merely imagine it? Yet surely the butler must guess the nature of the visit, and the request for a private audience? Even the most closely guarded debutante may receive a gentleman alone for the purpose of an offer of marriage, and Sara was very far from being an ingenue.

To Henry's surprise, she was not alone. She stood calmly in the midst of a veritable storm, as several men carried furniture about, and two housemaids on their knees rolled up the carpet.

"Henry!" she said, with a slight smile. "How charming to see you." Yet her voice was cool, and his heart sank.

She held out her hand, and with an answering smile he lifted it to his lips.

"How gallant you are today. I regret that I have nothing here to offer you. Shall I send for refreshments? Some tea? Or a glass of something more sustaining?"

He shook his head. "What are you about?" he said, moving aside to allow a chaise longue to be manoeuvred past him. "You are not moving into the Dower House yet, surely? You have weeks still before you need to leave, and I do not think Hope and Hugo will chase you out."

"Better not to put them in the position of chasing me out," she said. "Whatever happens next month, I must be gone from here, and there is no point in delay. I shall stay until Hope is wed, but then I will be gone and my new home must be ready for me. Come, let us sit in the window while the work is going on, and you may tell me what is so important that you need to see me privately."

"I should think you might guess that," he snapped, annoyed to find her so obtuse. It was hardly the romantic moment he had envisaged, with the housemaids practically crawling under his feet. "But we shall speak of it when we *are* private."

"Oh," she said. "Well, they will all be gone in a few moments."

She sat calmly in the window seat while the chaos reigned all around her, and Henry paced back and forth, and found himself in everybody's way. It did nothing to improve his mood.

Eventually, the last item of furniture was removed, and then the rolled-up carpet. The door clicked shut and the room fell into silence.

"Now then, Henry," Sara said placidly. "Come and sit beside me and tell me what is on your mind."

"Can you not guess?" he said irritably. But then good sense reasserted itself, and he chided himself for his short temper. He would never recommend himself to her by displaying such ill humour. So he sat, and continued more calmly, "Sara... you must be aware... it cannot be a surprise to you that..."

She patted his hand. "Come, come, Henry. You are not normally so incoherent."

He shook his head at his own stupidity. "I sound like a schoolboy. How foolish of me, and at my advanced age, too. But in truth, Sara, you cannot be unaware of my sentiments towards you. I have never stopped loving you, not for a moment, even when we were both married to other people. But now... now we are both free, and there is no obstacle."

"Henry, can it be possible that you are proposing marriage to me?"

"Of course I am! What else?" Again he had to breathe deeply to cool his rising irritation. "You must acknowledge how well-suited we are, and how perfectly we should deal together. Is it not the obvious solution to our difficulties?"

Her eyebrows lifted. "Our difficulties? What difficulties do we have?"

He frowned. "Why, we are both alone, of course. A man on his own is a sad enough case, but a woman alone is in dangerous waters, resented if she interferes too greatly with her daughters, eyed with suspicion by wives and with improper thoughts by men. This is patently obvious, Sara. And you are about to be exiled to the Dower House, and expected to live quietly, as any Dowager must. I can give you a position in society again."

A deep chuckle escaped her. "Live quietly? Exile? Great heavens, Henry, what century are we living in? What you see as a difficulty is to me a symbol of my freedom. I need no man to make me whole, or give me consequence. I am an earl's daughter, and the widow of a respectable gentleman, and I may move in society with my head high. I have my widow's portion, and may go where I please and do what I wish, and no man may stop me."

He was so taken aback that he could not say a word, only shake his head in disbelief.

More quietly, she went on, "I am very flattered, and honoured too, that you should consider me a suitable wife, but I must decline your most obliging offer."

Twice he opened his mouth to expostulate but could dredge up no words against her calm demeanour. What could be more impregnable than a woman determined to be independent? No argument of his could stand against it.

So he rose, and without a word strode to the door and left the room.

Outside, Young loitered. "May I announce you in the drawing room, sir?" he said imperturbably.

"Have my carriage brought round," Henry said, before stamping away down the stairs.

As he paced impatiently about the entrance hall, her words echoed in his head. *'I may go where I please and do what I wish.'* Just as she had done ever since William had died. Gadding about to London, and then to Shropshire... what did she get up to there? What friends did she have there who must be visited so frequently, yet never talked about? Nor did she take her maid with her, either, not at first. But then she had got rid of the maid she had had for years, and the new one went everywhere with her. So mysterious, so secretive, his Sara.

But she was not *his* Sara, of course. Still the same high-handed woman she always was, smiling, encouraging him — Lord, how she had encouraged him! — yet when it came to the point, no thank you, Henry, I manage perfectly well without you. *'I may go where I please and do what I wish.'* And where exactly did she go, and what precisely did she wish to do? If he knew that, he might, perhaps, be able to persuade her to give him a different answer.

His eye fell on the portrait of Lady Sara that hung on the wall of the entrance hall. Such a familiar face, and time had wrought few changes. Some tiny lines about the eyes, perhaps, and the lovely blonde hair had faded a little, but the figure was unchanged in twenty years and that smile—! Seldom seen, perhaps, in recent years, but no one, having once seen it, could ever forget that glorious smile.

And then he had a thought. From the pocket of his waistcoat he drew out the card that Mr Carpenter had given him. On the back, hastily scrawled with a badly made pen, the address of the interesting establishment where he had met the lady who looked so exactly like Sara. It had amused Henry, at first, that anyone should confuse the Lady Sara and a common brothel woman, but when he thought further on the matter, he realised that, while Mr Carpenter had appreciated his mistake, there could be other men who would be equally misguided, and it would become a great irritant.

Here at least was something he could do, a little service he could perform for Sara. If he could find this woman who looked so exactly like her, perhaps she could be persuaded to ply her disreputable trade elsewhere, and Sara would be free of impudent men who looked at her with lascivious eyes. And while he was in Shropshire, perhaps he might just discover what Sara got up to on her visits there.

10: The Last Day

As the days and weeks wore away, Hope began to feel as though the marriage would truly happen. The banns were called, the wedding clothes began to arrive and the whirl of excitement lifted her spirits. Even the fake Ernests and Franks faded away. There was still the fear at the back of her mind that the real Ernest would appear on the doorstep to claim his inheritance, but every day that passed made that less likely. A letter from Aunt Lucy revealed that she had had no success at all in tracing what had become of him. She now believed he must be dead, she explained. Perhaps he had gone to sea, as he had always wanted, and drowned far from home. She wished Hope and Hugo joy.

Hugo was exultant, but Hope was not quite so sanguine. "There is still time," she said repeatedly. "He may yet appear and snatch everything away from us."

Still, it was impossible to be downhearted with a wardrobe full of the most charming new gowns and bonnets and gloves and muffs, for her mama had spared no expense in outfitting her last daughter to be married. And then there was the joy of knowing that all her sisters were to be present for her wedding, even Dulcie, who was making the difficult journey from Scotland to attend.

'You are the last of us to become a wife and the last to receive your dowry,' she had written, her letters ill-formed in

her excitement, and spilling over two sheets of paper. *'Of course we must all be there to see you leave your old life behind and enter the new. And how glorious to think that you will now inherit the Hall and be mistress there and create a whole new family to play in the gardens and walk through the woods to the village. And they must have ponies to ride and a kindly governess and the boys must go to school and* <u>*everything*</u> *will be different. I cannot wait to see you again.'* She had underlined the word *'everything'* three times.

Hope suffered a few tremors of anxiety whenever she thought about the *'whole new family'* she was expected to provide to fill the emptiness of Allamont Hall, but Hugo had not mentioned the subject again, even in the most oblique way, so it was easy to set the question to the back of her mind.

A few days before Dulcie was expected, Amy and Belle arrived at the hall, separately, but clearly by design, for neither was surprised to see the other there.

"Now, sister, let us find a quiet room, away from all this chattering," Belle said. "Is the drawing room always so crowded these days?"

"Very much so," Hope said. "This spell of dry weather has brought everyone out of hiding, I believe. I do hope it lasts, so that Dulcie will not have too dreadful a journey. Where are you taking me?"

With Amy holding one hand and Belle the other, Hope allowed them to lead her to the morning room. A quick peek inside satisfied Belle that it was empty.

"Now we can have a comfortable coze."

"Could we not have done that in the drawing room?" Hope said, mystified.

Amy and Belle both giggled, and Amy blushed.

"Not really, sister," Belle said. "We need no audience for this subject."

"How ominous," Hope said, eyes wide.

Again they giggled.

"You see, you will soon be a married woman, and so there are matters which you will want to be informed upon beforehand."

"Oh, you mean about men? Mama has told me all about it."

Their mouths opened in astonishment. "Truly?" Belle said. "For she told us nothing at all. So then we decided to speak to Connie beforehand, because it is a great deal better to know something of the matter before one needs to. Mama told you everything?"

"Oh, yes. With pictures. She has a book with…" Here Hope blushed. "Well, I cannot describe it, but drawings of… of men. And women. It was… very surprising. And did you speak to Dulcie also?"

Amy blushed again, but Belle gave a deep-throated chuckle. "There was no need. Mr Drummond got to Dulcie before we did. And Grace was taken under Lady Graham's wing, so she did not need our advice either. But how strange Mama is! To say nothing at all to any of us, and then to decide that she will explain everything to you. Well, I am glad of it, dearest, but it is quite odd in Mama."

"But she is so different these days, not at all as stiff as she once was, you must have noticed it. She has been helpful with my wedding clothes, bringing a *modiste* from London, which she never did for either of you. She has found me a lady's maid, too, which I am most grateful for, because I should not at all know how to interview such a person or check references or anything of that sort, but Mama did everything."

Belle nodded. "She is certainly happier, I think. My suspicion was that it was due to Cousin Henry, for I was sure that they would make a match of it, but that prospect seems to have faded somewhat, and now he has gone away."

"I noticed he has not been to visit so often," Hope said. "Where has he gone to?"

"To Shropshire, according to my maid, who is friendly with one of the grooms," Belle said.

"Now, is that not the oddest thing?" Hope said softly. "Just when Mama seems to have lost interest in that county, Cousin Henry has developed an enthusiasm for the place. I wonder what the attraction is?"

But none of the sisters could answer.

~~~~~

With the arrival of Connie and Dulcie, all the daughters of Allamont Hall were reunited. Belle also stayed at the Hall, for Willowbye was too far away and the roads too mired in mud for easy travel. Amy and Grace visited every day, the sisters taking over the morning room as their private parlour, filling it with laughter and whispered secrets and excited chatter.

"Only a few more days, Hope, and then you will be mistress of all this," Amy sighed contentedly one day. "How fitting that one of us should live here, and not some horrid strangers. I am so glad for you."

"There is still time for Ernest to appear," Hope said. "I shall not feel secure until Mr Plumphett's office is closed on the fifteenth, for that is the last possible moment for Ernest to make a claim."

"Or Frank," added Belle. "Either of them could inherit."

Hope hesitated, but she could keep no secret from her sisters. "Frank will not claim the estate. He came here and told us so. He has a good career now, and has no wish to be a gentleman in society."

The others exclaimed in astonishment at this news, and Hope told them all about his visit.

"What is his career?" Connie said. "It must be very appealing if he turns down such a lucrative inheritance on that account."

Hope flushed uncomfortably. "I am ashamed to admit it of a brother, but he... he manages a number of gaming dens in Shropshire towns. Gentlemen's clubs, he called them, but Hugo says that such places are merely a front for gambling, where honest players are cheated and the wine is watered down."

"I believe there are respectable clubs, too," Connie said. "Lord Carrbridge and his brothers are members of White's, and there is any amount of gambling goes on there, but it is not in the least shady, I assure you."

"But there are others less scrupulous," Belle said. "The one in Market Clunbury in the house that Papa owned is just such a place. Mr Burford visited it with Lord Carrbridge and Mr Drummond three years ago, and they were quite sure that it was not as respectable as it appeared."

"Oh dear," Hope said. "I wonder if that is one of Frank's? He said he had such a place in every town of any size in the county."

"We should not sneer at such establishments," Dulcie said. "After all, that is where our dowries have come from, and while the rest of you have married wealthy husbands, Alex and I have been very glad to have such a healthy sum to supplement his income. Even though the school is doing very well, better than we could possibly have expected, his salary as a headteacher would not allow us to live so comfortably."

"We are all grateful to Aunt Lucy for setting up the dowry fund, I am sure," Connie said. "And to whoever has been conscientiously paying money into it week after week, although why anyone should do so for strangers I cannot imagine."

"Can you not?" Belle said, with a smile. "What if we were *not* strangers to this benevolent person?"

"But of course we are!" Amy cried.

"Oh, do you mean—?" Grace said. "Could it be possible?"

"I believe so," Belle said. "It makes sense, does it not?"

"Well, it does not make sense to *me*," Dulcie said crossly. "Would you care to be a *little* less enigmatic, sisters?"

"Just consider what we know," Grace said, jumping up excitedly to pace about the room. "Aunt Lucy set up the fund so that we should have dowries, and it originated in the Market Clunbury house, which belonged to Papa but which was also connected with Aunt Lucy through her less than respectable associates in Liverpool. That enabled her to make sure that whoever ran the gambling den there would put money into the account. But she was astonished at the amount we got, remember? When we told her it came to twenty thousand apiece, she was amazed. And in fact, I believe mine was even more than that, for George and his father were excessively pleased about it, as I recall. So someone made sure that there were large amounts of money put into it, over a number of years, and who else could it be?"

"That is just what we want to know," Amy said.

"Yes, do get on with it, Grace," Dulcie said.

"Why, is it not obvious? It could only be Frank!"

The sisters digested this in silence for some moments.

"That does make sense," Connie said slowly. "The Market Clunbury business was managed from Liverpool, Aunt Lucy told us that, so presumably that is how Frank came to leave Liverpool and found himself in Shropshire. And once he discovered that some of the profits were being set aside for our benefit, he may have decided to ensure that the sum would be a generous one."

"He has certainly shown kindness towards Hugo and me, by waiving his right to claim the Hall," Hope said. "Ensuring substantial dowries for us would be equally kind. He has been looking after our interests for years, it seems, without our knowing a thing about it."

"I think he must have been Mr Smith," Dulcie said suddenly. "Alex said that the Mr Smith they met there was a very young man, so most likely that was Frank. How amusing to think that they met him and did not even know it! But did he not mention the dowries when he was here, Hope?"

"Not a word, no. He said very little about his work, except the nature of it, and that his role was to travel to the various establishments in his control, and ensure that none of the customers were cheating. He makes himself very unobtrusive, he said, so that he moves about unnoticed, and then he can watch what goes on."

She did not attempt to describe the oddness of the conversation she and Hugo had had with Frank, nor the way he had altered his voice and his mannerisms and even his mouth, it seemed, so that he was like a different person. She had not known him even without such disguises, but with them he was a stranger.

"With the proper clothes, and a wig and so forth, even my own mother would not know me," he had said. Then, laughing, "To speak the honest truth, I am very sure that Mama would not recognise me anyway, so perhaps I should say that even my own brother and sisters would not know me."

Then he had demonstrated the different ways he could disguise himself. It was uncanny, and, having seen him at work, she believed him utterly, but she could not begin to explain that to her sisters.

"So at least he is honest," Amy said eagerly. "He does not cheat his customers, nor water down the wine."

"So he says," Hope said gloomily.

~~~~~

With the Hall full of visitors, the dull days and quiet evenings with just Hope and her mother were long gone. The servants' quarters were overflowing with valets and ladies' maids and grooms and coachmen, and extra help was sent for from the village. With the wedding fast approaching, there were dinners and evening parties and innumerable callers to be shown a glimpse of the wedding clothes. It was hard for Hope to find a moment to herself for quiet reflection. Perhaps it was just as well, for when she found herself alone, she was assailed by every kind of doubt.

Was she really doing the right thing? There was still time to draw back, and wait for a husband who made her heart leap for joy, a man with fire in his eyes, who smiled at her as she saw her brothers-in-law smile at her sisters. She liked Hugo well enough, and especially when he kissed her, or smiled at her in that lop-sided way he had, but he was not a man to set her heart alight. She did not skip in delight when he entered the room, or feel as if the world grew a little darker when he were not there.

But then she remembered his pleasure when she had finally accepted him, and his excitement at the prospect of owning the Hall and all its demesnes, and she knew she could not draw back now. It would hurt him too badly to turn away from him at this late stage. And then the Hall would have to go to the church after all, which she could not bear to see, nor could she condemn herself to living at the Dower House with her mama and some dreadful companion. Better by far to be mistress of Allamont Hall with Hugo.

So when the day came, she put on her finest gown and went to the church in Lower Brinford, there to stand beside

Hugo reciting the time-honoured words in front of Mr
Endercott. Most of the village squeezed into the pews to
witness it, or else stood outside in the bitter autumn wind to
wish her well.

That night she and Hugo each slept alone in their grand
new bedrooms, and the following day she and her sisters and all
their husbands drove to Brinchester, to sit in Mr Plumphett's
office until the hour he had deemed the final moment for any
claim to be made on the estate from either of the brothers.

The office was rather crowded, but Mr Plumphett and his
partners had provided tea and cakes for the ladies, and a decent
Madeira for the gentlemen, and it felt like a strange sort of
party. The others ate and drank and joked with each other, but
Hope was too nervous to enjoy the company, too aware that
even now it could all be lost. She could not be comfortable until
the hands on Mr Plumphett's ormolu clock had passed the
critical moment. Beside her, Hugo's knee twitched restlessly, as
he tapped his foot in a fidgety drumbeat.

As the minutes ticked away and the clock showed no more
than ten minutes remaining, the Marquess of Carrbridge poured
another round of Madeira and began describing the antics of his
youngest brother, currently engaged in terrorising Oxford in his
first term at university.

"He will never last," the marquess said sorrowfully. "Or
Oxford will never last, more likely. He will be rusticated by
Christmas, I am sure of it. Even in his first week, he was up to
mischief, for he went down to the river and—"

From the floor below, a sudden thump suggested that the
door to the street had blown open. They all fell silent,
wondering. Voices were heard, loud and abrupt.

Terror tore through Hope like a whirlwind, and she
reached for Hugo's hand, and squeezed it. He looked at her with
fearful eyes.

Footsteps pounded on the stairs, the door flew open and a man stood there, grinning wildly.

"I am Ernest Allamont and I claim my inheritance," he yelled into the shocked silence. "Am I in time? I am sure I am in time! Is it not a good joke?" He roared with laughter. "I have been here all week, you know, but I wanted to surprise you. Are you surprised? Is this not the perfect timing? Look, just three minutes to go!" He waved his pocket watch at them, rocking with merriment, as they stared at him, horrified.

"You are in time, sir," Mr Plumphett said, his voice flat.

Hope burst into tears.

11: The Day After

Because of the season and the lack of a full moon, a return to Lower Brinford was not possible that day, and they had all arranged to stay at the White Rose Hotel. The managers had arranged a celebratory dinner for their distinguished guests, but somehow it felt more like a wake. Ernest had to be invited too, and while he bubbled over with delight in his own cleverness in arriving at the very last moment to astonish them, the rest of the party sat and ate in near silence.

It was indeed Ernest, of that there could be no doubt. All six of the sisters recognised him, despite the whiskers on his face and a darkening of his complexion in the passage of eleven years, and although Hope would have denied it if she could, honesty compelled her to acknowledge her brother.

He had been in the West Indies, he told them, but a chance letter from Aunt Lucy to an acquaintance there, asking for information on Ernest's whereabouts, had alerted him to the situation, and he had returned on the first available ship, determined to claim his inheritance.

"How long have you been in the West Indies?" Mr Burford enquired politely.

"Seven years now, since I settled on Jamaica. It is a fine life out there, the climate favourable and every comfort provided. I have wanted for nothing, I assure you. We do not miss England in the least. Slaves are a far superior foundation for the life of a gentleman than paid workers, and the plantations so profitable that I am no longer employed as manager and junior partner, but have my own land. Now I shall be able to expand even further, no doubt." He grinned. "I shall be as rich as a nabob before long, you may be sure."

"If the life is so enticing, I wonder you wished to return to England at all," Burford said mildly.

"For myself, I should never have left, but my wife has a desire to be an English lady, and what Clarissa wants, Clarissa must have." He laughed. "It always pays to keep the ladies happy, eh, gentlemen?" And he winked broadly.

"Have you been married long?" Belle asked.

"Oh, not so long," he answered with a vague wave of the hand. "Long enough, yet not so long." And he laughed again, a strange, wild laugh that made Hope shiver.

"I am surprised to hear that there are English women in such a part of the world," Connie said. "Is the heat not disagreeable for Mrs Allamont?"

He cackled as if she had made a great joke. "She never complains of it." He clicked his fingers at the hotel manager attending them. "You there! More wine."

After that, the rest of the party lapsed back into silence, while Ernest rattled on at great length about his plantation and his journey back to England and his own deviousness in concealing his presence until the last possible moment.

Hugo had said next to nothing the whole evening, nor had he eaten anything, his countenance dark with anger. Hope had picked at her food, watching Hugo covertly, too distracted with waiting for the inevitable explosion to have any thought for her own feelings. When they at length retired to the room assigned to them, his wrath spilled out in a stream of invective against Ernest.

"How could he do this to us? He must have known, for he admitted that he made enquiries about the town. He *must* have known that we had married solely to keep the Hall out of the hands of the avaricious bishop. If he had only let us know, we need not have bothered. We could have been free as birds in the trees, instead of bound forever and with nothing, nothing at all to show for it."

He strode up and down the tiny room like a caged animal, his boiling anger too great to be contained. His hands stabbed the air for emphasis, the movement making the candles flicker, so that Hope was in terror of being plunged into darkness.

"Hugo—"

"A letter — is that so much to ask? He could have written from Liverpool when he first arrived to let us know. What a way to treat his own family! It is unforgivable! And to see his own stupidity as the greatest joke! How could he?"

"Hugo, please stop."

"Such a sly, nasty way to behave against those who have never offered him the slightest injury, or shown him anything but goodwill. I shall never forgive him, never."

"Hugo, you are frightening me."

He stopped abruptly. "Oh, Hope, I am so sorry. Please, you must not cry. No, no, hush now." He took her face in his hands with such gentleness that she could hardly believe the sudden switch in mood. "There, now, I did not mean to upset you with my ravings. Sshhh." Softly he wiped away each tear as it rolled down her cheeks. She had been so intent on him that she had not noticed her own weeping.

"Are you not angry?" he asked, still cradling her face. "You have lost everything, too."

"Of course, but... I still have you," she said quietly. "We still have each other."

"But you never wanted to marry me," he said, kissing her forehead. "How many times did you refuse me, and only agreed to it in the end to save the estate from being sold off? Two days earlier, and we could have called it off, and we would all have been happier."

"There is no point in thinking that way," she said. "It is done now, and cannot be helped, and we must learn to live with it. At least the Hall will not go to the church. Better by far that it should be Ernest and his wife. That is what we were trying to do, after all, to keep it in the family."

He nodded, and released her. "I know, but it is impossible not to rant about it." He sighed. "Well, I shall go and find a corner to sleep in, or rather to lie awake burning with resentment, I suppose. No doubt *he* will sleep like a babe. Perhaps I shall go and murder him in his bed. He deserves it, God knows." Another sigh, heavier, almost like a growl. "Shall I send your maid up to you?"

"Hugo…"

A thousand thoughts flitted through her mind like butterflies. The future was uncertain, and even their fine bedrooms at the Hall would have to be given up to Ernest and his wife. Where would they sleep? Where would they even live? And was there any point in maintaining separate lives now that the very reason for it was gone? She could not bear to sleep alone after all that had happened, and she dreaded what Hugo might do left to himself. Would he really murder Ernest? She could not answer the point with any certainty.

Above all, she needed the comfort of his arms around her and his kisses hot on her lips, and she remembered her mother's words when she spoke of men: *'There are times in every man's life when the world seems to be a harsh and unforgiving place, and then his wife may offer him the comfort of her arms.'* Tonight the world was indeed harsh, and perhaps Hugo needed her as much as she needed him.

"Hugo, will you kiss me?"

He smiled then, the first smile she had seen from him all day, and he scooped her into his arms and pressed her close to him, his mouth covering hers hungrily. Such warmth flooded through her! When, after an age, he shifted away a little, she sighed with pleasure and looked up at him hopefully.

Laughing, he tucked one arm under her legs and lifted her up. "Let us make ourselves comfortable, Mrs Allamont," he murmured into her hair.

She had no fault to find with this idea, giggling as he sat in a wing chair and pulled her onto his lap. Then they fell to kissing again, and she entered into it with as much enthusiasm as he did. Again he was the first to break away.

"Ah, Hope, you taste of sugar and syllabub," he whispered, running one finger over her lips so that they tingled most pleasurably. Sitting as they were, her face was level with his. It felt so intimate, curled up in the chair together. Tentatively she reached out a hand and stroked his hair. He smiled more broadly, but said nothing, gazing at her in the gloom of the candlelight as if memorising every contour of her face.

In that moment, the thought of a night of solitude was unbearable.

"Hugo..."

"Mmm?" His arms were tight around her, rocking her very gently.

"You will not leave me alone? You will stay with me tonight?"

He stilled, his eyes widening. "If that is your wish."

She nodded, and then, because she wanted to be sure that he understood her completely, she added, "I know we once talked about... about not being husband and wife, not properly, but... there is no need to hold to that, is there?"

He shook his head, his breathing ragged. "Is that—" He stopped, his voice not quite under control, then tried again. "Is that what you want?"

Again she nodded.

He hugged her tight. "Hope, you are the sweetest, most wonderful wife a man could wish for. Shall we... go to bed now?"

"You will have to unfasten my gown for me."

A sound that was half groan and half laugh escaped him. "With the greatest of pleasure, my little wife."

~~~~~

The next morning was grey with sheeting rain, the streets puddled and dreary, with only a few cloaked figures hurrying to shelter. No one was minded to stay another night in Brinchester, however, so after a hasty breakfast the carriages were summoned.

It had been agreed that Hope and Hugo would go ahead, to warn the servants of the change of plan. Connie and the marquess were to take up Ernest, as well as Dulcie and Alex Drummond, and follow on. The others had agreed that they would return to their own homes, and visit in a few days when Ernest had settled in.

Hope had been rather dreading the journey home, shut in the carriage with Hugo for perhaps two hours, if the road were to be as boggy as she expected. But this was a very different Hugo from the wild creature pacing back and forth the previous night. He held her hand and smiled a little, and several times he stroked her cheek and told her how lovely she was, how sweet, how perfect. Then he kissed her.

In between kisses, he talked calmly of what must be done to accommodate the new master of Allamont Hall. Perhaps he was reconciled to the new circumstances, but there was a sadness in his eyes when he talked of the Hall, or Mr Garmin's farm, or the tenant cottages — everything on the estate that had almost been his, but which now belonged to Ernest. Instead of ordering the building of the new glass houses, or the improvements to the cottages at High Brafton, or the new pear trees he wanted for the orchard, he would have to explain it all to Ernest, and justify the expense and then persuade him to agree to it.

The rain had stopped by the time they reached Lower Brinford, but there was another ordeal to be endured as the carriage rattled up the drive. All the servants, indoors and out, lined up to receive them formally, wreathed in smiles, and Hugo's first task was to tell them that they should return to their work, and save the reception for the arrival of Mr Ernest Allamont.

Lady Sara, they discovered, had already removed to the Dower House, where Cousin Henry was staying to ease her solitude, so the second task was to climb back into the carriage and go there at once to tell them both of the previous day's events.

"*Ernest?*" Lady Sara said, almost as if she had never heard the name before. "And he arrived at the very last moment? He was very lucky, then. Or you two were unlucky, perhaps."

"Luck had nothing to do with it," Hope said. "He planned to arrive just before the time ran out. To surprise us, he said."

Lady Sara's eyebrows snapped together. "He succeeded in *that* aim. But what shall you do now, Hugo? Everything is in pieces. How very unsettling."

"I shall see if Ernest needs an estate manager, or land agent, or some such," Hugo said with a creditable degree of composure. "An estate of this nature is very different from a sugar plantation, and he will need a little help, just at first. At least that way we can stay on in the house, for a while, anyway."

Hope was rather proud of her husband that day. It would have been too much to say that he accepted the situation without reservation, for there was no mistaking the catch in his voice sometimes as he gave orders in preparation for Ernest's arrival. Still, there was no rancour in his behaviour, and he did not hesitate to do everything that was needful. By the time the marquess's carriage appeared on the drive, the principal bedrooms had been stripped of Hope's and Hugo's things, and Lady Sara had been temporarily reinstalled as mistress of the house, until such time as Mrs Ernest Allamont should arrive.

In defiance of proper protocol, Ernest jumped out of the carriage first, not even waiting for the steps to be let down. He marched straight past the assembled staff without so much as a glance, and took the steps to the entrance two at a time. With a casual nod to his mother, he strode on into the house.

Inside, Cousin Henry lurked unobtrusively in a corner, not invited, but no doubt too curious to stay away. Lady Sara went to stand beside him as she followed Ernest into the house, her face cold.

Hope and Hugo waited in the centre of the entrance hall. They had not discussed how they would greet the new master of the Allamont estate, but as Hope made a formal obeisance to her brother, Hugo likewise bowed low beside her. Ernest grinned impudently at them.

"Well, well, well! This is very pleasant. I hope you have a good blaze going somewhere, for I am chilled to the bone. I had forgot how appalling the weather is here."

"There is a fire in the drawing room," Hope said. There was a fire in the book room, too, but that was still Hugo's domain, and she hoped Ernest would not want to use it. "Are you hungry, Ernest? Mrs Cooper can prepare a cold collation for you."

Young and the footman hovered nearby.

"No, something hot. I am frozen, did you not hear me say so?" He turned to the butler, waiting impassively. "You — fetch some soup."

"Very good, sir," Young said.

"And brandy."

"Certainly, sir."

"Bring it to the drawing room. I will eat beside the fire."

The butler and footman disappeared to attend to these instructions.

Lady Sara glided up behind him. "It is customary to eat in the dining room," she said coldly. "Unless one is ill, of course. Then one may eat from a tray in one's room."

"Well, listen to you, all hoity-toity. I'll have you remember that I am master here, Mother."

"Thank you for your advice, but I do not believe I shall forget it."

"What are you doing here anyway? Why are you not in the Dower House, like a good little Dowager? Clarissa will not want you in the house, you know, for all that you are my mother. Nor you two, either," he said, turning to look at Hope and Hugo. "You have no place here now that the Hall is mine."

"As you wish," Hugo said quietly, although his eyes flashed. "We can be gone in a few days, if that is convenient."

For a moment, the two men stared at each other, then Ernest laughed raucously. "No need, I am sure. Just my little joke. And Mother can stay until Clarissa gets here, if she wishes. I have no objection, so long as she does not countermand my orders."

Lady Sara looked him up and down composedly. "Is that what passes for humour in the West Indies? You will find society here rather different from what you are accustomed to, I daresay."

The smile was wiped out instantly, and his chin lifted belligerently. "Oh, are you teaching me how to behave, now? You had best be polite to your son and heir, madam, or else watch out for your allowance."

"The income from my jointure is mine until I die or remarry," she said composedly.

He glared at her, hands balled into fists, but whatever he was about to say was lost, as the door opened and Connie and Dulcie came in, smiling nervously, with their husbands.

"Well, how pleasant this is," the marquess said into the silence, rubbing his hands together. "Mother and son becoming reacquainted. What a charming picture of... um, a family reunited."

"Ernest is many things," Lady Sara said, her voice haughty. "He may even turn out to be a gentleman, in time. But a son of Allamont Hall he is not, or he could never have treated his family with all the consideration of a sewer rat. I acknowledge him as no son of mine. Ernest, you have your wish. I shall return to the Dower House forthwith."

She spun on her heel and marched out into the October gloom.

"Oh dear," the marquess said.

12: News From Shropshire

Hugo's life had been turned upside down. In that one moment when Ernest had burst into Mr Plumphett's office, Hugo had changed from a gentleman of wealth to a man with no home of his own, no income and no employment. The stream of well-wishers who arrived over the first few days to pay a congratulatory visit to the bride and groom in their new home now found them abruptly reduced to the role of poor relations, while a man no more than a distant memory to most and a complete stranger to some, ruled his new domain with many a smirk. So while the visitors smiled and drank tea and exclaimed in amazement at the return of the long-lost son and heir, many kissed Hope sadly and patted Hugo on the shoulder in silent commiseration.

There was little to be done, apart from trying to smile, and agreeing that yes, it was a great surprise, was it not? Who could have guessed it? And what astonishing timing to arrive at just the last moment. But inside Hugo seethed. As the youngest son, he had suffered all his life with having favourite books or toys or even a horse, once, commandeered by an older brother. Finally, he had fondly imagined, he would have his revenge for all those insults. While his oldest brother was married to a lowly farmer's daughter, and his middle brother was scraping a living as a schoolmaster, he would be a gentleman of means, the owner of a wealthy estate and a fine house. At last, he would be *somebody*. To have all that snatched away was intolerable. And yet he could say nothing. He must smile and nod and smile some more, and pretend to be happy for his cousin.

Hugo could perhaps salvage something from the disaster, however. His first task, as soon as Connie, Dulcie and their husbands had left and he felt Ernest was beginning to be settled, was to establish the terms under which he and Hope might stay on at the Hall. No further mention had been made of them moving out, and it was clear that Ernest had no idea how to manage his inheritance, so Hugo broached the idea of becoming the agent.

"Naturally it need only be a temporary arrangement if you wish it, just while you find your feet here, cousin," he said to Ernest. "I have had the management of affairs for three years now, so I have a fair idea of how matters go on and what needs to be done. I shall be happy to explain it all to you, but for now perhaps you might prefer a more formal arrangement."

"Oh, if you want to do it, I shall not stop you," Ernest said. He was huddled over the fire in the drawing room, a shawl around his shoulders. "Put another log on, will you? This room is so draughty."

"You might find the winter parlour more congenial," Hugo said. "Or the morning room, perhaps. They are small enough to be made cosy."

"Those are women's rooms," Ernest said loftily. "The book room is where I should be, although... I have no good memories of it. I suppose it has not changed since Papa had it?"

Hugo hesitated, unwilling to relinquish his own domain, but cognisant of Ernest's superior claim to it. "I have made a few changes since I have been using it. You might find it more comfortable." And when Ernest had inspected the room, and chased the dogs out, and examined the view from every window, and declared it not so bad, Hugo felt emboldened to ask, "What sort of salary did you have in mind?"

"Salary? For what purpose?"

"If I am to be agent officially, there should be a salary. Shall we say five hundred a year?" This was a wildly extravagant sum for an agent, but he felt he could not comfortably support Hope on less, and perhaps Ernest would not quibble.

"Why do you need a salary? You are family, you live under my roof, and eat at my table, so I do not see why I should pay you a salary like a servant."

"Very well. I am sure I can find employment elsewhere. There is an estate on the other side of Brinchester that—"

"Two hundred."

"Three."

"Two hundred and fifty, and not a penny more."

"Thank you, cousin, I accept."

It was a reasonable amount, but not such as could support a family, even without the expense of a separate establishment. Hope's dowry, which had always seemed of little consequence, was now become a matter of some import, and he wrote to Mr Plumphett to ask him to discover the amount. The addition of twenty thousand pounds, or perhaps more, if Grace's comments on the subject were accurate, would bring their income to almost a thousand a year, which he supposed they could live on comfortably enough, with care. He was glad now that he had not yet ordered the making of a carriage. A gig would be the most they could afford.

Somehow, he minded the necessary economies less than he might have supposed. Or rather, he minded only for Hope's sake, for he wanted her to have all the new gowns and bonnets and silk stockings her heart desired. Not that she had ever been profligate where money was concerned. Her father had been a tight-fisted man, and his daughters had long ago learned to make do, to patch pelisses and retrim bonnets. Hugo had hoped that his wife could enjoy a more lavish life now.

His wife! The thought made him smile. Every time he caught her eye across the dinner table, or during cards in the long evenings, or in the drawing room receiving guests, she looked a little conscious and his heart skipped a beat. In all his imaginings regarding his future existence as Mr Allamont of Allamont Hall, he had thought only of himself — striding about the house, or galloping here and there to oversee his lands, or driving to evening engagements in his fine new carriage. He had not thought much what it would be like to have a wife. Even when they had stood before Parson Endercott to be united, he had not seen Hope as anything more than a means of achieving his ambition.

Yet now, she was his comfort and his confidante, the friend of his heart, who delighted him every day. So pretty with her shy smile, so warm, so generous — how had he never seen all her good qualities before? She it was who had organised everything after Ernest's arrival. Hugo had been too despondent to consider where they were to sleep, knowing only that they had to move out of the two principal bedrooms. He had supposed that they would have one of the guest bedrooms, or perhaps one of the now empty children's rooms, but Hope had seen at once that it would not do.

"Ernest and Clarissa will want the full use of the house," she had said. "We cannot compromise their arrangements by taking any of the rooms in the main building. Besides, we may be family, but we are not here as guests. You are the agent and I am merely your wife. We will take some of those little rooms above the kitchen. They are hardly ever needed, except when the house is filled to overflowing, which last happened at Connie's wedding, I believe. There is a group of smaller rooms that can be combined to make a suite — a bedroom and dressing room, a sitting room and something that could be a small kitchen, with a little work. Then we could be independent if we wish to be. There is room for a nursery, too, in time." She coloured a little, and he smiled, lifting her hand to his lips.

"Our own little kingdom — that sounds delightful, Mrs Allamont. There is a back stair there, too, so we can come and go without constantly crossing the entrance hall."

"Exactly! And if Ernest wants the book room, you might establish your office in the old gun room. The dogs would be able to go out through the garden door."

"And so would I," he said. "Lord, that room has not been used since old Plumstead retired. What a clever little thing you are, wife."

And she had blushed so prettily at the compliment, that he had felt obliged to cover her rosy cheeks with kisses.

~~~~~

Henry returned home from his foray into Shropshire in an excessively bad temper. That evening was one of his regular engagements to dine at Willowbye with the Burfords, and he almost cried off, but decided in the end that roast mutton and perhaps some pigeon pie would suit him better than cold meat and cheese on a tray in front of the fire. Besides, sitting all alone in the Dower House would do nothing for his temper, but a little company, and the sensible conversation of Belle and John might lift his spirits. So it was that he walked up the drive, well wrapped against the chill autumn air, and was admitted to the house.

It still felt a trifle odd to enter his own house as a visitor, for the Burfords only leased it from him. His finances had been in such a dire state, and the house too, that he had had no choice in the matter. Now the refurbishments had all been completed and the rooms looked exactly as they should, which was very pleasing, but he still felt a pang seeing his own furniture, his pictures and even his servants here. He felt like a schoolboy gazing through the window of a shop, staring longingly at jars of sweets or desirable toys, none of which he could have.

But the Burfords were always very welcoming, and tonight there were interesting new faces, for John's brother, Mr Luke Burford, and his wife were visiting from Market Clunbury, one of the several towns in Shropshire Henry had passed through on his recent visit to the county. Not that he wished to discuss his business there, and so he carefully turned aside all questions on the subject. Now that all his children were settled, he had been minded for a change of scenery, he told them, and having heard the county described in glowing terms, he had decided to make a small tour before the winter set in. Yes, Market Clunbury was indeed a fine little town. No, he had not stayed there long.

"And what brings you away from home at this season?" he politely enquired of Mr Luke Burford as they awaited the summons to dinner, expecting the usual bland responses about visiting family or admiring the baby.

"I have business in Brinchester," he replied. "Indeed, it is business in which you have a keen interest, Mr Allamont, for it concerns the final settlement of the dowries for the Miss Allamonts, a fund which has been under the management of my partner since its inception some years ago. Now that the last of the Miss Allamonts has entered the state of matrimony, the fund is being wound up and the final portion transferred here to the benefit of Mr and Mrs Hugo Allamont."

"Hugo will be very happy to have it, now that his expectations have been reduced," Henry said. "Instead of an income of three thousand a year, he now has no more than five hundred pounds a year, with the allowance I make him and his salary as agent for the Allamont estate. Hope's dowry will bring in another seven or eight hundred a year, I imagine, which will lift them out of poverty."

Mr Luke rubbed at his nose, looking uncomfortable. "Indeed. But there is a small problem, and the blame lies, I regret to say, with my partner, Mr Hillsharrop. Who is also my father-in-law," he added, with a wry glance at his wife.

"You need not scruple to express your opinion on the matter, Mr Burford," she said. "Papa has admitted his fault, and yet I do not quite see what could have been done about it, for how could he know which of the Miss Allamonts would marry, or when?"

"This is all very mysterious," Belle said. "Can you enlighten us, or is it terribly secret?"

"Since you all have an interest in the matter, I will speak plain," Mr Luke said. "In that way, you may appreciate the problem, and advise what, if anything, may be done about it. The fund has the unusual characteristic that it continued to be added to as each month and year passed, and this was not merely the result of investment in the three per cents, which sums would not cause any great difficulty. Each week a sum of two or three hundred was paid into the bank, with the result that the total fund increased by some ten thousand pounds or more with each year that passed."

"This we have known for a long time," his brother said. "It does not materially alter the situation, except that the earlier sisters to marry would receive a smaller sum than the later. Belle received a little more than Amy and a little less than Connie."

"Indeed, but this is the very heart of the difficulty," Mr Luke said. "A little more — a few hundred, perhaps — is of no consequence, but as each sister is removed from the calculation, and the increased amounts are divided into fewer portions, the amount grows alarmingly. Miss Dulcie received somewhat in excess of twenty three thousand, but Miss Grace's portion was thirty five thousand and the sum remaining for Miss Hope is close to fifty thousand."

Henry gasped in amazement. "Fifty thousand! That is enough to allow Hugo to live as a gentleman, even without the salary from Ernest."

Mr Luke said nothing, and it was John Burford who stated the obvious. "Unfortunately, the question naturally arises as to whether such a division is a fair one. Is it right that one sister should receive so much more than the others? Or should the fund be divided equally amongst them, now that the final amount is known."

Henry's pleasure dissipated at once. Of course it was not fair. It was a disappointment, but Hope should not receive so much more than her due.

"But suppose Hope had never married?" Belle said in her calm way. "The fund would have continued to increase over the years to become a great fortune. What would have happened to it then? And besides, most of us do not need the extra money, whereas it will add materially to the comfort of Hope and Hugo."

"You are very perceptive, madam," Mr Luke said, smiling at her. "Mr Hillsharrop and I are of one mind on the subject — the will was excessively badly worded, and the intentions of the deceased are by no means clear. It will not be easy to concoct an equitable arrangement that does not disadvantage Mr and Mrs Hugo."

"I imagine Dulcie and Alex Drummond would also be glad of the income from a few extra thousands," Henry said. "What would the sum be if the entire fund were to be divided equally amongst the girls?"

"Around twenty-eight thousand," Mr Luke said. "But that presents a second difficulty, for Miss Grace — Mrs Graham, I should say — has already received in excess of that sum, and we can hardly ask for it back now. So you see the problem, and understand why I am bound for the office of the Allamont family solicitor in Brinchester to see how we may disentangle this unfortunate affair."

"You will not find Plumphett much help, I fear," Henry said with a smile. "He is a perfectly competent lawyer in his way, but not clever, I should say. Not clever at all. But I assume that Hope's settlement cannot be made until the legal minds have determined the best way forward?"

"I fear you are right," Mr Luke said. "It is most unfortunate, but your son will have to wait a little longer to benefit from his wife's wealth."

The uncertainty of Hugo's prospects distracted Henry for the rest of the evening. Having seen his youngest son married and, as it seemed, prosperously situated, to have the Hall in other hands, Hugo with no more than a salaried post and now even Hope's dowry out of reach for the moment was excessively disappointing. None of his children's lives had quite gone as he had hoped. Mary was advantageously married, but little better than a nursemaid to her sick husband. James, his eldest son who should by rights have married an heiress and restored the family's fortunes, had been forced by imprudent behaviour to marry a farmer's daughter. Mark had got into deep water with a plausible rogue, and was now struggling to make a career for himself as a lowly schoolmaster. And as for Henry himself, he was a widower and quite alone in the world, and that was not his natural state.

But that brought him round to his travels through Shropshire and the Lady Sara Allamont, and by the time he had walked the short distance from Willowbye back to his house, his ill-temper had returned in full force. What was he to do? He could hardly ignore what he had learned, but it may be that she could provide some explanation beyond the obvious. Certainly he must give her the chance to do so.

As soon as he had breakfasted the following morning, he sent for his horse and rode as fast as the muddy fields allowed to Allamont Hall. Outside the Dower House, he jumped to the ground, tossed his horse's reins over a convenient bush and strode to the front door. His impatient ringing and knocking was answered by a familiar face.

"Young? What are you doing here? I thought you were a permanent fixture at the main house."

"Mr Ernest Allamont preferred to engage a new butler, sir."

"Good God! How long have you been at the Hall, Young?"

"It is thirty nine years, sir, since Mrs Walter Allamont engaged me as a page boy at the age of eleven. Were you wishing to see her ladyship, sir? I regret that she is not at home."

"Not at home? She will be at home to me, surely!"

"Her ladyship truly is not at home, sir. I believe you will find her at the Hall."

"Ah. Then I shall go there. Thank you, Young, and I am glad that you are still serving the Allamont family."

"As am I, sir."

Remounting his horse, Henry rode slowly up the drive, much of his anger displaced by confusion over Ernest's actions. What sort of man would dismiss an excellent butler like Young on a whim? It was madness.

The house seemed to be full, despite the early hour. Raucous laughter emanated from the book room as he handed his hat, coat and gloves to the footman — he, at least, had not been displaced.

"I am very pleased to see a familiar face, William," Henry murmured. "You have a new superior, I understand."

"Yes, sir. A Mr Corning from Liverpool, sir."

"And why is he not here to greet arriving visitors?"

William made no reply, merely twitching his head towards the door of the book room, where more masculine laughter could be heard.

"Ah. Where may I find the Lady Sara Allamont?"

"In the book room, sir. Everyone is in the book room. Shall I announce you, sir?"

Henry hesitated. Being family, he was not accustomed to being announced here, although Young had usually insisted if there were morning callers present. But Ernest was almost a stranger, and judging by the noise from the book room, there were those present who might not know Henry, so it was as well to be formal, for once. He nodded his assent and William laid down the outer garments he was holding and threw open the door of the book room.

"Mr Henry Allamont."

13: A Question Of Servants

The room fell silent. Some twenty pairs of eyes turned towards Henry. Heat assaulted him from a roaring blaze in the fireplace. Clustered in the bay window, as far from the raging fire as they could get, he saw Hugo and Hope, Sara, Mr and Miss Endercott and the Amblesides. In the middle of the room, two card tables had been set up where Ernest and a number of men unknown to Henry were engaged in card games. Judging by the money heaped about, they were gambling heavily. His cousin's desk, no doubt too heavy to move elsewhere, had been put to use as an impromptu sideboard, littered with decanters and bottles and used glasses and plates.

Ernest waved cheerfully from the card table, without rising. "Cousin Henry! Good of you to call. Hope, give him a drink."

Hope jumped up, but Henry said, "You have servants to attend to guests, Ernest. You need not call on your sister to wait upon me. Where is your new butler?"

"New butler? Oh, you mean Corning. True, I had forgot you are the butler now, Corning." He slapped one of his gambling cronies on the back. "As you can see, cousin, he is busy here with me. Hope will attend to you, or send for that sour-faced housekeeper. She's always skulking in the kitchens, never around when she's wanted."

"I am sure Mrs Miller has much to attend to below stairs," Henry said. "I will pour my own refreshments, since you have thoughtfully brought half the cellar up here. Goodness, this is a prime vintage. My cousin used to keep this for special occasions only."

"Pruett here wanted to try it," Ernest shrugged. "I like to be hospitable towards my guests."

"And towards your butler, I observe," Henry said, seeing a glass in Corning's hand.

But Ernest had lost interest in the conversation, and turned back to the game. Frowning, Henry turned to the decanters, but Hope was there before him.

"What will you have, Cousin Henry? This is a very good Madeira, worth a try."

"You are not a housemaid, Hope."

"No, indeed, but I am happy to be of service while my brother settles in," she said quietly. "May I pour you something?"

"Certainly not. And it is too hot to breathe in here." He ran a finger inside his collar, his throat already sweating. "This is insupportable."

Abruptly he made for the door, but Hope was there before him, holding it open for him. As he passed through, she closed it behind her.

"It *is* cooler out here," she said. "He will get used to English weather soon enough, I daresay, but just now he is running through the coal supplies rather quickly."

"Who are his gaming chums? Apart from the butler, that is."

"All fellow plantation owners or ship owners, it seems, invited to try out his new establishment. One of them had a wish to try his hand as a butler, and Ernest thought it a very good joke. He thinks everything a good joke."

"You and Hugo should leave here while you can. Once your dowry is settled, Hugo will have a modest competence to support you until he finds employment elsewhere."

"I daresay we will do that in time, but we have decided to stay at least for the winter, for Ernest has not the least idea how to manage an estate like this. He is used to slaves, you know, who may be disposed of however their owner wishes. He is no longer used to the ways of English servants. After Young was dismissed, half the staff would have walked out at once if Hugo and I had not been here. I do not quite like to leave my brother to fend for himself. His wife has landed on English soil, although at Southampton, not Liverpool, for they were diverted by a storm. She is on her way here as we speak. Everything will be more settled with a mistress in the house. It is always so, is it not? Men can never manage so well on their own."

He smiled at this, wondering how it was that the army coped and even thrived without the guiding hand of women, but forbore to tease her on the subject. She was coping very well with the abrupt change in circumstances, and clearly it was her influence which had induced Hugo to accept it so calmly. He had had his doubts about the strength of a marriage founded only on a mutual desire to inherit a handsome estate, but clearly it was working out better than he had dared to hope.

Taking his leave shortly after, he was half way home before he realised that he had not fulfilled the original purpose of his visit, to talk to Sara.

~~~~~

Hope was beginning to be optimistic about the future. The abruptness of the change had been a great shock, but she discovered she had responsibilities now that kept her from repining too greatly about the direness of her future. Ernest and his wife would certainly need her help to adjust to the ways of society, the servants needed her as a steadying influence in a time of turmoil, and Hugo — above all, Hugo needed her to be calm and reassuring. With Mama gone to the Dower House, Hope was mistress of Allamont Hall, a position she quietly enjoyed.

Ernest was not at all what she had expected, but he had lived abroad for some years, and clearly he would adapt to English customs in time. His wife, when she arrived, would be a soothing influence on him, and while they might need to order more coals and restock the wine cellar, by the time the warmer weather arrived, all would be well. They would probably want to spend some months of every year in London, and for that time she and Hugo would be *the* Mr and Mrs Allamont of Allamont Hall.

She wondered greatly about Ernest's wife. Clarissa, her name was, and apart from the plain facts that she had been born on one of the plantations, was rather taller than Hope and was very pretty, she could discover nothing else about her or her family. Whenever she made some polite enquiry, no matter how discreetly worded, Ernest would laugh and shake his head.

"No, no, no, you shall not weasel anything out of me, sister! You must wait until the lady herself arrives, and then all your questions shall be answered.

It was not very satisfactory, but nevertheless, she began to form a picture in her mind of Mrs Ernest Allamont. She would be fair-haired, Hope decided, for she and her sisters were all dark-haired and Hope greatly admired her mother's cool, blonde beauty. Fair hair which curled naturally, and a sweet face peeping out from beneath a wide-brimmed bonnet. The sun in the West Indies would make a wide brim an absolute necessity, so surely all Clarissa's bonnets would be so.

And here was where the picture began to include Hope herself, for it was a certainty that a lady in the West Indies would not have information on the latest fashions. Even if she were a close follower of the London styles, the journals could not reach her for many months, whereas Hope had the benefit of several sisters who went regularly to London and brought back great mounds of journals, and had subscriptions to several of them. So now the picture involved Clarissa and Hope herself, heads bent together over the fashion plates, as Hope gently steered her new sister towards the most elegant style of a sleeve or skirt.

How pleasant it would be to offer the hand of friendship to a lady who would have no idea how to go on in society. She would blush and simper and say coyly, "Oh Hope, what a charming sister you are! What on earth should I do without you?" And Hope would smile and demur and know that whenever the beautiful young Mrs Allamont was admired, it would all be due to Hope's ministrations.

And so the days passed, and more coals were ordered, and replenishments to the wine cellar were sent for, and letters arrived from a series of inns as Clarissa made her ponderous journey north.

~~~~~

Hugo received Mr Plumphett's response to his enquiry about Hope's dowry with some pleasure, but there was just enough oddity in the wording to give him pause. He talked of discussion and matters of interest and approaches to the question, rather than of settlements and transfers of funds. So when he entered Plumphett's office, he was not entirely surprised to see Mr Ambleside, Mr Burford and George Graham there too. And when everything was explained about the unexpected growth of the dowry fund, he could see the force of the argument.

"How disappointing that I should agree with you on the inequitable distribution of the fund," he said with a wry smile. "For I daresay I could have argued the point for some time, had I set my mind to it."

Burford and Graham smiled at this, but Ambleside answered seriously, "For myself, I should have been disappointed had you viewed the matter in any other light. But the question remains as to what is to be done?"

"It seems to me," Burford said, "that several of us do not need any addition to the dowry that was provided at the time. Mrs Burford's jointure was very generous, and I have added somewhat to it, so that she is amply provided for. Mrs Ambleside and the Marchioness of Carrbridge are in the same case, I make no doubt."

"My wife, also, is perfectly well provided for," Graham said. "It is only Drummond who might feel the pinch, and be glad of some extra income. Might we not adjust the amount for Hugo, so that the excess is divided between the two of them?"

Ambleside frowned. "We do not, I feel, have the right to make such a decision. It is a question of what it would be proper to do, which is fair to all parties and yet complies fully with the provisions of the will. It is the greatest pity this outcome was not anticipated from the start and due allowance made for it, instead of trying to thrash out a solution after the event. What does Carrbridge have to say on the matter, Plumphett?"

"His lordship is content to leave the final distribution in my capable hands, if I may quote his lordship's most flattering words," the solicitor said. "Mr Drummond, too, writes that he will accept whatever I deem to be fair."

"Then we can leave it to Mr Plumphett," Graham said, half rising.

"We can *not* so leave it," Ambleside said in quelling tones. "It is for the law to determine what should happen here, not one individual."

"Mr Plumphett, what precisely does the will say?" Hugo said. "Let us start there, and see if perhaps the solution may be clear."

With a rustle of papers, Plumphett produced the document. "Let me see... no, not that passage... where is it? Ah! Here it is. It reads as follows: *'To my daughters, should any survive me and be not yet married, I leave to each the contents of the box engraved with her initial, which boxes may be found in my book room. In addition, from the account...'* And here he gives the details of the account at Market Clunbury. Where was I? Ah, here: *'...one sixth of the total to be given to each on the occasion of her marriage. In order to instil the proper degree of meekness...'* But that part, about the order in which the Miss Allamonts must marry, is no longer relevant to the case."

"One sixth of the total," Hugo said. "But which total? The total at the time of each marriage, or the overall total?"

"It is ambiguous," Burford said with a smile.

"Then we are no further forward," Hugo said gloomily.

~~~~~

The day arrived when Clarissa might be expected to reach her destination. The house had been scrubbed from top to bottom, the servants put on their best uniforms, an unusually good dinner was ordered and Hope positioned herself in the morning room, where the window seat overlooking the drive would give her the earliest intimation of the arrival. Yet the hours ticked away, one by one, and darkness fell with no sign of the lady. A second day passed in the same way, and a third.

But then, finally, an enormous travelling coach lumbered up the drive, and behind it a second almost as large, then a third, smaller, vehicle, and at the rear no fewer than four wagons filled with boxes of all shapes and sizes, and even items of furniture shrouded in sacking. The servants took up their positions to greet their new mistress, while Hope and Hugo waited at the top of the steps as William rushed out to open the door of the coach. Of Ernest, his friends and the new butler there was no sign.

They all stood in the blustery wind for some time before anyone emerged from the coach. William, holding the door, was motionless. Voices could be heard from within, as if some debate were underway, and Hope wondered briefly if Clarissa would decide that she did not like the look of the place and drive away again.

But then a figure appeared, wreathed from head to foot in heavy furs, the head so swathed that only a tiny bit of the lady's face could be discerned. She stood at the foot of the coach steps, so close that the other occupants could not themselves descend, and stared up at the porticoed frontage of the house. For some time, she stayed thus.

Hope looked at Hugo, but he merely shrugged. At length, fearing for everyone's health if they could not soon escape from the penetrating wind, Hope descended the entrance steps and crossed the drive to the coach.

"Clarissa? Welcome to Allamont Hall. I am—"

"Where is Ernest?" Her voice wavered slightly, then she added more firmly, "Why is he not here to greet me?"

"He has been sent for. I am sure he will be here directly. Will you not come into the house to warm yourself?"

"Nowhere is warm in this God-forsaken country."

"But the inside of the house is warmer than the outside, and we shall all freeze to death if we stand about in this wind much longer."

Perhaps the sharpness of the tone registered, for she turned fully towards Hope then, her dark eyes looking her up and down. Without a word, Clarissa began to move towards the house, although very slowly, as if she could hardly lift her feet to place one in front of the other.

To Hope's relief, Ernest and several of his friends emerged from the house.

"Clarry!" Ernest yelled, and leapt down the steps to meet her, sweeping her off her feet and swinging her round. "At last! Whatever took you so long? The roads are not so bad, surely?"

"The roads are bad, the inns are bad, everything is bad in this miserable country of yours. The books I have read missed out a great deal, I feel — they talk about roads and populations and taxes and kings, but they do not mention that the entire country is axle deep in mud. Is this your house, Ernie? Truly? Must we stay here? It looks so dreary and dismal."

"It is quite comfortable inside, I assure you. Come on in. My father kept an indifferent cellar, but there are a few decent bottles to keep us going until the vintner's cart gets here."

From the coach emerged three more figures, a black man and woman, with the look of high-ranked servants, and a small black child, with the sweetest face imaginable.

"Oh, you have a little black page boy!" Hope cried. "How charming!"

Ernest turned to her, his face expressionless.

"That is my son, Edward."

14: Ladies

As soon as they were all indoors, and Clarissa had loosened the furs around her head a little, Hope could see that all her imaginings about her new sister-in-law were false. Clarissa was mulatto, with black hair curling abundantly around her face in the most entrancing way. She was quite the most ravishingly beautiful woman Hope had ever seen, and she entirely understood why Ernest had married her.

Clarissa wanted neither tea nor coffee nor food, but a glass of Madeira brought a smile to her lips and the blazing fire in the book room made her sigh with pleasure. Ernest brought a chair almost to the hearth for her, and she half reclined there, still in her furs, glass in hand, gazing about the room.

"This is not so terrible after all. What do we eat tonight? You have promised me the best of English food, Ernie, so I expect something extraordinary. Where is that housekeeper? You there!" she said, her eye falling on Hope. "What is for dinner?"

"Goose, duck, pheasant and pork, but I am not—"

"Pheasant! I have never had pheasant in my life! That will be interesting. And something sweet, I trust. I am very fond of fruit."

"Apple pie and apricots, but—"

"No pineapple, I suppose." She sighed deeply. "I daresay I shall never taste pineapple again. More wine."

She waved her glass at Hope, but with a frown and a shake of his head, Hugo stayed her impulse to comply. He fetched the decanter himself.

"There you are, Mrs Allamont. May I be permitted to introduce myself? I am Hugo Allamont, cousin to your husband and agent here. The lady over there is my wife, and your husband's sister, Hope. The housekeeper, Miller, is standing by the door."

His voice was level, but there was an edge of anger flashing in his eyes that made Hope rather proud. How pleasant to have a husband ready to spring to her defence at the slightest insult! Not that she had minded, for it was a natural mistake to make, but Clarissa should have waited to be formally introduced before jumping to conclusions. Had she come straight into the house, as any normal person would have done in such inclement weather, there would have been leisure for the proprieties.

Clarissa's eyes followed as he pointed out the two women. For a moment she seemed nonplussed, but, catching sight of Ernest sniggering behind his hand, she started to laugh too. "Oh dear! You are affronted because I mistook your wife for the housekeeper. I beg your pardon! And hers, of course. But when she dresses like such a dowd you cannot be surprised at it. Why does she wear a cap if she is not a servant?"

"She is a married woman, and that is the custom here," Hugo said stiffly, eyebrows raised.

But Clarissa and her husband laughed long and hard at this strange idea.

The three coaches had disgorged some dozen servants, in addition to Clarissa and her son, not to mention the coachmen, postilions and grooms, several of whom were in Clarissa's employ and not merely hired for the journey. Two of the coaches also were hers, and there was a great deal of furniture to be disposed about a house already amply supplied. Since none of this had been communicated in advance, despite the many letters flying back and forth between husband and wife, a great deal of disruption was caused to the servants in unloading the goods, arranging suitable accommodation for people, coaches and horses alike, and managing the feeding of the same.

Hope was kept busy with Miller and Mrs Cooper, the cook, soothing their agitation and trying to find a way to settle the new arrivals with the minimum of fuss. Fortunately, the drive being visible from the Dower House, and the number of vehicles arriving and the smaller number departing being likewise visible, Lady Sara had sent most of her household to help out with the sudden influx. The newcomers, too, proved helpful, although inclined to stand about the corridors chattering excitedly unless directed. But Hope soon found that if she told them what to do, they set about it willingly enough.

With so much bustle, it was late in the afternoon before Hope had a chance to change her dress and attend to Ernest and Clarissa. She found them in the drawing room this time, a rather overheated room, with the fire blazing away. Ernest, his wife and his friends were at the card tables, and now that the furs had been cast aside, Hope could see that Clarissa's gown was of the first stare of fashion, no doubt wildly expensive.

Meanwhile Lady Sara, the Amblesides and a bemused Lady Graham with her two daughters, Alice and Joan, sat neglected on the other side of the room. Mr Ambleside's face looked as stormy as a thundercloud. He was a great stickler for protocol, and would not overlook such discourtesy. Hugo was nowhere to be seen. William was in attendance, since the supposed butler was playing cards. The child was engaged in carrying decanters of wine and brandy to the players, to their great entertainment.

Amy smiled to see Hope, and waved her across to the seat beside her. "How are you coping?" she whispered. "Six coaches, I hear, and a score of servants."

Mrs Graham moved to sit on Hope's other side. "Where is your butler today? Not ill, I hope, at such a moment?"

Hope tried to explain, but it was difficult to account for something which she did not herself understand. It was fortunate that some twist of the game led Clarissa to throw down her cards and rise from the table. Looking round at the guests as if seeing them for the first time, she lifted her little boy into her arms and swayed languidly across the room, a smile playing about her lips.

"So many visitors," she said. "Have you come to see me?"

Hope jumped to her feet. "Clarissa, allow me to make everyone known to you. Mama, this is Ernest's wife. Clarissa, this is—"

"*Lady* Clarissa," called Ernest from the card table.

Hope's hand shot to her mouth in dismay. "Oh, I am so sorry! I had no idea your father was titled. Pray forgive me. Perhaps I should have introduced Mama to you, then?"

Lady Sara, never at a loss in society, smiled. "Let us not worry too much about the nuances of introductions, since we are both family. I am Ernest's mother, Lady Clarissa. How do you do."

Hope moved on from this tricky meeting of ladies as quickly as she could. "May I introduce Lady Graham to you, Lady Clarissa. Sir Matthew is a near neighbour of ours in the village. This is Miss Graham, and Miss Joan Graham. Lady Clarissa Allamont."

"Welcome to Lower Brinford, Lady Clarissa," Lady Graham said. "What a charming little boy you have. May you all be very happy here."

Clarissa looked them over in silence. Her eye settled on Alice, the older daughter. "She is very pale," she said to Lady Graham. "Such white skin, such yellow hair, and far too thin. A great shame. Not the fashion these days, is it not so?"

"My daughters have more to recommend them than mere looks," Lady Graham said at once. "They are most accomplished."

Clarissa tittered. "Looks are better for getting a husband than painting or embroidery. Do you imagine I would have been of interest to Ernest if I looked like that? No, men like a bit of colour, and a bit of flesh, too, and none of them care if a woman can decorate a screen."

Lady Graham went puce but was too polite to answer.

"Do come and meet another of Ernest's sisters," Hope said quickly, tugging at Clarissa's still fur-clad arm. "May I present to you Mr and Mrs Ambleside, of Higher Brinford. Amy is the eldest of all of us, Lady Clarissa."

"How lovely to meet you at last, Lady Clarissa," Amy said with her gentle smile. "You must forgive us for knowing nothing at all about you, for Ernest has told us not a thing. Pray excuse our rudeness in not appreciating your rank."

"Civility works both ways," Mr Ambleside said, his face not welcoming at all. "It is the height of bad manners to conceal your rank, and thus allow those who wish you well to fall into humiliating error. Even now, we do not know who your father is."

"Does it matter?" she said sulkily.

Hope gasped at the ignorance contained in that simple question, and she saw the shock on the faces of the others.

"*Does it matter?*" Ambleside repeated, his voice rising. "Of course it matters! How else is anyone to know how to address you correctly? Why, you may meet people in society to whom you are related, with no one will be any the wiser. I must insist on knowing the name and rank of your father."

"It is just a courtesy title," she said, holding the child a little tighter. "You make such a *fuss* about such a small thing."

"Well, of course it is a courtesy title, for very few ladies hold titles in their own right. At least inform us as to whether your father is a duke or a marquess or an earl."

Hope, beginning to understand, leaned across Amy to murmur to Mr Ambleside, "I believe my sister-in-law means that it is just an amusing epithet, and not a matter of rank."

"Then she has no business to employ it," he said haughtily. "Whatever may be the custom in the colonies, in this country we respect the time-honoured traditions of high rank and the rules of entitlement. Come, Mrs Ambleside, we have stayed long enough. Good day to you, Lady Sara. Lady Graham. Miss Graham. Miss Joan. Pray give my good wishes to your husband, Mrs Allamont." Then, to Hope, he said, "Will you be so good as to see us out, Mrs Allamont?"

In the entrance hall, William scuttling behind them to fetch coats and hats, they stood in silence until the footman had gone off to order the carriage to be brought round.

"This is awkward for you, Mrs Allamont," Mr Ambleside said. "Nothing here is as it ought to be. If you should wish to leave, for any reason, you may be sure of a safe haven with us."

"Oh yes, you may stay with us for as long as you want," Amy added. "For I do not think Ernest and his wife are quite the thing."

"Far from it," her husband said. "Ernest is a gentleman by birth, but his wife..." He frowned, hesitating. "I did not at all believe that she could bear a title. She is mulatto, and although there are many such in society, they are generally natural children. We would surely have heard if any peer of the realm had married a negress. It was quite wrong in her to give herself airs in that way. I cannot abide such presumption."

"No indeed," Amy said. "It was very bad of her to pretend to be titled."

"I do not think she quite knows how to go on in English society," Hope said. "It must all be so strange to her."

"Then she should display some humility," Mr Ambleside snapped. "Or her husband should teach her. I do not like to leave you here, exposed to their odd ways."

"You are very kind," Hope said. "We must stay for the winter, at least, I believe. We cannot simply abandon them, and there are the servants to consider, too. "

"Hmm. As you wish, but do not hesitate if things get difficult. Mrs Ernest Allamont must be the recipient of good will at present, but unless she learns the ways of society very quickly she is liable to find herself friendless, and then she may work out her displeasure on you and your husband. So have a care."

~~~~~

When the visitors had gone, and Clarissa had drifted back to the card tables with the child on her knee, Hope found Hugo in his new office, hard at work on the accounts. She liked the way he had fitted out the room, with his desk under the window, but a pair of chairs beside the fire, too, and some rugs for comfort. It was a small, plain room, but with the addition of some wood panelling and a few pictures, it would be very cosy. When he saw her, he tossed down his pen, and ran his hands through his hair.

"Can you believe it?" he said. "So many extra servants! And the horses! Have you any idea how many pecks of oats and trusses of hay a horse needs per week in the winter? They sit in those stables, with nothing at all to do, eating their heads off."

"The estate can afford it, surely? You have always insisted that we needed more servants — a second footman, another housemaid and scullery maid, and at least two more gardeners, or so you said only a few weeks ago."

"Oh indeed, we do need more, but acquired slowly, here and there, not all at once, and with not the least idea of what work they might be capable of. And there is no necessity for so many coach horses, for no one can use so many carriages all at once, not in the usual way. Nor do we need so many travelling coaches. One is enough, and something smarter for paying morning calls or going to Brinchester, but one set of horses would do for both, you know. And lately Ernest has been making noises about a hunter and a hacking horse, and if *she* wants to ride, too, that will be a great deal of expense."

"It is his estate now, and if he wants to spend his money that way, he may do so, I suppose. He has three thousand a year, after all. He *ought* to live in some style."

"Two thousand eight hundred," Hugo said automatically, then, as Hope giggled, he added, "What is so funny?"

"You always say that — whenever anyone says *'three thousand'*, you say *'no, it is only two thousand eight hundred'*, as if it is vastly different."

"It will do no good, however great his income is, if he is planning to feed an army of extra servants and horses, not to mention the consumption of coal and wine. And above all, it is outrageous to do all this without the slightest notice, not a word so that we might have prepared adequately, and he must have known for weeks. It is too bad of Ernest, truly it is. But he sees no difficulty! He says blithely that it is a large house, as if the walls might expand and the number of rooms multiply overnight to accommodate all his friends and his wife's servants. If they *are* all servants, for who can tell? They have no proper uniforms, or any sense of hierarchy. It is the outside of enough! We are doing our best for him, but he is not helping, not in the slightest."

Hope could see that he would run on in this vein for some time, arms waving wildly. She hated it when he became so agitated, for he never seemed to know when to stop, and accept the situation in resignation. Instead, he *would* rant about it, working himself up into a lather of indignation that lasted for days, sometimes. It unnerved her, and she knew of only one way to settle him.

"Shhh," she said, bending down over his chair to put her arms around him and kiss the top of his head. "Do not let him make you angry, for I am sure he finds that very humorous. Everything is a great joke to him."

"He is too frivolous by far," Hugo said, but his tone was calmer.

"I know. He will begin to appreciate the importance of his position in society in time, by your example."

She kissed the top of his head again, and then, finding him compliant, his forehead and nose and mouth. He smiled then, lifting his face to hers, and reaching with one hand to play with a stray curl that fell over her cheek. "Ah, my little wife, come and sit on my knee so that I may kiss you properly."

She was very happy to comply, and for a while no words were spoken, and the only sound was the gentle crackle of the fire, and the tick of a small clock on the mantel. Even the dogs were quiet, dozing in front of the fire.

"What do you think of her?" he said after a while.

"Clarissa? She has not been here above four hours. I may perhaps have formed an opinion of her by Christmas."

"Hmm. It seems to me that people reveal their innermost natures very soon, even when they try to hide behind a mask of goodness," he said seriously. "Which she does not, at all. You must surely have been shocked by her manners, or rather, her lack of them."

"It would be unkind to make an instant judgement of someone who has been torn away from her home, and forced to journey, entirely alone, through a country quite alien to her. I make allowances, for now."

"Not *entirely* alone," he said, pointing to his list of the servants she had brought with her. "You are all generosity, Hope, but confess it, for all she is married to a gentleman, Clarissa is no lady."

She laughed, telling him the story of *'Lady Clarissa'*, but he saw no humour in it.

"I am entirely with Ambleside on the point," he said, his face darkening. "She is as bad as Ernest for not taking anything seriously. One cannot call oneself whatever one wishes. It is just as well that she has been corrected at the outset, for think how awkward it would be to introduce her all around the neighbourhood as Lady Clarissa, and have everyone bowing and curtsying to her, and then to find out it was no such thing!"

"It was awkward enough as it was, for I was in the middle of introducing her to Mama, and then I did not know whether I ought to be introducing Mama to *her*. It was very distressing. I was quite at a loss, for I needed to know if she was the daughter of a duke or a marquess, and therefore outranked Mama, and if she were an earl's daughter, I should have needed to find her father in Debrett's to see if his title was older than Grandpapa's. So perplexing! Fortunately, Mama was equal to it, and managed it very tactfully. I thought Mr Ambleside was quite rude at first, when he insisted on knowing who her father was, but he was perfectly right, it turns out."

"And who *is* her father?" Hugo said. "One of the plantation owners, I expect, and I am very sure he never married her mother. It is not uncommon in the West Indies, so I have heard. The mulatto children are treated well by their fathers, just as natural children often are here, and settled in respectable trades and useful occupations. Some are raised as ladies and gentlemen."

"That is true," Hope said. "Connie has seen several mulatto ladies in town, and they are just as fashionable and accomplished and well-educated as any other lady. Clarissa is certainly fashionable and educated, and her accent is very good, with only an occasional word wrong. And she is very beautiful, I think."

"I daresay, but beauty is not the primary prerequisite for the mistress of an establishment such as this. Her manners leave a great deal to be desired."

"She was very rude about Alice Graham, too, and that I do *not* condone," Hope said. "Clarissa will need the support of people like Lady Graham if she is to establish herself creditably here, and insulting her daughter is not the way to achieve that. Although Alice *is* very thin and pale," she added fairly.

He laughed at that, and gave her a squeeze. "You are very calm about all this, little wife. You were so worried about the possibility of Ernest appearing at the last minute, yet now that he has, you are not weeping and wailing, as might be expected." He nuzzled her neck gently. "I am very proud of you."

The compliment made her glow with pride, but she lowered her head diffidently. "I suppose now that the worst has happened, there is not much left to worry about. Being married makes a difference, though. I have you to think about now, and therefore I cannot spare so much thought for Ernest and Clarissa. I am very afraid of what will happen to us, that cannot be denied, for everything is uncertain, but whatever the future brings, we will face it together."

He stroked her face gently, smiling at her. "I like being married to you, Hope. You are warm and generous and kind and thoughtful and, no matter how bad everything seems, you always make me feel better. You are everything a wife should be, and I am a very lucky man."

He pulled her close for another kiss.

15: Paying Calls

The first evening with Clarissa was the strangest Hugo could ever recall. The new butler seemed to have no idea of his duties, and sat in the drawing room before dinner with Ernest. When they went through to the dining room, he helped to hand round the soup, to the great amusement of his friends, and then took his place at the table in the manner of any regular guest. Fortunately, William had brought in a couple of grooms to act as extra footmen, which concealed any deficiency.

By some quirk of the seats, Hugo found himself sitting next to Ernest, and having had little opportunity to talk to him socially, he now began to ask the questions that burned in his mind. One of his greatest curiosities was to discover, if he could, what had caused the quarrel between Ernest and Frank, a quarrel so violent and final that Ernest had resorted to forcing his brother aboard a ship. But Ernest's face darkened to an angry red when Frank's name was mentioned.

"Him!" he said, throwing down his fork. "You will not talk to me of that man, not if you have any compassion for my feelings. He betrayed me utterly, and although it worked out well for me in the end, his action was still most foul. But he has paid for his wickedness, for he is dead now, and serve him right!"

Hugo could not hide his surprise at this, so very different from the story he had heard from Frank himself, who was very much alive.

"Ah, you may well look shocked," Ernest went on, mistaking Hugo's reaction. "We were so close as boys. No two brothers could ever have been closer, and even though we were never alike in looks or wit — poor Frank was second in those areas, as in age, being the younger by ten minutes or so — still, I regarded him as my closest and dearest friend. But in Liverpool, he was drawn into bad company. I am ashamed to say such things of a brother, but he frequented the gaming hells with the sole intent of defrauding honest players of their money by sharp practices. I did everything I could to deter him, and to prevent him from employing his nefarious techniques, and he grew angry with me."

Here he was distracted by the appearance of the pheasant, and for several minutes he was engaged in shouting down the table to his wife at the far end, encouraging her to try it and shrieking with laughter as she pulled a face and declared it to be the foulest meat she had ever eaten. Then all the others had to try it too, and a lively discussion ensued between those who thought it divine and worthy of the King's own table, and those who thought it fit only for the pigswill. In the end, Ernest ordered it sent back to the kitchen, together with another dish that had failed to please Clarissa. It was some time before Hugo could attract Ernest's attention again.

"You were telling me about Frank, and his evil ways," he said, as soon as an opportunity arose.

"Was I? So I was! Well then, I had always had it in mind that we should go to sea, for that would have been the greatest adventure, as it seemed to my boyish self. But in Liverpool we heard so many dire tales of the misfortunes likely to befall even the best of ships, that we decided not to risk it. Then the next idea was that we would go into cotton, and perhaps establish a mill or two, for Lancashire is a perfect place for spinning and weaving of all varieties, and Aunt Lucy had associates who would have helped us get a foothold. But that would not do for Frank. His cheating ways were too profitable for him to give up. In the end I wore him down, and he agreed to it, or so I thought. But the night before we were to leave, he took me out to the theatre to celebrate, and as we made our way home, we were set upon by his cronies, who kidnapped me and carried me away to a ship which immediately set sail for the West Indies."

"Good God!" Hugo said. "But how do you know that the dreadful deed was executed by Frank's cronies? It could have been any group of villains, surely?"

"Any normal group of villains would have taken both of us, which these did not. No, it was all arranged by Frank, with the complicity of Aunt Lucy, for I discovered later that the mill to which she planned to send us did not exist. Frank was ever her favourite, for he followed her lead in everything. They wanted to get me out of the way so that Frank could continue their wicked ways, and if I had died on the journey I daresay it would have been all the same to him. It is a dreadful feeling to be betrayed by your own brother, Hugo."

"I can well imagine it. But you said that Frank died? You went back to Liverpool to look for him, then?"

"Not at all. I discovered that sea travel was just as uncomfortable and dangerous as I had feared, so when I arrived safely in the West Indies, my gratitude was so great that I swore never to leave again, nor did I until this year. I moved here and there, and eventually settled on Jamaica. But I had many friends there, amongst them a number of ship's captains who plied back and forth to Liverpool, so I was able to make enquiries through them. Frank had cheated once too often, it seemed, for a customer pulled a knife on him one day and took revenge for his losses. Frank is dead, and just as well for him, for if I had ever met him again, I should have killed him myself."

Hugo was too discomfited to make any response, and Ernest turned back to his friends.

Later, when Ernest and Clarissa were established for a night at the card tables, Hugo returned with Hope to their little apartment, and there, settled in front of their own fire with cups of tea, he told her the story.

"Is it possible we were deceived?" he said to her. "Perhaps Frank truly is dead, and we were taken in by a clever impostor."

"One who answered all the test questions?" she said. "Impossible! It could only have been Frank."

"Yet you did not recognise him."

"He was always the nondescript one, the one no one remembered," she said, thoughtfully. "Ernest was much more memorable — no one could forget that nose! He was very much the leader of the two, always first into whatever mischief they got up to. Although to be sure, it was Frank who was the inventive mind behind most of their schemes, yet everyone assumed it was Ernest. He got the credit, but he also got the blame, and he never could lie convincingly, whereas Frank could say the sky was green and everyone would believe him. His face was all innocence, with just a hint of being hurt that you would even consider questioning his word. Frank got away with a great deal."

"Then he is well-cast as a card sharp, if that is what he is," Hugo said. "For myself, I think that more likely than this talk of making sure the customers are not cheating the club. He has drawn a handsome picture of himself as a respectable man of business, but gaming dens are always on the take, if you ask me."

"It is Papa's naming curse at work," Hope said, giggling. "We are all named for virtues, but we each turned out to be quite the opposite. Amy is supposed to be so amiable, but she was so shy that she never said a word, or else panicked and was rude to people. Belle — poor Belle! — was hardly the beauty her name implied. Connie should be the faithful, constant one, yet she could never make up her mind about anything. And as for not-so-sweet Dulcie! And then Grace is so clumsy, and I am always worrying, and anything but hopeful. Now we know that Frank is a liar and a cheat, and Ernest is not at all serious. He thinks life is nothing but a joke provided for his entertainment."

"Well, I was named after one of Mama's brothers, who was a dreadful wastrel, by all accounts," Hugo said. "Life is a great deal easier when nothing very much is expected of one."

~~~~~

Hope was afraid that Clarissa would not like the idea of paying morning calls on their neighbours, and expected that she would have to work hard to convince her of the necessity. To her surprise, Clarissa was eager to participate.

"Oh, I want to be a real English lady, so of course I must pay calls. You may tell me who we should go to see, and when we must stay at the house to receive callers in our turn. We did something of the sort at home, you know, although it was not quite so formal, and the hours were different. We would go out in the early morning, and then be back home before noon to avoid the worst of the heat. But here it will take me hours, I daresay, to wrap myself in enough furs to keep out the frost."

"The weather is quite mild at the moment," Hope said.

But Clarissa laughed loudly at this. "Mild? What a divine sense of humour you have, my dear. Mild? There was ice on the inside of my window this morning. Ice! On the inside!"

Hope said nothing more, but she wondered how Clarissa was to get through the winter if she thought a crisp autumn morning anything extraordinary.

On several days each week, therefore, one of Clarissa's huge carriages was called into service, and Clarissa, Hope and

Lady Sara drove out into the countryside to pay calls on the gentry in their part of Brinshire.

All Hope's fears regarding the unfashionable nature of Clarissa's gowns were quite swept away. Every day she emerged from her room attired in the first style of fashion, as if she had stepped directly from the pages of one of the London journals, and Hope felt like a country dowd beside her. And yet she could not quite understand how it was that a lady from such a hot climate could have so many woollen dresses and tweed pelisses and fur-lined muffs.

"Did you buy some clothes in Southampton?" she asked one day, as they bounced over the frost-hardened ruts in the road. "For these are too warm for the West Indies, I suspect."

Clarissa laughed, a deep, fruity laugh that made her whole body quiver. She was a generously-proportioned woman, with a shapely figure that slender Hope could only envy. "I bought myself a seamstress in Southampton," Clarissa said. "I told her I wanted to be as well-dressed as any great English lady, and she chose the materials and made everything as we travelled north."

"She sewed in the coach?" Hope squeaked, astonished.

"Sometimes, if it was work that needed no great precision, like hemming. But we would stop for a day or two here and there, for travel is so fatiguing, is it not? And then she would be working away, stitch, stitch, stitch, and so each garment was made."

"Ah, so that is why your journey was so slow," Hope said. "How clever of you!"

Lady Sara gazed out of the carriage window and said nothing.

If Clarissa had taken great pains to look the part of a lady, she took less trouble to behave that way. She would stride into a room without waiting to be introduced and hold out her hand to everyone there as if she were an intimate friend of many years' standing instead of a newcomer. Then she would sit and make the most blatant comments about the room, pointing out deficiencies and offering advice about improvements, until Hope was quite crushed with mortification. Once or twice Hope had tentatively tried to offer a hint, but Clarissa had laughed and said that Ernest liked her to be herself and not be shy in company, and there was no use arguing with the wishes of a lady's husband.

Sometimes Ernest went with them, and that was, if anything, worse, for he laughed uproariously at everything his wife said, and would turn to his nearest neighbour and whisper, "Is she not wonderful? No false praise from my Clarissa. She says exactly what she thinks."

But no one quite liked to cut her, so the calls were returned and dinner invitations issued and everyone treated her as they would any other newcomer to the neighbourhood, although Hope could only imagine the comments they made about Mr and Mrs Ernest Allamont when they were alone.

When the time came for the first assembly since her arrival, Clarissa was wild to go. Ernest having no desire to deny his wife any pleasure that the county could afford, the subscription was paid, hotel rooms booked for Ernest and his wife and all their many friends, and the number of carriages to be employed calculated.

The day before, when Hugo was explaining the disposition of hotel rooms, Clarissa said, "But what about Jacob? Where is he to sleep?"

"Jacob?" Hugo said. "Who is Jacob? I thought we had all Ernest's friends accounted for."

"Jacob is one of the servants," Hope said. "The big, handsome fellow. He is a groom, I believe."

"He is *not* a groom," Clarissa said haughtily. "He is my brother."

Hope's hands flew to her mouth in horror. "Oh no! But he has been housed in the servants' quarters! How dreadful! I am so sorry, Clarissa, I had no idea."

Hugo tutted in annoyance. "Well, of course you had no idea, for no one informed us of Jacob's rank or the correct level of accommodation for him," he said. "How on earth are we supposed to know? We have no power to divine these things, Mrs Allamont. We depend upon you and Ernest to inform us of the appropriate arrangements."

Ernest had been struggling not to laugh throughout this exchange. "You people make so much *fuss* over these things. Jacob is only Clarissa's half-brother. He is a slave, Hugo, or he was in Jamaica — I suppose he is a free man here — but even so, the servants' quarters are plenty good enough for him. But he is a great dancer, and always attends the dances and balls at home. He is a great favourite with the ladies, as you may imagine, a fine, strong man like that. We have promised to take him to this assembly of yours, so I am sure you will squeeze him in somewhere. He can share with the valets, for I am sure it is of no consequence to him."

"It might be of consequence to the valets, however," Hugo said at once. "Whatever Jacob's relationship with Mrs Allamont, and however he was treated in the West Indies, here he is a groom, and grooms do *not* dance at assemblies. If he goes to this assembly, he goes as a groom, and sleeps over the stables with all the other grooms, and he does *not* participate in the dancing."

"He is *not* a groom, and he wants to dance," Clarissa said. "How stuffy you are, Hugo! I will not have my brother treated as if he is nobody!"

"If he is not nobody, then he must be somebody," Hugo cried. "By all means let him come to the assembly and dance and be a gentleman, but we must treat him that way here, too. He must have a bedroom in the house, and he must dress like a gentleman, and have a valet to attend him, and he must take his meals with the family and not with the servants. Everyone must have his proper place in society, Mrs Allamont, or we shall have anarchy and chaos and civilisation will collapse."

Ernest and Clarissa shrieked with laughter, but Ernest said, "Have it your way, Hugo. Let Jacob be a gentleman, if that is your wish. For we would not wish to be responsible for the collapse of civilisation, would we?"

And they laughed so hard that tears squeezed from their eyes, and no sense could be got out of either of them.

16: The Card Room

Hope generally enjoyed the monthly assemblies at Brinchester, and as she had been too busy at the Hall to attend the last two, she was especially looking forward to this one. Or she would have been, if only she could quell her worries over Ernest and Clarissa.

"Clarissa has not the least idea how to go on," she had wailed to Hugo. "She will tell all the ladies how badly they are dressed, criticise the number of chandeliers or supper dishes, and I cannot bear to think what she might say about the dancing. I like a forthright person as much as anyone, but a little discretion never went amiss. And as for Ernest—"

"No need to worry about him," Hugo had said quickly. "I shall introduce him in the card rooms, and he will spend the evening there, and his friends with him. We might even get Clarissa to play, if she tires of the dancing. They will be safe enough in there, you know."

So Hope had tried to set aside her fears. On the tedious journey to Brinchester, the huge coach crawling through axle-deep mud all the way to the turn-pike road, Clarissa chattered away excitedly to no one in particular. Ernest laughed greatly at every remark, from time to time patting his wife's knee and saying, "You will enjoy it excessively, Clarry, and you will outshine all the other ladies, I know it." Lady Sara, Hugo and Hope said nothing at all.

The other occupant of the coach, the former groom, Jacob, now resplendent in the attire of a gentleman, was equally silent, an enigmatic smile playing about his lips. He was a fine looking man, Hope conceded, tall and well built, the immaculately tailored coat fitting him as closely as a glove, and his breeches clinging to shapely legs. Unlike the softer colouring of his sister, Jacob was a full negro, his skin the colour of burnished mahogany, his countenance most pleasing. He carried his transformation lightly, his manners at dinner the night before such as would meet with approval anywhere. Hope wondered at his wishing to play the role of groom, but perhaps that was merely a natural diffidence about mingling in good society.

Another cause for satisfaction on Hope's part emerged as her maid dressed her for the evening. This was her first opportunity to wear one of the new ball gowns provided for her marriage, and she would not have been human had she not smiled to see herself in the glass.

"You look very beautiful, madam," Flora said.

Hope blushed, but answered composedly, "You have turned me out very well, Flora. I like this way you have with my hair."

"It is her ladyship who chose this headdress, and the gown, too, madam. Her ladyship has excellent taste."

"True, and she took the greatest interest in all my wedding clothes, far more than with my sisters. But it is very nice not to be confined to pale colours, or simple muslins and silks. This gown is the most ravishing colour. I adore it."

"That shade of blue sets off your beauty to perfection, madam."

Such a conversation could not fail to send Hope off for the evening in the most pleasant frame of mind, which happy state was increased when she saw the look of frank admiration in Hugo's eyes.

"Well, Mrs Allamont, you will set the assembly rooms on fire tonight. How delightfully you look! Shall we go down to dinner?"

And he offered her his arm, the light in his eyes easy to read as he gazed at her.

As soon as they reached the hotel dining room, Hope's pleasure was somewhat diminished by the sight of Clarissa in the most exquisite dress of gold thread, which shimmered as she moved in an entrancing way. With her hair and ears and throat likewise laden with gold, she looked like a princess.

"How lovely she is!" she said impulsively to Hugo.

He shrugged. "Overdressed, if you ask me. *You* are the prettiest woman here."

Which made her blush all over again.

Their party was the gayest in the room. At one end of the table, Ernest and his friends paid noisy court to Clarissa, designating her their queen for the night and addressing her, with much laughter, as 'your majesty'. At the other, Hope and Hugo were joined by Amy, Belle, Grace and Mary, and various members of their families, making a lively party. Only Sir Osborne Hardy was absent, too ill to attend. Between the two groups, Jacob sat eating his dinner stolidly without conversation.

The night was cold but dry, so most of the party walked the short distance to the assembly rooms. Only one or two of the ladies, fearful of the freezing night air, took sedan chairs. They had taken so long over dinner that the assembly rooms were already crowded, the dancing well underway. Hugo, as he had promised, whisked Ernest and his cronies off to the card rooms, while Hope was immediately invited to dance by one of her former admirers, his face alight with pleasure. As they danced, he watched her with such intensity that she was almost tempted to laugh, except that it would have been abominably rude.

"You were very much missed at the assembly last month, Mrs Allamont," he said. "The room was a little less bright without your presence, and the dancing much less pleasing to the eye."

He had always talked such nonsense, and when she had been unmarried and trying very gently to discourage him, she had found it difficult to answer him at all. If she adopted the same tone, he might think she was flirting with him, yet she could not quite bring herself to be direct. Now, knowing herself to be protected from his unwanted attentions, it was easy to smile and say lightly, "Why, Mr Mann, are you trying to get up a flirtation with a married woman? I wonder what my husband would say about that?"

And he laughed and answered in the same jocular tone, and it was all pleasantly enjoyable, and perfectly safe, because there could be no impassioned declarations of love, no embarrassing offers to be tactfully refused and no tears afterwards at the thought of hurt feelings and disappointment. She could at last savour the gentle compliments and admiring glances, knowing they meant nothing. And at the end of the evening, there would be Hugo by her side to escort her home and keep her warm during the long, cold night. So she danced and smiled and flirted just a little, and was glad she was a married woman now.

~~~~~

Hugo took longer than he had anticipated to settle Ernest and his friends into the card rooms. There were introductions to be made, and then, not unnaturally, the gentry and burghers of Brinchester wanted to know more of the West Indies, so there were many questions to be answered, and it was not easy to keep Ernest sweet-tempered during this interrogation, for he was wild for his glass of brandy and his cards and the pile of coins on the table.

Eventually, the newcomers were disposed to the satisfaction of all, and Hugo made his way thankfully back towards the dance floor. He paused on the balcony with its vista over the whole room, and his eye searched first for a certain blue gown. There she was, going down the set with Mr Verdun, who was a fine dancer, a worthy partner for her. How gracefully she moved, her head so charmingly tilted, and her pretty features alight with the energy of the dance. He sighed with pleasure as he watched her. His wife! It still gave him a thrill to look at her and realise that she was entirely his, and that however admiringly other men might look at Hope, they could not have her. How unexpected to encounter such feelings now, after he had known Hope for his whole life and never thought twice about her, except as the provider of a splendid inheritance. And even though the inheritance was now denied him, he was very content with his choice.

After a while, it began to dawn on him that he would look like a love-struck gudgeon standing watching his own wife dance, so he allowed his gaze to roam. The first dancer to attract his notice was Jacob, and the second was Clarissa, for they were dancing together with great vivacity, their steps and arm movements livelier and more forceful than anyone else's. He had never seen Clarissa so sprightly. Many eyes were on them, Hugo saw, and the matrons were whispering behind their fans. He could not wonder at it, for it was the oddest sight in the world, a woman dancing with her own brother, and with such energy. It was no surprise that the couple should attract attention.

He became curious to know what was being said about them, so he made his way down the stairs, where the view was less good, but perhaps he might overhear the comments as he moved about the room. This plan fell to pieces immediately, as he was hailed by some of his acquaintance and congratulated on his recent marriage.

"You have not been near us these three months, Mr Allamont," the lady said archly. "We feel quite neglected, is it not so, my dears?" Her companions all acknowledged their feelings of neglect.

"I must beg to be forgiven, ladies, but as you may imagine, I have been much occupied with the unexpected return of my cousin and his wife."

It was just the opening they wanted. "Oh indeed, such a surprise!" the speaker trilled. "Who could have guessed that Mr Ernest Allamont would contrive to return at the very last moment, as we have all heard. Such very *fortunate* timing, would you not agree, Mr Allamont?"

Hugo could not agree to any such thing, so he made some noncommittal remark, but he found he was not to escape so easily. They wanted all the details of Ernest's long stay away from his home, and then they plied him with questions about Clarissa, most of which he could not answer.

"I have not had the pleasure of being informed upon the matter," became his repeated answer. And eventually, "Upon my word, you will have to ask the lady herself, for I know nothing about her."

"And the gentleman with whom she dances so energetically?" She smiled sweetly at him, the very picture of innocence, although he was tolerably sure that she already knew perfectly well who it was.

"That is her brother, Jacob Wellman."

"Oh, indeed? Her brother? How interesting." She turned to him expectantly for more details.

What was he to say about Jacob? That he had been a slave until he arrived in England? That he was in reality a groom except that his sister had insisted he must attend the assembly? And beyond that, he knew nothing at all about him. It was a strange feeling to look at a man in such company and yet have not the slightest idea of his history. Amongst the nobility, family lines could be traced back centuries, and even respectable burghers and bankers had deep local roots. If a man moved into a neighbourhood, he would bring letters of introduction or would call upon mutual acquaintance to vouch for him. Even Ernest had three generations of Allamonts at Lower Brinford to support his claim to be a gentleman. Yet nothing was known of Clarissa or Jacob except what they chose to reveal, and she at least had already demonstrated her willingness to bend the truth if it suited her.

"It will not astonish you to hear that I know nothing about Mr Wellman," Hugo said eventually, with a wry smile.

"You are disappointingly ill-informed," the lady said, although she smiled as she spoke. "There is nothing for it but to ask the lady and gentleman directly. Perhaps you would be so good as to introduce us, Mr Allamont? Oh — too late, there they go again."

While they had been talking, the sets had broken up and the next were forming, and Jacob again led Clarissa onto the floor.

"How many dances is that?" he asked.

"That is the third," the lady said, and the disapproval in her voice was unmistakable. And then, with a gasp, "What *are* they doing?"

It was no dance that Hugo had ever seen before. So close that they were touching, their arms around each other in the most shocking manner, Clarissa and Jacob swayed and slowly revolved, just the two of them, quite separate from the sets. If the matrons had been whispering discreetly, now there was no mistaking the outrage on their faces. Even the dancers in the sets were becoming distracted and missing their steps.

Something had to be done, at once, before the damage was irrevocable, and Hugo did not hesitate. Striding across the dance floor, weaving between and through the sets, he reached the oblivious couple, still entwined and gazing rapturously into each other's eyes like lovers.

"Mrs Allamont?" Hugo began. "Best to stop now."

Her smile broadened, if that were possible, but she made no answer and continued to writhe sinuously.

"No," he said more forcefully. "This is not how we dance here. You must not do this."

She laughed in his face at that. "*Must* not, Hugo? Does no one dance the waltz here?" But at least she had disentangled herself from Jacob.

"Is that what it is? No, we do not, and you are attracting most unwelcome notice to yourself by doing so."

She looked around her, and, seeing the number of onlookers staring at them with shocked faces, her eyes dropped. But then, lifting her chin defiantly, she smirked at Hugo. "How parochial you are. How provincial. How extraordinarily backward. How... how *stuffy*."

"Yes, we are all those things, I daresay, but if you wish to move in this society, you would be well advised to accord with the prevailing rules of propriety. The sets are all made up now, but perhaps you would like a glass of wine? Champagne, perhaps?"

Her face brightened at the thought. "Well, if I am not permitted to dance, I shall have to find something else to do. Where is Ernie?"

"He is in the card rooms. Should you like a little card play? Or dice, perhaps?"

"Oh yes! Come along, Jake. Let us leave the provincials to their country dances."

Hugo led the way, and she followed slowly, hips swaying, her languorous pace at great odds with her energetic mode of dancing. Jacob silently brought up the rear. Hugo tried to ignore the many eyes following their progress, and the fans held up to hide the words of censure he felt sure were on every pair of lips. Upstairs, Hugo showed Clarissa where her husband sat, too engrossed to notice her.

"Is there another card room? I do not like this one."

"Yes, several. Try this one."

There was less ritual involved in introducing a lady into such a room, especially one dressed in the first stare of fashion, who was both beautiful and openly friendly. A few smiles saw Clarissa settled at a faro table, Jacob at her elbow. After seeing them both supplied with drinks, Hugo felt it was safe to leave them, for they could come to no harm in the card room.

He made his way back to the dance floor, but found he was too late to secure Hope's hand, for she was engaged for every dance. He did not mind, for he was not himself a great dancer, and much preferred to watch and listen and move around the room meeting up with his acquaintance. He was much sought after, for many there had business with Allamont Hall, or the tenant farms and properties associated with it, and there was much concern about the future.

"We have every confidence in *you*," one said. "Been dealing with you for long enough now to know your cut. But this fellow is a stranger, and I hear nothing good of him."

"Nothing bad, either, I trust," Hugo said.

"Not yet," the man said repressively.

It was not encouraging. But a gentle hand at his elbow drew his attention to Hope's smiling face.

"Are you going to take me in to supper, Mr Allamont? The others are going now, and I should like to find a seat near them, if I can."

He made his excuses and moved away, his wife on his arm. "Are you enjoying yourself?" he said.

"Oh yes, although... should I have saved a dance for you? I was not sure if you would want to stand up with me, or if perhaps you would be obliged to trail about after Ernest and Clarissa all evening. Where are they, by the way?"

"In the card rooms, and if they stay there all evening it will suit me very well."

She was silent as they followed the crowds up the stairs. Outside the supper rooms, the press of people was so great that they halted altogether. "It was very embarrassing," she said quietly. "When they were dancing alone. I did not know where to look."

"It is the waltz, apparently."

"Oh. Connie said she had seen it danced once or twice, at private balls, though, not in public."

"And did she participate?" Hugo said.

"Oh no, she said it was too shocking for words. So much touching! She thinks it will be quite acceptable, in time, but I am not sure."

They finally managed to squeeze into the supper room, but Ernest, Clarissa and Jacob were not there.

Hugo gave a cluck of annoyance. "I suppose I had better go and find them. They may not realise that all the best food will be gone if they are late."

In the first card room, Hugo dragged a reluctant Ernest away from the table.

"Well, a man must eat, I suppose. And a woman, too, no doubt. Where is that wife of mine?"

"In the next card room, playing faro."

But when they opened the door, a dreadful sight greeted them. Jacob was the one sitting playing cards, while Clarissa perched on his knee in a shockingly improper manner. Hugo was becoming used to Clarissa's unseemly behaviour, but this was beyond anything.

Ernest gave a great shriek and tore across the room, as Clarissa screamed, scrambling away from Jacob. And then the room fell into chaos, Ernest and Jacob pushing and shoving each other, Ernest yelling, Clarissa screaming and everyone else jumping clear of the fracas. It was as well that there were few people in the room, and although curious onlookers appeared at the door, Hugo shut it firmly, and wedged a chair back under it to prevent anyone else entering.

After a few preliminary sallies, Ernest and Jacob began a more determined fight, fists raised, faces taut with concentration. Back and forth they went, with more shoving and feinting than solid hits. A small table came near to toppling, but someone whisked it away at the last moment. Then the pair were across the room and almost in the hearth, scattering onlookers. Jacob jabbed at Ernest and caught him close to one eye, leaving a trail of blood. Ernest pushed Jacob so hard they both staggered.

"Excellent mill, eh?" said a stout burgher to Hugo, one of the small crowd of onlookers, while a steward was engaged in rescuing the bottles, glasses and decanters from harm's way. One decanter had already been smashed to pieces.

"Why is no one doing anything?" Hugo murmured, about to step into the fray to separate the combatants, even though he knew it was probably futile and he would end up with a bloody nose for his pains.

But then, with a mighty swing and a shriek of pure rage, Ernest's fist caught Jacob clean on the side of his head, and he went crashing down amidst a cluster of chairs, and lay still.

17: Blood

Ernest would have fallen on his opponent to continue pounding him with blows, but Hugo and another man jumped in front of him.

"That is enough!" Hugo said, grabbing Ernest's arm. "Remember where you are, for heaven's sake!"

"He is a damned snake!" Ernest said, struggling to free himself. "I'll kill him, I swear it!"

"No, you will not, and remember your language. There is a lady present."

"Lady? Ha!" He started to laugh then, a strange, high laugh that edged towards hysteria. "Do you think *she* is a lady?" He pointed a shaking finger at Clarissa. "Ha!"

He had stopped struggling, and Hugo looked about him for the familiar faces of Ernest's cronies. He recognised two, although in the heat of the moment their names escaped him. "You, sir, and you there — get him out of here, will you? Carry him, if you have to, but get him back to the hotel and lock him in."

Ernest raised his hands in surrender. He was breathing heavily, but he seemed more controlled. "No, no, no! No one need carry me. I appreciate your concern, cousin, but I am perfectly capable of walking. Unlike *him*." He laughed abruptly, pointing at Jacob. "I put *him* in his place and no mistake. My God, I am famished. Is there food here?"

"The supper room, but..." Hugo hesitated to inflict Ernest on a crowded supper room, but he and Clarissa did seem calmer. "Very well. But please... be circumspect. And... you have blood on your cravat, cousin."

Clarissa sniggered. "So *stuffy*," she hissed, as she passed by on Ernest's arm. Hugo released the door and they moved out into the passageway with most of the onlookers. Only the steward and one other man remained in the room.

"Nicely managed," said the man who had helped to restrain Ernest. He knelt down beside the unconscious Jacob, mopping away blood with a handkerchief. "His heart is beating soundly and his breathing is good, so I think he will recover well. Now, what are we to do with him? He cannot lie here all night."

"I know a fellow with a cart just the right size for an insensible gentleman, even one so tall and well-built as this man," said the steward. "I'll fetch another man to help me carry him downstairs—"

"We will do the carrying," said the stranger. "The cart will be useful, however, to convey him to the White Rose. I am sure that Mr Hugo Allamont will reimburse you in due course for the damage caused tonight."

Hugo was happy to agree to it. With some difficulty, for Jacob was a big man, they raised their cargo from the floor, Hugo with the legs and the stranger with the shoulders. In this manner, and with the guidance of the steward, they manoeuvred the unconscious form of Jacob down the service stairs and through the basement kitchens to the small yard at the back, where a cart, clearly kept for the purpose, already stood awaiting them.

"This is not an unusual occurrence, then," Hugo said, as they heaved Jacob into the cart and tucked in his dangling arms.

"Very common, sir," the steward said, with a smile. "You'd be surprised how often a gentleman takes a drop too much Madeira and finds it a mite tricky to walk home."

"Not many have been knocked out cold by a fist, I wager."

"Oh, a few, sir, a few."

"Thank you for your assistance," said the stranger, with a flash of silver pressed into the steward's hand. "We will manage now."

The steward, well pleased, disappeared.

"We?" Hugo said with a smile. "You have done more than enough, my good sir. I shall see this fellow safely back to the hotel."

"Easier with two," the stranger said mildly, and set off with the cart before Hugo could stop him. It was not far by the back alleys to the rear entrance of the hotel's stable yard, where Hugo tracked down one of the Allamont grooms and left Jacob in his care, to recover his senses in the straw.

The two men walked side by side back to the assembly rooms, rather briskly, for it was bitterly cold. The stranger seemed disinclined for conversation, and Hugo was sunk in despondency again. A thousand times he had cursed his cousin for stealing the Hall away from him, and probably he would curse him a thousand times more, and had Ernest been the kindest and best of men, Hugo would still have chafed under his superiority, and wished him far away. It was the most wretched ill-fortune. Hugo should have been master of the Allamont estate, his days filled with plans for improvements and good works, and instead he had to take orders from his buffoon of a cousin, and tidy up his messes. It was most unsatisfactory.

On reaching the assembly rooms again, Hugo was obliged to exert himself. "I cannot thank you enough for your assistance, sir," he said, as they were about to re-enter the crowded ballroom. "May I know to whom I am so deeply obliged?"

"Erasmus Kent at your service. Here…" He fished in a pocket. "My card."

"And mine," Hugo said, "although you seem to know my name already. You have my very sincere thanks, Mr Kent."

"You are most welcome, Mr Allamont. I have heard much of your recent sudden change of circumstances, and the tale has aroused all my sympathies on your behalf. Indeed, the events of this evening have only served to increase those feelings. It delights me to be of assistance to you, sir, and if ever you should need my services again for any matter, large or small, you may write to me at that address. I should be happy to oblige you in any way that I can."

"You are very good, but I hope that will not be necessary, Mr Kent."

"We are agreed on that point, but remember that you are by no means friendless, Mr Allamont."

He smiled, and with a wave of his hand, Mr Kent disappeared into the throng.

~~~~~

Hope could not eat a thing at supper. She was frantic with worry about Hugo, who had surely been in the midst of everything when the screaming and crashing had begun. No one in the supper room had seemed unduly alarmed, and the stewards had passed through the room assuring everyone that a little disagreement over the cards had been settled without much difficulty and all was well. Even so, when Ernest and Clarissa had sauntered in, arm in arm, laughing as if nothing untoward had occurred, Hope had scurried across to ask about Hugo.

Ernest had shrugged, but Clarissa said, "He is helping the stewards to sweep up the mess." Then they had both roared with laughter.

Mr Burford appeared at Hope's side. "Are you concerned, Mrs Allamont? Shall I go and find him for you?"

"Oh, would you? That would be a kindness indeed. I am sure he is perfectly unharmed but I cannot help worrying, you know."

He patted her hand genially. "You were ever a worrier. Do you sit down with Belle and eat your supper, and I will find out where Hugo has got to."

He was back very soon.

"Hugo is indeed helping the stewards. He is completely unharmed, and is just seeing the big negro fellow back to the hotel."

"Oh, Jacob? I mean Mr Wellman... is he ill?"

"I daresay he is unused to the strength of the drink here."

"Ah, of course. Thank you, Mr Burford, you are kindness itself."

"Delighted to be able to set your mind at rest, Mrs Allamont."

Even with this reassurance, Hope left her supper plate untouched and could not be easy until she saw Hugo stroll back into the ballroom after the first dance had begun. She left the set to rush to his side.

"Are you all right?" she said, taking his hand and pressing it to her cheek. "Oh, so cold! You did not go outside without your greatcoat?"

"It was only a short distance." He lifted her gloved hand to his lips. "I am perfectly well, as you see, and I shall tell you all about it later. Go back to your partner, little wife."

She smiled at him, blushing slightly at his use of the affectionate term in such a public place, but not at all displeased. It was not until she had returned to the dance and moved up the set several times that she realised that all her feelings that evening had been directed at Hugo. Not long ago, she would have been all aflutter to be the recipient of Mr Burford's attentions, yet tonight she had had no thought for anyone but her husband. Hugo had entirely replaced Mr Burford in her affections.

That was as it should be, of course. A wife's care should always be for her husband, and no other man should ever intrude upon that closeness. And yet she was not in love with Hugo. Her heart never danced about wildly when he entered the room or came to sit beside her. She liked it when he was attentive to her, naturally, and she liked his kisses very much indeed — they made her feel warm all over. And sometimes, when he looked at her with open admiration and told her how much he enjoyed being married to her, she felt... *something*. A glow of happiness, perhaps. But it was not love, and sometimes, when she saw her sisters so happy, and the way their husbands looked at them, their eyes burning with adoration, she was a little downhearted that she would never have the joy of such a deep love. Still, there was no use in pining for something that could never be hers. She must find what enjoyment she could in her life.

So she danced until her feet were almost worn out, and then walked the short distance back to the hotel on Hugo's arm, telling him of how one partner had stepped on her feet, and another had been so tongue-tied that he had said not a word for the whole time they stood up together. He laughed at her little jokes, and it was the most companionable thing in the world, making their way through the deserted streets, the lamps flickering and their breath clouding in the frosty air.

"And there was another man who thought he recognised Mama," she said, as they reached their room. "Is that not the oddest thing? He called her *'Maud'*, too, just as the other one did, do you remember? We met him outside the hotel."

"I remember," Hugo said. "Odd, but of no consequence, I believe. Shall I send for your maid?" He reached for the clasp of her cloak, unfastening it so that the garment slithered to the floor.

"I told her to go to bed. You will not mind unfastening my gown for me?"

"Not in the least," he said softly. "Come here, little wife." He pulled her into his arms for a warm kiss.

When they parted, she said, "You were very brave tonight, my husband."

"Me? Brave?"

"You told Clarissa not to do that... *thing* that they were doing. And you stayed to help clean up after the trouble. What did happen in there? Was Jacob causing trouble? Was that why he left?"

"No, he left unconscious in a handcart because Ernest had hit him."

"Oh!" She jumped back, hands to her mouth in horror. "Is *that* what was going on? But why?"

"Because his wife was sitting on Jacob's knee, and that is not the worst of it."

"What could possibly be worse?"

He led her to a chair beside the fire and pulled her onto his knee. "This is bad enough, is it not? For a woman to sit so, in company, is most improper, and one can quite understand why Ernest was so upset. But even worse is that his hand was resting on her leg, like this."

"Oh!" Hope huffed a shocked breath, as he slid his hand under her skirt. "Oh, that is... that is..."

"Quite so. But that is not all. He was also kissing her... just here." He bent his head to demonstrate, his lips brushing her bare flesh, and Hope was shocked into silence. When Hugo looked up at her wide eyes, he whispered, "That was very bad of him, was it not?"

"And very bad of *her*, to permit it," Hope said with asperity. "That is something for the bedroom, and a husband's enjoyment only."

"Or a lover, perhaps," Hugo said quietly.

"But he is her brother..." Then she understood. "You mean, he is *not* her brother, but something... quite different. Oh, but..." She could not find words for the situation that was now being unfolded before her eyes. "Poor Ernest!"

Hugo laughed. "Poor Ernest indeed. What a wife! I am very thankful that I am married to you, my little wife, and not a woman like Clarissa."

~~~~~

It was customary after an assembly, or a ball of any sort, for the ladies of Higher and Lower Brinford to meet at the earliest opportunity to discuss events. However dilatory they might otherwise be in the matter of morning calls given and received, such an occasion required unusual exertion, so that those who had not attended could learn what they had missed, and those who had could convey the success of the evening.

In this particular case, however, there was only one topic of conversation in the crowded drawing room at Allamont Hall, where Hope and Hugo presided.

"It was a waltz," Mary said firmly.

Several people said 'Ah!' in unison.

"I thought it must be, from the description of it," Miss Endercott said. "I believe it is quite the thing in some circles. Have you danced it yourself, Lady Hardy?"

"Only in private," Mary said. "Sir Osborne was so good as to teach me the movements, for he feels it is sure to be accepted in the highest levels of society before long. It is widespread on the continent, so it cannot be long before it is danced at Almacks."

"I did not like it at all," Lady Graham said. "I should not wish to see any of my daughters participate in such an intimate dance."

"Your feelings do you credit," Mary said. "I think it will not soon be accepted in Brinchester, whatever may go on in the great houses of England. I must assume, however, that it is considered quite normal in the ballrooms of the West Indies, or else Mrs Ernest Allamont would not have attempted it."

The room fell silent.

Miss Endercott coughed discreetly. "Where is dear Mrs Ernest Allamont, I wonder? And Mr Allamont? I hope they took no chill from the night air after the assembly? It was a very cold night."

"They are perfectly well, I believe," Hope said. "They... they generally rise late."

"It is three o'clock," Miss Endercott said acidly. But then, in more doubtful tones, "I daresay we must make allowances for the very great differences of climate and customs between the West Indies and here. And how is Sir Osborne, Lady Hardy?"

The discussion of Sir Osborne's health occupied the room for some time, until Mr Wills, his mother, his aunts and his cousin, the physician, arrived, causing a general change of seats. Mary rose to leave, and indicated to Hope that she should accompany her to the door.

"I did not like to mention it in company," Mary said, as they waited for her carriage to be brought round. "However, I must tell *you*, at least, that Sir Osborne was most distressed to hear of the events of the other night."

"The waltz?" Hope said, surprised.

"Partly that, but also... the rumours of other difficulties, involving Ernest and his wife, and another man. Blood was spilled, it seems, and the lady was not entirely blameless in the affair. I will not ask the truth of the matter, although I can see by your face that there is something to it. You must know, Hope, that Sir Osborne has a position to maintain in the county. In this neighbourhood, he has the highest rank of anyone except Lady Humbleforth and Lady Sara, and he must set the standard of acceptable behaviour, and not be seen to condone wildness or wantonness. This puts him in a very difficult position. For the moment, he is prepared to make allowances for newcomers who may not be fully cognisant of our ways, nor does he wish to cut the connection between our families, but if there is any repetition..."

"I understand you," Hope said, hanging her head in mortification. "Although I do not know what I can do to curb their excesses. They are not like us, Mary. Ernest is a stranger, and nothing like the boy I remember."

"Perhaps if Hugo has a word with him, as one man to another, he may appreciate the precipice upon which he stands. We are not the only ones considering whether Mr and Mrs Ernest Allamont are quite the thing."

Hope saw Mary safely bestowed in her carriage, and then turned back to the drawing room. As she spun round, she caught a glimpse of a small face disappearing behind a pillar, making her smile. How delightful to have a child in the house again! Although, despite the angelic face, he was always into mischief — why, only a few days earlier, he had escaped from his mama and found his way to the stairs that led to the roof. Yet Clarissa would not hear of handing him into the care of a nurse, and carried him everywhere with her.

"Edward? I know you are there. Will you come out?"

Shyly the head of dark hair reappeared.

"Where is your mama? Have you given her the slip again?"

He nodded, grinning.

"You must not, you know. And if you do, you absolutely must not go up onto the roof again, understand? It is very dangerous up there for little boys. Even your papa never went up there before he was old enough to appreciate how high it was, and how far to fall."

He looked surprised at that. "Papa went up there? When he was little?"

"Not very little, no. He must have been... oh, nine or ten, perhaps. So you have a few years to wait yet, and then he will take you, I am sure. Now, would you like to come and say hello to all the ladies and gentlemen? There is cake, and apple juice."

He smiled and nodded, and she took his hand, dark in her pale fingers, and led him into the drawing room. The ladies all exclaimed in delight.

"This is Edward Allamont," she said quickly, before anyone could make the mistake of thinking him a page boy, as she once had. "He is Mr Ernest Allamont's son."

"Eh, what's that?" Mr Torrington said. "Mr Ernest's son? Don't think so, my dear Mrs Hugo. Not possible."

The silence was so profound that Edward's foot scuffing the rug could be clearly heard.

"Whatever do you mean, Mr Torrington?" Hope said, her voice quivering.

"Colour's all wrong," Mr Torrington said. "I may be only a country physician, but I know something of how these matters work, and no English gentleman ever produced a child as dark of feature as that. Just never happens. That is a negro child through and through."

18: Quarrels

Hope cried for an hour after all the visitors had left, sobbing uncontrollably on their bed. Hugo had watched helplessly at first, and then, not knowing how else to comfort her, had held her in his arms and let her weep all over his second-best waistcoat.

"What are we to do?" she wailed. "Everyone will cut us, and we will be cast out of society. What is Clarissa thinking about, to be behaving in such a way, and trying to pass him off as Ernest's child? She is a wicked, wicked woman."

"She has not done anything that is not regularly seen in the highest levels of society," he said. "Connie is forever telling us of such people and the astonishing things they get up to."

"Yes, but they are not Allamonts! We have always been a respectable family, and now Clarissa is setting everyone by the ears, and I hate it! I *hate* it, Hugo! I cannot bear to be in the same house as her."

"I hate it, too!" he said, more sharply than he intended. "You are not the only one affected by this, Hope. Nevertheless, she is Ernest's wife. I have agreed to stay as agent until the spring, at any rate, so we are stuck here until then, and we will just have to make the best of it."

She lifted her head and looked him full in the face. "Make the best of it? Impossible! I wanted so much to like them, and help them establish their family here, and now everything is ruined and we will not be able to show our faces anywhere. We have to leave, at once!"

"Stop being so melodramatic!" he snapped, then, seeing the tears trickling down again, forced himself to speak more calmly. "We cannot leave. It would be wrong to abandon them now."

She gave a low moan of frustration. "Oh, you are *hopeless,* Hugo! What about me? I believe you care more about *them* than your own wife! How can you be so unfeeling?"

"Because I must be practical. We are dependent on Ernest's goodwill, at least until your dowry is released. He provides our home, our income and the food on our table. Paid servants cannot afford to question the antics of their superiors."

"But family can and should!" she cried, pushing herself away from him to sit upright. "If *we* do not advise him how to go on, who will? He can recover from this, but only if he controls his wife and behaves with dignity himself. You must talk to him, Hugo."

"*Must*? Do not tell me what I *must* do! It would be the grossest impertinence for me to comment on the way a gentleman conducts himself. That is a task for a father, or perhaps an older brother, not a mere younger cousin and dependent. It is not for you to give me orders or criticise my decisions."

There was a long silence as she stared at him in angry defiance. Then her face crumpled.

"I beg your pardon," she said, lowering her head, and he saw tears welling up again. "It was not my intention to criticise you."

"There, there," he said, helpless again in the face of her tears. "I will talk to him, if you wish it. No harm can come of a few words of... of clarification, shall we say, of the situation that now faces Ernest."

"Thank you, Hugo!" She looked up with a tremulous smile. "Are we entirely dependent on Ernest? We have my dowry, do we not? Or we will have it, very shortly."

Hugo heaved a sigh. "The money is awaiting release by Mr Plumphett, and he will not do that until we agree how the excess shall be divided. The problem is — we cannot agree. Five of us would be quite happy to share the surplus just with Dulcie, for the Drummonds need it more than the others do. But Ambleside finds that too informal a business by far. He wants the money divided by law, and is quite prepared to take to the courts to have it settled officially."

"Does that matter? I suppose it delays everything abominably."

"Not only that, but once the law is involved, the lawyers eat up money the way normal people eat mutton chops, so the likelihood is that by the time they have finished, there will be nothing at all left."

"Oh." And that started the tears all over again, and Hugo could to nothing to comfort her but hold her tight and rock her and kiss the top of her head.

When he had finally seen Hope more composed, and summoned her maid to help her dress for dinner, he went in search of Ernest. He found him in the book room with his cronies, not gaming, for once. Two more had arrived just the previous day, and all the guest bedrooms were now occupied. If any more arrived, Hugo and Hope would be in danger of losing their little set of rooms above the kitchen.

"Oh, here comes Mr Long-face," Ernest said, as Hugo crept into the room. "What do you want? Is there some crisis in the still room? Laundry maid failing to scrub the sheets, eh?" He laughed immoderately at his own wit, and his friends all joined in.

"Such matters are for the housekeeper," Hugo said. "Might I talk to you in private?"

"Oooh, serious business," Ernest said. "Are you going to scold me for thumping Jacob the other night? Or tell me to chastise my wife for liking a little flirtation? Should I beat her to instil more demure behaviour in her, do you think?"

"Oh, you should certainly beat the wench," one of his friends said.

Another added, "I'd pay good money to watch *that*!" to general laughter.

"In private, cousin?" Hugo said quietly.

"Oh, spit it out, for God's sake, and don't be so prim."

"As you please. A number of today's callers made adverse comments about the events of the other night."

"I can imagine. Is this all?" He grinned at Hugo in the most irritating way.

"And the child... Ernest, you really wish me to say this publicly?" Hugo said. At a nod from Ernest, he went on, "Mr Torrington says that Edward cannot be yours."

To his astonishment, Ernest and his friends all roared with laughter.

"Of course not!" Ernest said between bouts of hilarity. "Jacob's, I expect, although it's impossible to be sure."

Hugo was too much taken aback to say a word.

"What, did you think I didn't know? What kind of a flat do you take me for? It was amusing to see you treat him like royalty, but you were bound to work it out sooner or later. Surprised it took so long, frankly. Don't look so shocked, coz. Just my little joke. A man has to amuse himself somehow in this frozen waste you call England, for there's nothing at all to do here."

Hugo cast about desperately for something to suggest. "Perhaps you would like to look over the estate? Meet your tenants and so forth, before the winter sets in."

"*Before* the winter? You do not call this freezing foulness winter?"

Hugo could not help a wry smile. "No, this is just autumn, cousin. There will be much colder weather after Christmas, and snow too."

Ernest shuddered. "Very well. Let us wrap ourselves in furs and venture forth to meet the peasants. *My* peasants."

That started them laughing all over again.

~~~~~

The following morning, Hugo and Ernest and three of his friends who felt venturesome rode out to inspect the Allamont estate, the dogs racing ahead and then gambolling back before tearing off in a different direction, tongues lolling. Hugo punctiliously pointed out the nature of each field to Ernest, and the uses to which each might be put through the varying seasons of the year, and tried not to be offended when Ernest merely laughed at him.

"Do you think I know nothing, cousin?" Ernest said. "I grew up here, remember? I understand something of English farming."

"My apologies, cousin," Hugo said stiffly.

Ernest shook his head. "Ah, Hugo, you despise me, I know it."

"Why should you think such a thing?"

"I see it in your face, the disdain, the contempt. You hate me because I stole away your chance to be a gentleman."

Hugo pulled his horse up sharply. "I am already a gentleman, sir. You stole away the house in which I might have lived as one, that is all."

His cousin stopped, too, his smile never wavering. "You like the house, do you?"

"I love it," Hugo said passionately. "It is everything a house should be — elegant, spacious, well-proportioned, with every room superbly designed for its purpose. You were lucky to grow up in such a place. The house where *I* grew up is nothing but a jumble of mismatched wings, where the floors are uneven, the windows rattle and every door is different from every other. But Allamont Hall is perfect. I envied you that house when I was a boy, and I do so still."

He kicked his horse into motion again, annoyed with himself for allowing Ernest's needling to goad him into a response. Behind him he heard the murmur of voices and bursts of laughter, aimed at him, no doubt. What a fusty simpleton they must think him. If only he and Ernest could have been friends, as cousins should be — how pleasant that would have been!

The first destination was the home farm of the Garmin family, and they were so fortunate as to spy Mr Garmin not far away as they crossed his fields. Hugo hailed him, and the farmer rode towards them.

"Why, Mr Hugo, what a pleasure!" Garmin shouted, as he approached. "Do you and your friends want some rough shooting?" But he looked surprised, for they bore no guns.

"I have brought Mr Ernest Allamont to meet you, Garmin. He is minded to take a look at the farm."

"Why, I am very honoured, sir, I am sure, and I beg leave to assure you that you will find all in order and nothing deficient, I flatter myself."

Ernest nodded, but said nothing, so Hugo said, "I can vouch for Mr Garmin's excellent management."

"Would you be wishful to step into the house, Mr Allamont, sir?" Garmin said. "It would be a privilege to offer you the hospitality of my humble abode. Mrs Garmin's cook makes an excellent cherry cake."

Ernest graciously agreed, and they rode in leisurely fashion across two ploughed fields and one of pasture to reach the farmhouse. It was a snug little property, with gardens at the front and vegetables at the rear, and a yard in remarkably good order for the time of year. Just as they arrived, a neat little carriage bowled in from the opposite direction, disgorging Mrs Garmin and her unmarried daughter. With the briefest of delays for introductions and deep curtsies, they scurried indoors to set all in order to receive their guests.

"The farmer keeps a carriage, does he?" Ernest said. "With a coachman and a groom and two horses, and no expense spared."

"It is a prosperous farm," Hugo said mildly.

"I daresay it is, such prime land as this, but its prosperity should flow to the owner and not the farmer and his wife."

Garmin would have spoken, but Hugo waved him to silence. "The arrangement we have is that Mr Garmin has the land at no rent in exchange for the provision of whatever meat, game, potatoes and grains the Hall requires. Any surplus he is at liberty to sell at market prices."

"So he is lining his own pockets at my expense, is he? A havey-cavey business, I call it."

"It is a very standard arrangement, cousin, nothing underhand about it. We have never gone short, and Garmin only sells what we do not need."

"Well, I won't have it," Ernest said, his voice rising in anger. "What kind of society is it where farmers keep a carriage and live like gentlemen?"

"It is English society," Hugo said icily. "This is how we do things here."

"It is not how *I* do things," Ernest said. "On *my* estate, field workers know their place and don't try to ape their betters. I want him gone. See to it, cousin."

"Gone?" Hugo said. "What nonsense is this? There have been Garmins on the home farm since before the Allamonts moved here. You cannot just throw him out."

"I am not doing the throwing, cousin, you are. You are my agent, and as such I order you to get rid of him. I want him and his fine carriage and all his fashionably dressed women out of here by the end of the week. See to it. Come on, fellows, let us ride on to West Brafton."

With a great clatter of hooves on the cobbles of the yard, Ernest and his friends rode out of the gate through which the carriage had driven, and disappeared down the lane, leaving Hugo and Mr Garmin staring at each other in shock.

"I cannot believe... My God, I am so sorry," Hugo burst out. "I will try to get him to change his mind."

"No," Garmin said, his face ashen. "He has the right. We'll go as soon as we can. Molly's sister will put us up for now, until we can find another place."

"I cannot tell you how grieved this makes me," Hugo said quietly.

~~~~~

Henry Allamont rode slowly across the bare fields. His anger against Sara had long since trickled away to nothing. She had been in his heart for so long and he understood her so well that he could forgive her anything, if only she would be his. If only!

Such little words, and yet filled with so much sorrow and longing. He still planned to marry her, for he could not take her rejection seriously. Why would she refuse to countenance the match when she showed him so much affection? Her coldness had all but vanished these days, and surely it could be only a matter of time before she was ready to hear his offer again, and would give him the answer he longed for.

So he waited, and tried to be patient. He had another reason for waiting, too, for the *avocat* had not yet notified him of the sum left to him by his late wife. A large sum would certainly help him to keep Sara in the manner she deserved. Yet here he was, already out of mourning, and thinking of marriage again, and still his late wife's affairs were unresolved. And thus the days and weeks had drifted past.

But then, at the assembly, a man had come up to Sara and addressed her as a close acquaintance. Just like the first man, he had called her *'Maud'* and was astonished when she professed not to know him. Henry knew he could no longer keep silence, but must act, and quickly.

He was lost in his own thoughts, and noticed nothing around him until his horse shied suddenly. Abruptly brought to his senses, he quickly brought the horse under control, then looked about him for the cause of the mischief. A rustling and panting under a nearby hedge revealed itself as a familiar shape.

"Well, old girl, what are you doing out here? And where is your master, eh?"

The dog bounded off again, and Henry turned his horse to follow. Jumping the gate at the end of the field he saw Hugo not far away, riding slowly, head down.

Cantering up to him, Henry said, "Well met, Hugo! What are you doing so far from home?"

"Father! Good morning! If it is a good morning."

"That sounds bad. What now has happened? You have not quarrelled with Hope?"

"Oh no! Well, nothing to speak of."

"It is natural, with so much turmoil about you. But you cannot be disappointed in your marriage, I am sure."

"Not in the least," Hugo said, with the glimmer of a smile. "Who could be disappointed with Hope? She is the sweetest little thing. No, it is Ernest. It seemed a good moment to introduce him to the estate, show him around and so forth, but he has gone and thrown off the Garmins."

"Good God! Whatever for?"

"Because they keep a carriage, and that is too grand for a farmer, apparently. And now the wretched man has gone off to West Brafton and I dread to think what havoc he might wreak there."

"I will say to you again, Hugo, I believe you should leave here. You would have no trouble securing another position, in time, and you will have Hope's dowry to live on in the meantime."

Hugo pulled a face. "That could be tied up for years. Ambleside is determined to take it to law, and you know what he is like — there is no moving him at all."

"Ambleside has many fine qualities," Henry said, "but he is damnably particular about correct procedure. As if he has not dark moments in his own history! You would think a man with a natural daughter would show more understanding, and not be so scrupulous about the proper form."

"Is that true?" Hugo said. "I have heard the rumours about Miss Firth, but nothing to verify it."

"Except her looks," Henry said, smiling. "She is exactly like him. But he has dealt kindly with her and her mother, and many young men make such mistakes, so I do not condemn him for that. It would be well if he could deal so generously with you."

"Indeed, but he will not give way, and so I have nothing except my salary from Ernest to live on."

"And your allowance. I have not stopped that yet, nor will I until you no longer have need of it."

"Thank you, Father!" That brought a wider smile. "You are very good. Are you bound to the Hall? I will ride with you."

Henry parted from his son just inside the gates of Allamont Hall, and rode down the short drive that led to the Dower House. It had its own grounds, walled about to separate it from the Hall's parkland, although the gardens were still in some disarray after the renovations. No doubt in the spring, Sara would engage a gardener to restore order. Or perhaps she would not be here in the spring? His heart gave a little leap of hope. He quelled it immediately. He had tried a direct approach, now it was time to be more equivocal.

She was at home, and that was a good sign. He was admitted to the morning room, and, despite its dark aspect, overshadowed as it was by a gigantic tree on the lawn outside, she had made it a very pretty room. With the fire blazing merrily, several lamps lit, some pale rugs and the lightest of furniture, it had become a charming boudoir.

Sara received him composedly, and for a while they talked only of the family — of Ernest and Clarissa, of Hugo and Hope, and all the difficulties and tribulations inflicted by the former upon the latter. But eventually the talk came round to the assembly at Brinchester, and this was Henry's opening.

"It was a strange business, that man who called you *'Maud'* and claimed to know you," he began.

Was it his imagination or did she look the tiniest bit conscious? "Not so strange," she said with an indifferent shrug.

"People make mistakes all the time. Sometimes it is just a ploy, to inveigle an introduction to someone of rank."

"But it is not the first time someone has called you by that name," he went on. "An odd coincidence, for both to make the same mistake."

"Not in the least," she said, with a touch of asperity. "No doubt there is a Maud somewhere who looks very like me. Perhaps she is accosted in the same way by persons who address her as Lady Sara."

He was glad that he had allowed his anger to cool, for he needed to tread with the greatest care from now on. "That is what I thought also, when I pondered the matter. And Mr Carpenter — the first man who thought he recognised you — said that he met Maud in a brothel, and obviously the Lady Sara Allamont, the daughter of the Earl of Harkwood, would never be found in a brothel."

"Obviously," she said coldly.

"But it seemed to me that this was a problem that would recur, so it occurred to me that if, perhaps, this Maud could be found and persuaded to move to a different part of the country, it would make your life a little easier."

"You are all consideration for my welfare, Henry." But he thought her manner was wary.

"On that account, I went into Shropshire, to the brothel that Mr Carpenter was so obliging as to give me the direction of, and there enquired after a lady called Maud. She was not there, although they knew of her, for she had been there on numerous occasions in the past, plying her trade. Where might she be found, I asked the lady in charge. Maud lives in Brinshire, I was told, and they have no address for her, since she arrives and leaves as she pleases. But she is very grand, they told me, for she arrives in a hired post chaise, and latterly she has brought her own maid with her."

Sara jumped up and moved to the window, her back to Henry.

"Do you want to know the maid's name, Sara?" he said softly. "It might be familiar to—"

"Stop this!" she said, spinning round to face him, her eyes flashing. "What business is any of this to you?"

"What business is it? You are family, Sara, and that alone would be reason enough for my concern. But you are also the woman I love, the woman I hope one day will make my life complete by becoming my wife. Do you really imagine I want a succession of men turning up who once shared the delights of your body in a brothel?"

"Do not judge me! Do not you *dare* to judge me!"

"I do not judge," he said quietly. "But I should like to understand."

For a moment, she stood, chest heaving, eyes sparkling, her colour high as anger roiled inside her, and he caught his breath to see her so gloriously beautiful. She was magnificent.

Then she seemed to sag. "Very well. Sit and let me try to explain."

19: Leaving

Henry sat, and to his disappointment Sara sat as far from him as possible. He made no comment, however, as she began to talk.

"Can you imagine what my life was like with *him*? My husband. Ha! My dear, dear husband. You cannot imagine it, of course, for you are a man, and for you, freedom is your natural state of being. A man can always do what he wishes, with no thought of the consequences. But for me, it was as if I had been shut in a small cage. I was quite sure I had died and this was my personal Hell. So it was, I suppose — punishment for my wicked excesses as a young woman. Well, you know about those for you were very much part of them. But you took fright and fled, and I was in the deepest trouble. No, no!" She raised a hand as he began to speak. "I do not blame you, not in the slightest."

He subsided, and sat back to listen.

She heaved a sigh. "The trouble with having an identical twin is that it is so easy to play tricks on people, so easy to make them doubt. Tilly and I had been making mischief in that way for so long it was as natural as breathing. How many times had we changed places, worn each other's gowns, pretended to be the other? Even the coloured ribbons on our wrists that we wore so that anyone might tell us apart — yes, we swapped those, too, sometimes. When you were courting me so assiduously, Tilly and I often exchanged ribbons in the retiring rooms so that I could dance with you again."

"Did you?" he breathed, enchanted with this unsuspected sign of affection.

"It was a long time ago," Sara said coldly. "I was young and foolish, too foolish to keep hold of you in case the worst happened and I needed a husband in a hurry. You would have married me, I make no doubt."

"Of course I would. That was all I wanted."

"It was not what I wanted, but it would have done, in a crisis."

"Good God, Sara, you are as cold and unfeeling as a piece of glass," he cried. "*'It would have done!'* Is that all I was to you, someone who could be brought up to the mark if your reputation was at risk?"

Her face softened. "You were far more than that, Henry, but you never actually offered for me, you know."

"I planned to, indeed I tried to, but your father always looked down his nose at me. Mr Henry Allamont of Brinshire was never going to be good enough for the Earl of Harkwood's daughter. But then…"

"Then I made you doubt whether you were with me or Tilly, and so you flew away, and the blame for that was entirely mine. And Maxwell was born… my son." For a moment her face softened. "I could not keep him with me, of course, it was impossible, but at least he was given a home and a respectable upbringing in Scotland, and I was grateful for that. My sister wrote to tell me of his progress, which was something, even if I could not watch him grow up myself. But my father insisted I marry, and the man he offered me was the last person I expected — your cousin. It seemed like a piece of good fortune, at the time, for surely he would be something like you. Perhaps not in looks, for he was not handsome, but I was certain he would have something of your passionate nature."

Henry said nothing, seeing the tragedy unfolding as she spoke. He had always wondered why she had married his cousin William, with his regularity of habit and his ascetic ways, but now he could see why she had misunderstood his nature.

"I felt as if I could not breathe," she said. "He stifled me, every day, in every moment. Meals precisely on time, the fires to be lit at the exact hour specified, and allowed just so much coal, according to the season but with no regard for the vagaries of the weather. Even his visits to my bedroom were by strict timetable. Dear God, I was suffocating! And then the children! Every one of them exactly like their father, with the same lank, dark hair, the same brown eyes, the same thin face. I could not bear to look at them, and so timid as they were! Such spineless creatures, utterly cowed by him. Yet there was no escape. My father had agreed to conceal my unhappy history, but I was forbidden from all better society in case I should fall from grace again. Even my own family home was closed to me at first, until I pleaded for a reprieve, for the sake of my sanity. As for London — I was not permitted anywhere near Tilly, in case she corrupted me again."

"Tilly went in a different direction," Henry said sadly.

"Oh yes. Her lover protected her, for a while, and then there was another, and yet another. When she tired of that circus, she set herself up with a discreet little brothel, very exclusive. But I was respectable, and not to be tainted by my sister. I felt as if I were in prison, Henry. It was hideous. But then, most unexpectedly, William took a chill and died and I was free. Can you imagine how I rejoiced? And do you blame me? The first place I went to was London, to see Tilly. Oh, the joy of being with my sister again! I cannot tell you how wonderful it was, for we were like two sides of the same coin and separation was as dreadful to each of us as losing a limb. But there she was, laughing and crying and kissing me, and it was wonderful."

"That I am glad of," Henry said. "But you were not friendless, Sara. I hope I was always a friend to you."

"Perhaps, but when you first came back you had a wife and child, and you were so wrapped up in them that there was no place for a mere friend. And when Elizabeth died, you married Vivienne almost at once."

"Only because you were spoken for," he said quietly.

She gave a half smile then. "So I was. And you were too stuffy... or respectable, perhaps, to consider anything less than marriage, even when eventually I was free."

"But I was not free, not then."

"True. And when I was at Tilly's, rediscovering my sister, I rediscovered also my joy in the pleasures of the flesh."

"So Tilly *was* a corrupting influence."

She laughed then, but it was a harsh, brittle sound. "You say that as if there is something evil about it, but it is not so, Henry." She raised a hand to forestall his protests. "No, let us not argue about it. I was very happy when I went to stay with Tilly, but London is a long journey away and when I discovered that William's house in Shropshire was being used as a gambling den and brothel, that gave me an idea. Shropshire is very much closer than London, much more convenient. It seemed like such a good plan. You remember my friend Mr Eddington? He helped me set up a place, and he runs it in the usual manner of brothels, but one I could visit easily when I felt the need for some diversion."

When she laughed again, it was a merry sound that made him smile too. But he said nothing, not wanting to interrupt the flow of confidences.

"Not that I was liberal with my favours, I assure you!" she went on. "I modelled myself on Tilly, creating a fashionable little salon, choosing the women carefully, making sure they were well treated and the men were the respectable sort, not drunk or ill-mannered. It was all very elegant and refined, you may be sure. And from time to time I would choose a favourite for some amusement of my own. At first I left my maid behind, which was most inconvenient, but I could not trust her. Eventually I replaced her. The new one is not so good, but very discreet. Very, very discreet. I should have remembered to change her name as well as my own. Ah well. So what are you going to do now that you know my little secret, Henry?"

"Nothing."

Her eyebrows lifted. "Nothing?"

"It would be unforgivable in me to reveal any of this to the world, so you may depend on my silence."

"And?"

"And what?"

"There is a catch, I am sure."

"No catch," he said. "The danger of your position will occur to you soon enough. Two men have already identified you as '*Maud*', and undoubtedly more will do so. Your so convenient little brothel is no more than half a day's drive from Brinchester, and there is a great deal of interchange between the two counties. How long do you think it will be before people begin to notice these men, and draw the obvious conclusion?"

"I cannot imagine anyone would connect the very proper and respectable Lady Sara Allamont with a woman from a brothel, Henry. Did you believe it until you heard the maid's name?"

"No, but I wondered, and all it takes is one person wondering to a dozen or two of her acquaintance. You cannot stay here, Sara. Your position will become untenable, especially without a husband to protect you."

"Ah, I thought we would come to that before too long."

"My offer has been made, and I will not bore you with repetition. You know my feelings, Sara, and nothing has changed on my part. One word from you will be enough to bring

195

me to your side. However, if you do not wish to marry, then I think it imperative that you should move away from Brinshire. If not London, then Bath might suit you, or Brighton, perhaps. Or go further north, to York or Harrogate. But do not stay here, under any circumstances. You are not happy here, in any event, are you?"

"You think I would be happier in Bath? Or less inclined to stray from the path of respectability? And the cost would be beyond my means. My little brothel was expensive to establish, for I wished it to be very exclusive, like Tilly's. Much of my widow's portion is gone to the venture. Here I have a good house provided, stabling for my carriage and horses, and half my dinners at the Hall. My expenses are very low."

"Then find yourself a husband. With your looks, a few months in Bath would give you ample choice."

She shuddered visibly. "No husband, I beg you! I want to be free, Henry, not suffocating under the rule of a man."

For a moment grief overcame him. Here was the end of all his fine hopes and dreams! William had ruined her, so that she saw every man as an oppressor of the worst kind. She could not even imagine a husband who would treat her gently and cherish her for ever.

"Then I cannot help you," he said sadly. "Sooner or later your reputation will be ruined, and nothing can prevent it."

~~~~~

The house was quiet when Hugo reached home. When he took his horse to the stables, he discovered that one of the carriages was out, as the ladies had gone to call on some of their acquaintance. He shut himself in the gun room with a plate of cold meat and some ale, and settled down with the accounts, trying to work out how they might make do until a new farmer was installed at the home farm. As if life were not difficult enough, without Ernest making everything ten times worse.

He had not been there long when he heard raised voices in the entrance hall, then loud footsteps and doors banging. He waited, but it became quiet again. Just as he bent his head to the account books once more, a timid scratching on the door was followed immediately by Hope's face, very pale, still bonneted.

"Am I disturbing you? May I come in?"

"Of course you may! Whatever is going on out there?"

"It is Clarissa," she said, tugging at the ribbons of her bonnet and succeeding only in tangling them into a knot. "Oh! Hugo, would you be so obliging as to unravel this for me?" While he did so, she went on, "We have been everywhere this morning, and no one is at home! It is so... so *lowering*, Hugo, to be ostracised in such a way. I had hoped that our neighbours would be tolerant of someone new to the county, someone not yet accustomed to our ways— oh, thank you! How did they ever get into such a tangle?" She cast the bonnet aside impatiently. "We tried the Grahams and Lady Humbleforth and the Willses, and then — oh, Hugo, I cannot believe it, but even Amy would not receive us! And now Clarissa is in *such* a temper, and swears she will not stay here to be insulted. She has gone to pack already."

"Well, good riddance if she does go," he said, unfastening her pelisse. "Goodness, but there are a lot of buttons on this. But frankly I suspect she will change her mind about that. Where will she go? And so close to Christmas, too. She will not want to be travelling at this time of year."

"Oh, you are quite right. I had not thought of that. Although I do not think she is very settled here."

He gave a bark of laughter. "You mean she is not quite the demure wife that a respectable English gentleman should have? But then Ernest is not quite the respectable English gentleman one might have hoped for. You will not believe what he has done today."

He told her the whole story, and her hands flew to her mouth in shock. "Oh, poor Mr Garmin! And Mrs and Miss Garmin, too. Such a dreadful thing to do, to turn them off in such a high-handed manner, and with no notice, either."

"He does have the right," Hugo said slowly. "The land is his, after all. Perhaps he will install one of his friends as farmer there, as he set one of them up as butler."

"A fine butler he makes, too," Hope said disgustedly. "He poured wine three times and served the soup twice, and since then he has done nothing at all. Everything is left to William. But if the Garmins are to leave, someone will have to manage the farm — the animals, and so on."

"He has workers who can keep things going for a while, but—"

A burst of angry voices distracted them. They crept to the door and opened it a fraction. The gun room lay in the corridor to the kitchen wing, but it was near enough to the main house that they could identify the voices of Ernest and Clarissa, one loud and rough, the other shrieking like a demented woman. And then there was the crash of something breaking, followed by another, and yet another.

"The figurines on the console at the top of the stairs," Hope whispered. "Oh dear!"

Hugo pulled her back into the room. "We should keep out of their way for a while, or we might get porcelain thrown at us, too."

~~~~~

Later, when the house had fallen into its usual afternoon quiet, Hope felt it was safe to creep out to the drawing room. As she was passing the door to the north gallery, she heard a gentle sniffling sound, like someone weeping. One of the housemaids, she guessed, for it would not be the first time Ernest had shouted at one or other of them and reduced her to tears. She

198

could not ignore it, so she peeped round the half-open door into the dusk-shadowed gloom.

At first, she could see no one, but then another sniff revealed Clarissa sitting hunched up on the floor in one corner, little Edward asleep in her arms.

"Oh, Clarissa! I did not see you at first, behind that urn," Hope said. Then, seeing the tears coursing down Clarissa's cheeks, she added softly, "Oh dear! Whatever is the matter? May I fetch you something? Some brandy perhaps?"

Silently, Clarissa shook her head.

"But there must be something I can do for you. May I fetch Ernest—"

"No!" Her head shot up. "Not him! Anyone but him."

"Your maid, then. Jacob?" she added tentatively.

Clarissa smiled. "Thank you, Hope, but no one can help me. It is all over. I so wanted to be an English lady, but it is impossible."

Hope dragged a stool nearer so that she might sit down. "Do not despair. You can still come about, if you begin anew. You have made a few mistakes, but—"

"Ha! A few! I have done everything wrong, and it is all *his* fault."

"Ernest's?" Hope said in surprise.

"Oh, yes. It is all his doing. *'How shall I go on in England?'* I asked him, for I had heard how particular English society is, but I had no notion of the proper way to behave, since I had no one to teach me. My father was a good man, Hope, and had me well taught, as far as he was able, and raised me as a lady — so much so that everyone called me *'Lady Clarissa'* — but he could not impart the rules of English society to me for he had never lived here. So I asked Ernest to help me. *'You need only be yourself and everyone will love you,'* he said. *'But you must on* no account be reserved or demure, for then everyone will despise you. Be forthright and bold, and you will be a great leader of society, and the ton will follow your every whim.' But he lied to me, Hope. He thought it the greatest joke in the world to set me loose with such advice and watch me be rejected by everyone. He it was who told me to dance the waltz with Jacob. *'Brinshire is too timid to try it. They await only one bold advocate to begin the fashion, and the whole county will follow. They will be delighted by your courageous leadership.'* He allowed me to make a fool of myself, and afterwards I was so angry with him, all I wanted was to pay him back. But that only made it worse, and now everyone despises me even more."

Another tear rolled down her cheek.

Hope had no idea what she might say to comfort her sister-in-law, but she had to try. "Clarissa, if you will put yourself in my hands, I can advise you better than Ernest. We can recruit my sisters to the cause, too. If you will allow me to tell them all that you have confided to me, they will want to help you. It will not be easy, but I believe, in time, we can persuade Brinshire to accept you."

"You are kind to say such things, but I doubt my reputation can be salvaged now," Clarissa said with a wan smile. "Nor do I want that, not really. English society is so... so *confining*, Hope, that I wonder you can bear it. So many things that one must never do, or must do in the only acceptable way, with no variation. No one here is permitted to be true to themselves, or to break out of the little box in which society has placed them, and that is as much so for the scullery maid as the duchess. Well, it does not suit me, and nor does this miserable weather, so I am going home to Jamaica where I can be free again. I am just waiting for the carriage to be brought round."

"I am so sorry," Hope whispered. "I very much wanted us to be sisters — to be friends."

"Did you indeed?" Clarissa said, with a hint of acid in her voice. "I doubt that. You always despised me, I believe. Not good enough for Allamont Hall."

"No, I—"

"Do not deny it, little sister-in-law, or otherwise I should be forced to admit to your good qualities and mourn the loss of your company. Better if I leave here without any regrets. Here, give me a hand up, will you?" Hope pulled her to her feet, and Edward stirred in his mother's arms. She smiled down at his sleeping face. "Ah, at least there is one good thing in my life. Farewell, Hope. We shall not meet again. Tell Ernest that he is a devious, conniving devil, and I hate him."

So saying she swept out of the room.

20: A Clever Scheme

Hope retreated to her bedroom to weep a little, and pace about, and weep some more. She was almost too distressed to leave her room that evening. Her charming vision of Allamont Hall becoming a happy family home was dashed to pieces, and now there was only Ernest and his peculiar friends, with their endless gambling and drinking and quarrelling. And they shouted at the servants so! There was no bearing it.

When her maid came to dress her, she said mournfully, "I shall not go down tonight, Flora. Pray tell my husband so."

But Hugo himself came to see her. "What is it? Are you ill?" he said abruptly.

"No, no, nothing like that. I just... do not want to spend any more time in Ernest's company. I wish he would go away, Hugo! If only he would leave us in peace again, for everything is spoiled now and I hate it!"

"Really, Hope, are you a child or a grown woman? We cannot always have things just the way we like them. I am disappointed in you."

Then she collapsed into a chair and wept in good earnest, for it was a dreadful thing to have one's husband of only a few weeks disappointed in one. But Hugo knelt at her feet and chafed her hands and told her not to cry.

"I am sorry I spoke so to you," he said. "I hate it when you cry. It makes me feel like such a worm."

"We must not quarrel, Hugo," she said through her tears. "It is worse than anything when we quarrel."

"I know," he said. "You need not come down for dinner if you dislike it so much, but I should be very glad if you could make the effort. Ernest is so provoking, and your presence is a calming influence."

So she dressed in her finery, and let her maid powder her tear-stained cheeks and arrange her hair in one of the fetching styles that she liked so much, and descended the stairs on Hugo's arm with some measure of composure.

Ernest was in a strange mood when they gathered before dinner. He said nothing about Clarissa's hasty departure, greeting Hope affably enough, calling her his dear sister, and giving her the best chair beside the fire. It was the one Clarissa had habitually used, and was therefore too close to the fire to be comfortable, but Hope was too subdued to make any protest. Then Ernest insisted on giving her a glass of brandy, which was not a favoured drink of hers, but she sipped it dutifully to please him. Hugo received no such distinguishing attention, and Hope saw him slip into the shadows on the far side of the room, avoiding notice.

When William announced dinner, Ernest offered Hope his arm. She could not refuse, as she was the only lady present, but she was by no means pleased to be led to Clarissa's chair at the foot of the table, as if she were the mistress of the house. Luckily, Ernest's friends clustered around him, so that the chair nearest to Hope was left free for Hugo. She did not much care for Ernest's friends, who were careless with their language, even with ladies in the room.

The meal passed off reasonably well, and with Clarissa gone, no dishes were sent back to the kitchen. Ernest and his friends drank too much and became rowdy, but Hope was used to that by now, and she had Hugo for rational conversation. It was only when she rose to leave the gentlemen that Ernest took notice of her again.

"Going away, little lady?"

"The meal is finished, brother. I shall leave you all to your port and your male discussions."

"Our male discussions, eh? What might they be?"

Hope's immediate thought was to say, *'How should I know, since I am not male?'* but she quelled the impulse. There was an odd glitter in Ernest's eye that made her quake. So she answered in mild tones, "Politics and so forth, I imagine."

Ernest and his friends roared with laughter. "Politics? You can keep your damned politics. We talk about women, little lady. Women we've bedded, women we might like to bed, if we can persuade them, eh, fellows? Or if we find them all alone and unprotected."

Hope coloured and made for the door. She dared not look at Hugo's face, but perhaps she could escape before Ernest said anything too despicable for Hugo to ignore.

"Stay here, woman!" Ernest yelled. "I did not give you permission to go! Sit down." Meekly, Hope returned to her chair, demurely lowering her eyes. "There, that is better," Ernest went on. "You are the mistress of the house now, you know, with my dear wife gone. Yes, you like that, don't you? You like being in charge. I daresay you'd like me gone, too, eh? Well, maybe I will go. What do you say to that, little lady?"

Hope licked her lips. He was clearly right on the edge of control, and any small thing could ignite an explosion. What could she say that would not antagonise him further?

"It makes me sad that Clarissa was not happy here," she said carefully. "I had hoped the two of you would make this house the wonderful family home it ought to be. But if you cannot find contentment here, perhaps it would be better for you to go back to the life you loved in the West Indies."

"You're right," Ernest said. "I shall leave this God-forsaken house and go home, where at least the sun shines occasionally and the air is warm and the fruit is full of the sweetest juice, and the women are warm and sweet too. But what shall I do with this house, eh?"

She said nothing, but she felt Hugo stiffen beside her. She could only trust him to say nothing that would inflame Ernest even more.

"Well?" Ernest said. "Cat got your tongue, little lady? What shall I do with this place?"

"I... I cannot advise you. It is your house, you must do as you think best."

Ernest jumped to his feet, face suddenly red with anger. He rested his fists on the table, as a wineglass slowly toppled.

"*Yes!*" he yelled. "*My* house. *Mine!* Every evil stone of it is mine now, every rug and table and pane of glass is mine, yet still filled with my father's wickedness. It cannot be made clean. Nothing can scour away the foulness that lives here. So as soon as I have made my travel arrangements, I shall burn it to the ground."

~~~~~

Hope had never seen Hugo so still and silent. He was not even angry, for the wound went too deep for that. He had sat motionless all evening, responding when anyone spoke, but in such a thread of a voice that her heart wept for him, sunk in despair as he was.

Across the drawing room, Ernest and his cronies were engaged in one of their endless card games, all the while discussing the best way to burn a stone-built house to the ground. It would not be easy, so she gathered, and there was much talk of filling the ground floor rooms with wood, perhaps by chopping all the furniture into pieces, or else piling linens into a bonfire heap. But however difficult, they were determined to do it, and in such a way as to make the conflagration as spectacular as possible.

While she fretted over Hugo and half-attended to Ernest's conversation, Hope's mind mulled over possibilities. Would Ernest really do it, that was the first question, and she could not in all conscience give a negative answer. He was certainly wild enough for anything, and after such a public declaration and with his friends urging him on, he was not likely to go back on his given word.

What could change his mind? This was more problematic, because she did not know Ernest very well, and she had no idea what might tempt him to abandon his plan. She wished she were clever, like Belle or Grace, and could think up some ingenious scheme.

When she and Hugo retired to their rooms that night, she said, "What shall we do? Can you think of anything? I have been racking my brains all evening to think of something but nothing comes to mind. What is your opinion? What can we do?"

He looked at her vaguely, almost as if he hardly recognised her. "Do? There is nothing to be done, nothing at all. Everything is finished, do you understand? It is all over. We have lost the house, I have no employment and even your dowry is to be snatched away from us, to line the pockets of greedy lawyers. What is left for us now except misery and a life of dependence on kindly relations?"

"Hugo…"

"We should never have married, and that is all there is to be said about it. You would have been better off without me, that much is certain."

And nothing she said could convince him otherwise.

But Hope was not so cast down. So long as the house still stood, there was a chance of rescuing it from disaster. Even so, she woke from a long restless night no nearer to a solution. Hugo disappeared with the dogs at first light, but Hope rose and dressed slowly, pondering the possibilities. Only one option was unacceptable to her, that of doing nothing at all. She had come up with no clever scheme, so she resolved to approach the case in the most straightforward manner possible — by talking directly with Ernest. She would not argue or plead or become angry or cry. She would talk to him, sister to brother, and see if there was a way to resolve the situation to the satisfaction of all parties.

First she had to find him, and this was more difficult than she had supposed. Generally he rose late, so all that was needed was to set one of the servants to watch his bedchamber and send word whenever he drifted from his bed. But today, for some unfathomable reason, he had risen early and vanished. Hope began a systematic scouring of the house, first the ground floor, and when that proved fruitless, the upper level.

She ran him to earth in the schoolroom, sitting at the table, head down, and he looked so glum that, despite all, she could not help saying, "Oh, what is the matter? May I get you anything?" But even as she spoke, she noticed the decanter of wine and a half-full glass within his reach.

"What is the matter?" he said without lifting his head. "Well, let me consider the question. Firstly, there is the trifling matter that my wife has left me. Then there is the minor detail that everyone in Brinshire despises me. And then, there is this place. Look around you, sister. Can you be in this room without feeling as if a thousand snakes were crawling over your skin?"

"I never minded this room," she said. "At least *he* hardly ever came here. Most of the time it was just us, and Miss Bellows. I learned to draw in this room, and to understand numbers, and to dance. We were happy enough — were we not?"

He raised his head to look directly into her eyes. "*Never!*"

"But I recall you laughing and teasing us," she said, before she remembered that she had intended not to argue with him. "You enjoyed some of the lessons. You liked making things, do you remember? The wooden tree you carved—"

"That Grace broke," he said, rolling his eyes.

"Well, Grace broke a great many things over the years," Hope said, with a laugh. "The one I liked was the model of the house. You had the proportions to perfection."

His lips twitched in the hint of a smile. "I daresay Grace broke that, too."

"No, I am sure it is still here, somewhere." She ran off to the far end of the room, opening cupboard after cupboard. "Ah, here it is! See how fine a piece it is. Do you still carve?"

"Not for years." He picked up the model and turned it this way and that. "It *is* a good piece, my best, I think. When I was working on a carving, I could forget everything else — the world was gone, and all that existed besides myself was this block of wood and the shape that was inside it, waiting to be released."

"Is that how you saw it — a shape inside?"

"Like a nut inside the shell, and just like the nut, the trick is to get the shell off without damaging the nut inside. Perhaps people are like that, too — a clean, sweet nut buried deep, and if the shell is hammered too hard, then the nut will break along with the shell. And once it is broken, it cannot be repaired." He looked up at her then, and she saw that his eyes were glittering again in the way that made her shake. He leaned forward, catching her hand and squeezing it tight. "And sometimes..." A harder squeeze. "Sometimes the pleasure is in crushing nut and shell and all." Another, painfully tight squeeze, before he let her go. "So much philosophy before breakfast. What do you want, sister?"

Hope rubbed her sore hand, trying not to cry. She would *not* cry. She was almost too distressed by his abrupt changes of mood to answer, but this was the opening she had been waiting for and she was determined not to waste the opportunity.

"I... I hoped to talk to you about this plan of yours to burn the Hall."

At once his face lit up with amusement. "Ah, so you think to change my mind, eh? Well, have at it, little sister. Let me see what arguments you can muster."

"It would be futile to attempt such a thing. I suspect that once you have decided upon a course of action, no power on earth can stop you."

"That is very true. I am quite immovable. So what is there to talk about?"

"I want only to understand why you would destroy something so valuable. Even if you do not want to live here, many other people would be delighted to have such an imposing residence, and would pay you a great deal of money for the privilege."

"Are you offering to buy it?"

"I? By no means. Neither Hugo nor I has enough money for such a scheme. I merely wondered why you would turn down a fortune, and destroy the house utterly."

"Pfft. Buying and selling property — that is such a mundane piece of business, is it not? Where is the fun in that? Far more amusing to set a fire here. At least there would be something to watch, instead of leaving it all to the scratching pens of the lawyers."

"Oh, I see. You want to dispose of the house in an entertaining way? You could hold an auction, then. That would be amusing, I should think, to have a room full of people bidding more and more outrageous amounts of money."

"Possibly, possibly. But there is no part for me to play in this delightful scene. I do not want to be a mere spectator, I want to be the centre of attention."

And that was the moment when Hope conceived her ingenious scheme.

"You could allow people to gamble for it," she said. "Anyone who wishes to buy the house may play cards with you. If they win, they get to buy it. If *you* win, you get to burn it down."

Ernest looked at her in silence. Very slowly, a grin spread across his features.

"That would be *very* amusing," he said.

21: *Games Of Chance*

"You did *what?*" Hugo could scarcely believe it. They were eating breakfast in the dining room, alone, for Ernest's friends were not yet abroad, and Ernest himself had vanished again.

"I persuaded him to let people gamble for it. I could not think what to do, so it occurred to me that if only I could just talk to him, then perhaps he would be more understanding, for people are always more reasonable if one talks to them sensibly, are they not? He said he wanted some scheme to amuse him, and gambling always amuses him, does it not? So he is to allow anyone who wishes to play cards with him. If they win, they can buy the house from him."

"And how on earth does that help us?"

She blinked. "Why are you so angry? Is it not better for someone to buy the Hall from Ernest instead of having it burned to the ground? The new owner will undoubtedly want an agent to manage the estate for him, so we shall get to stay here, at least. And the Hall will survive, that is the most important aspect. These lovely rooms, the sweep of the staircase, the painted ceilings in the galleries — they will not now be lost. This is what we always wanted."

"What *I* wanted was to own it, Hope, to be master of all this. Being just the agent, on a salary of a few hundred a year — what is that to me? No one respects an agent. It is only one step above the likes of Garmin, and just as uncertain. I want this house to be *mine*, so that I can keep you in a manner befitting a lady, and not skulking in poky little rooms above the kitchen. That is not what you were born to, and not what you deserve."

"I do not mind that," she said, smiling shyly. "It would not suit me to be married to a great lord, like Connie. We have been happy enough in our poky little rooms, have we not? Let someone else own the Hall, and perhaps he will be kinder than Ernest."

Hugo had to acknowledge that the scheme was better than nothing. At least there might still be a home for them, and employment for him. Yes, it was very much better than nothing.

So when Ernest came in, grinning from ear to ear, Hugo felt able to say with tolerable calmness, "I hear you have a new idea for disposing of your unwanted property."

"Indeed I have, thanks to your charming wife. Might I trouble you for the marmalade? Thank you. Hope, you will be delighted to hear that I have thought of a way to make the whole enterprise even more amusing."

"Oh. I am very happy for you."

He laughed hard at that. "No, you are not. You despise everything I do, but let it pass. Your plan had a small deficiency, my dear. The winner simply had the right to buy the house, and that is not very amusing at all. Buying and selling, lawyers, documents, money in the bank — no, that was too dull for words. The new plan is to gamble for the house itself, and I will throw the game open to anyone. Anyone who wishes to try will have to put a thousand pounds on the table to play, and my wager will be the house. There! Is that not the most delicious scheme? And very fair, for the house is worth a great deal more than a thousand pounds. Best of all, you will be able to play, too. Think you can beat me at the card table, eh, Hugo?"

"I should like to try, but I have not even a thousand pounds to my name," he said morosely.

"But I have, Hugo," Hope said eagerly. "Papa left a box of money for each of us, in addition to the proper dowry, remember? There was a little over a thousand in each."

"That is your money, not mine. I have nothing of my own."

"Hope's dowry is yours, cousin," Ernest said, taking a bite of bread.

"But I cannot get my hands on it."

"Well, better see about it, then. I will set a date a week or ten days from now, so that there is plenty of time to spread the word. Get the dowry in your pocket before then, and you might yet take the house away from me."

This exchange galvanised Hugo into action. He needed Hope's dowry, now, immediately, and there was not a moment to be lost. Ambleside's excessive sense of propriety had kept Hugo penniless for too long, but now that money was his only chance to win back the Hall. How like Ernest, to treat the matter so frivolously! Yet it gave Hugo a sliver of hope at last. It was the tiniest sliver, but it was a great deal better than no hope at all. So he sent for his horse and rode at a fast pace out of the gates towards Higher Brinford, where the Amblesides' house was situated.

He was so sunk in his own thoughts that he scarcely noticed his surroundings until the dogs barked and his horse shied a little as they rounded the bend at the end of the woods. As he pulled up, a lady hailed him from the side of the road.

"Good day to you, Mr Allamont!"

The school teacher, Margaret Firth. Seeing her face, with its striking resemblance to Ambleside's, reminded him afresh of all the rumours. He had laughed about it a thousand times, that a man as correct as Ambleside should have a natural daughter, but today he could not laugh. How dared he claim moral justification for withholding the fortune that was Hugo's by right, when his own morals were so suspect? It was insufferable in the man!

He greeted Miss Firth with civility, for she was a pleasant young woman who ran the school admirably, but inside he boiled with anger, and after an exchange of civilities, he rode off determined to confront Ambleside with every argument at his disposal, and not to back down until he had achieved his aim.

It was fortunate that Ambleside was at home and disposed to see him, or otherwise he might have returned home with his anger unabated, or else ridden his horse until exhaustion overtook rider and animal both. But Ambleside came to the door himself to greet his visitor, receiving him with every appearance of pleasure.

"Come in, Allamont, come in. I should have come to see you soon in any event, for I have good news for you."

"Oh?" Hugo said, as he was ushered into Ambleside's cosy little book room.

"Indeed. For I have found a lawyer who is prepared to take on the case of the dowries, and see the matter through the courts. It remains only for all parties to agree, and then we may engage his services and set the process in motion."

Hugo had to use every ounce of willpower not to explode in anger. But he thought of Hope, and the house, and all that was at stake, and forced himself to be calm. "It is about the dowries that I wish to talk to you, but I have no desire to discuss lawyers, as I have already explained."

"I cannot see how it can be avoided."

"It can be avoided very easily, as you well know. Let us speak plainly, Ambleside. You are keeping me from money that is rightfully mine, money which I should by now have the full enjoyment of, and which I have the greatest need of, if I am to keep my wife in any degree of comfort. What do you say to agreeing to release the sum of twenty thousand immediately, and arguing about the rest at leisure? With lawyers, if you insist, although no doubt they will swallow most of the sum remaining."

Ambleside frowned. "I cannot see that it would be proper—"

"Proper!" Hugo spat. "You and your propriety!" But then he reminded himself that anger would not advance his case so well as reasoned argument, so with an effort he reined in his temper. "It is a weakness to put all one's dependence in the most absolute rule of correct behaviour. A man of understanding must use his judgement and make decisions for each case on its own merits, and not merely by rule, would you not agree?"

"Rules are there to guide our behaviour into proper channels and avoid the least impropriety. With the application of rules, a gentleman knows how to behave on every occasion, Allamont."

"There is little point in speaking so of propriety when the whole world knows that you were not always so correct in your behaviour."

"What do you mean?" Ambleside said, but his cheeks reddened.

"I am sure you understand me," Hugo said quietly. "Miss Firth is a charming young woman, but her looks are very much from her father, I would say."

There was a long silence. "We all make mistakes in our youth, Allamont," Ambleside said, but his tone was softer. "That is mine, and I regret it deeply. Why do you think I strive to the utmost now to maintain every propriety?"

"I know," Hugo said gently. "God knows that I have made more than my share of mistakes, too. But it is possible to swerve too far in the other direction, and to use propriety as a method of avoiding difficult decisions. Then it becomes a cage.

Our wives are sisters, so we are like brothers, Ambleside, and I am asking you, as a brother, to treat this matter with the kindness of family, not the coldness of the law courts."

Another long silence, then, "Perhaps you are right about leaving the lawyers out of this, for they are expensive, no doubt about it. Very well, it shall be as you wish. I shall write to Plumphett at once to release twenty thousand to you, and agreeing to whatever division of the rest he deems fair. But you should perhaps understand, Allamont, that had it been agreed to divide this extra money evenly between the six sisters, I should immediately have handed Mrs Ambleside's share back to you and to Mr Drummond. Mr Burford planned to do the same. So you would not have lost out."

"You are too good, Ambleside," Hugo said stiffly. "I appreciate your generosity."

He was left wondering how it was that he had achieved exactly what he set out to do, yet was made to feel like a selfish, whining child in the company of his betters. Ambleside was a good enough sort of fellow, and an excellent husband for Amy, but his style of morality somehow left an unpleasant taste in the mouth.

~~~~~

Henry's grasp of French was excellent, but even so the letter was hard to understand. The florid style of the *avocat* and the excessive amount of congratulatory language made it almost impossible to tease out the most important nugget of information. But when he found it at last, he smiled. He sent for his horse and rode the whole way to the Allamont Dower House with a smile on his face.

Sara received him with a sigh. "This is becoming a habit, Henry."

He was in too good a humour to be offended by her tone. "My circumstances have altered, Sara. We now have more options at our disposal."

"We?"

"Here, read this."

He passed her the letter and she read it, frowning, for some minutes. "Well, I see that you are to be congratulated, but I am sure I cannot tell the reason for it."

He chuckled. "Indeed, the Frenchman's style is somewhat overwrought. Here — this is the point of it, this line here. Vivienne was a wealthy woman, Sara, and she has left me everything, no less than eighty gold *louis*, so the *avocat* says."

"*Louis?* Do they still use the term? Is it not *Napoleans*, now?"

"Oh, probably. The *avocat* is old style, I would guess. But the money seems to be in the bank in London already. What a piece of good fortune, and so unexpected. Vivienne always told me she was penniless, having given her fortune away to a half-sister, or some such, years ago. But clearly it was not so." He laughed again.

Sara smiled at him, laying the letter in her lap. "But you have not yet been in touch with the bank?"

"Not yet, but the money is there, the *avocat* says so. Is it not the most wonderful news? Now we can do as we please, Sara."

"We?" she said again.

"Yes, we," he said impatiently. "Unless you have someone else in mind to pay your expenses. Look, with this much money, we may go anywhere, do what we wish."

She was silent, reading the letter over again. "You think it means *louis*?" she said eventually.

All his excitement vanished in an instant. "You do not?" he said in a small voice.

"The 'l' could be pounds. Eighty pounds would not stretch very far, would it?"

He jumped up from his chair and strode across to the window, staring unseeingly through the panes. Such evil luck he had! Surely she was right, and he had made a fool of himself again, allowing his wishes to lead him astray. No, eighty pounds would not do to keep his Sara in the manner she deserved. He had a vision of himself, dwindling into old age at Willowbye, with Sara such a short distance away, yet never to be his.

"Thirty years, Sara," he said despairingly. "Thirty years I have loved you and desired you, watching that evil man douse the flames of your spirit until I doubted even one spark remained. Thirty years, yet always hoping there would come a time when we would both be free and you would turn to me so that I could ignite those flames again. Have you forgotten what we once were to each other, and those endless nights at Hepplestone when we never slept at all? Our love lifted us from the realm of mortal weakness so that nothing could touch us — not hunger nor thirst nor exhaustion. We needed only each other. *I* have not forgotten it, even if you have. This last year, I had finally begun to hope that there might be a future for us, that finally my heart's desire was within reach. And to have it snatched away—! My cursed life! Nothing has ever gone right for me — *nothing* — except that one sweet summer of desire, when you were mine. Oh God, Sara, what am I to do without you? How can I possibly go on like this? My life is a torment to me."

She came to stand beside him, not touching him, but close enough that he could smell her perfume. "Is this truly how you feel? I had no idea you felt so passionately about it."

"Passionately! Who would not be passionate about you? But forgive me, I have allowed my distress to overcome propriety."

"Do not apologise," she said, laughing suddenly. "I thought you were offering me a prudent match — a widow and a widower, stepping into companionable old age side by side."

"Good God, what do you take me for?" he cried. "Prudent? Companionable? Lord, how dreary that sounds! No, I want a lover, Sara, someone to set me on fire with one touch of her fingers, someone who makes me dizzy with happiness. You do not have to marry me if you have no stomach for it, but at least let me be a part of your life. I am only sorry that I have so little to offer you. It seemed so providential, this money of Vivienne's, a way I could take you away so you could be whatever you want to be, but I fear that will not be possible." He heaved a sigh. "It seems I am destined never to be a rich man."

"But I, it seems, am destined to be a rich woman. That little... um, business I started in Shropshire has begun to earn me some profit. I have received notice of a very handsome amount deposited in my bank account."

He laughed suddenly at the delicious irony of it. "Then let me take you away from here, somewhere safe from anyone who might know you from Shropshire. That way you may be as free as you want without the risk of distressing your family."

"Is that truly what you want, Henry?"

"I want only two things — for you to be happy, and to be by your side."

"You would not mind living on such a dubious income?"

"Not in the least. If brothels are so profitable, perhaps we should consider expanding the business."

She laughed at that. "And you will not press me to marry you?"

"Not in the least. I do not care whether we are married or not. That sort of thing matters if we are to stay here, and it would protect you if ever a scandal breaks out, but if we can leave this miserable corner of England behind us, then it hardly matters whether we are married or not. I do not want to keep you in a cage like some exotic song bird."

"And I thought you were so bound by propriety, Henry, dear."

He laughed. "I could never afford not to be. It was my ill-luck to inherit an expensive house with a very modest fortune, and neither of my wives brought any money to the marriage. Then there were the children to consider. But now, our children are settled and neither of us is constrained. What do you say? Should we make a new life for ourselves?"

She was silent, but a smile played about her lips. "Perhaps the time has come for me to leave this stifling life once and for all. But will you give me a little more time? I need to see how matters play out at the Hall before I can think about my own future."

"Of course. At least that is not a refusal."

"It is not a refusal," she agreed.

22: A Final Throw

The day appointed for the final disposal of Allamont Hall drew near. Or rather, the night drew near, for Ernest had decided that the gambling would continue from dusk until the following dawn. Whoever held the house at that point would keep it. He and his friends had assiduously spread the word in Brinchester and the villages round about, to ensure that as many people as possible knew of the event. Those who wished to participate must arrive at the Hall before dusk with a promissory note from a bank for one thousand pounds, to be exchanged for fish to play with. Ernest himself would always be the banker, in games where such was needed, and would decide which games were to be played.

Hope dressed with unusual care that day. In the end, she chose one of her finest new gowns, something worthy of the occasion, for this was the day which would change their futures utterly. By the next dawn, there would be a new owner of the Hall, someone who was not an Allamont, or else it would burn to the ground. Whichever it was, everything would be different.

She had always been a worrying sort, fretting constantly about the various ways in which things might go awry. No longer. Ernest's erratic behaviour had swept it all away. What was the point of worrying about the future now? Let it happen as it would, and she and Hugo would cope with it.

Because of course now she had Hugo. By tomorrow she might not have a home, and he might not have employment, but they still had each other. That was a surprise, that she cared so much about Hugo. What had started as just a marriage of convenience had become something far more precious to her, something more than the slightly uneasy accord of cousinship, something more, even, than friendship. He was not always the easiest of men, but she was coming to understand his ways and know how to cool his anger and lift his mood. She wanted to make him happy, and when she was with him, shut away in their own little apartment, she felt safe and cherished.

It was not love, and a tiny part of her regretted that she would never again see a man look at her with such longing, such ardour, such fire in his eyes. A man who burned for her love, and for whom she was the whole world. What she had with Hugo was a quieter, steadier sort of affection, strong enough to build a life together. So she told herself.

The carriages began to arrive shortly before noon, disgorging a variety of men with avaricious eyes, looking up at the front elevation of the house as if weighing up the value of it. Was it worth a thousand pound wager? A great many men apparently thought it was.

But amongst the cold visages of strangers, there were some arrivals that Hope was delighted to see. Mr Ambleside and Mr Burford arrived together, and George Graham came with his father, Sir Matthew, and his uncle, Mr Bertram Graham. Sir Osborne Hardy's friend, Mr Merton, came too, sent by Sir Osborne to play on his behalf.

Cousin Henry arrived with Lady Sara on his arm.

"Only those gambling are permitted inside, Mama," Hope said.

"I have my promissory note," she said with grim determination. "With enough of us, surely one of us will win it from Ernest."

Hope took them through to the book room, where Ernest was accepting promissory notes and issuing fish. He was sitting at his father's huge desk, the surface littered with papers, boxes of fish, decanters, plates and wine glasses.

"Well, well, well," he said, leaning back in his chair and smirking at them. "Not too grand for a little faro, Mama?"

"Is that what it is to be?" she said languidly. "It is all the same to me."

"And Cousin Henry. What a delightful family gathering. Ready to play, cousin?"

"If necessary, but this whole sordid affair could be avoided if you were minded to sell the place. How much would you take for it?"

Ernest laughed uproariously at this. "You are the fifth... no, the sixth to offer, for I have just been given a letter from Sir Osborne Hardy stating his willingness to purchase, at whatever price I care to name. It astonishes me to find so many people wishful to live here. Or to sell it for profit, I daresay. Here, cousin, twenty fish for your note."

"Is that the rate of exchange? One fish is worth fifty pounds?"

"That should give us some lively play, would you not agree?" And he laughed and laughed again. As they left the room and another gambler went in, that wild laughter followed them all the way across the entrance hall.

As the stream of arrivals slowed to a trickle and dusk fell, Ernest ordered the doors closed and everyone moved through to the dining room, which contained the only table large enough to accommodate the expected number of players. There was to be no formal dinner, but food and drink was laid out on the sideboards, to be replenished as needed.

The room was crowded. Apart from Ernest and the ten or so who qualified as family, and Mr Plumphett, there to witness the transfer of ownership of the estate, there were some thirty other men there. Some Hope recognised, familiar faces from the assemblies at Brinchester or from balls and other gatherings around the county. Several of Ernest's friends were there also. But most were strangers drawn out of the dark holes where they lived, attracted by the prospect of high-stake gambling and the opportunity of winning a fine estate. Some were undoubtedly gentlemen, but there were others of whose origins she could be less certain. One or two looked hard-faced, as if they would not hesitate to wield a knife to protect themselves if need be.

"Why is it so dark in here?" Lady Sara said.

"Ernest ordered that only every third candle be lit," Hope said. "That way, when they burn down, the next set may be lit and so on, to save the servants from needing to replenish the candles if the play goes on all night."

Ernest took his place in the centre of one side of the table, setting his wine glass down carefully. In front of him he placed his stake, the wooden model of the house that he himself had carved as a boy. It seemed appropriate. "I will allow the family to play first, if they wish," he said. "It is only right that those with a connection to the Allamont name should have the first chance to secure Allamont Hall for themselves. And it would be courteous, I feel, to allow the ladies to go first. Hope, will you begin?"

Her stomach somersaulted. First? She had hoped for some time to watch the play before joining in herself. But she could not refuse, and perhaps the whole foolish charade could be laid to rest straight away, if she were to win. All it would take would be a modest run of luck, for Ernest had only his single basket of fish to bet with, and once they were gone, it would have to be the house. She took the seat opposite him, her bowl of fish

224

beside her. He smiled, and laid down a pack of cards beside his own fish. "Piquet?"

"I… I am not sure. Piquet is complicated and I am unused to playing for high stakes," she said. "May we just throw dice? Something simple?"

He laughed at her. "Of course, sister dear. Here…" He fished two dice from his pocket. "Let me see… is this simple enough? We each stake one fish, and take turns to guess what the score will be with both dice."

"Both dice? Very well."

She put one fish into the centre of the table. "Seven." Then she threw the dice. A five and a six came up.

"Bad luck." He scooped up the fallen fish. "My turn. Nine." This time it was two fives.

"Do I win?" she said.

"No, the fish stay on the table. Your turn."

Hope discovered that twenty fish lasted a surprising length of time. At first, her basket emptied quite quickly, and for every turn she won there were three or four that she lost, until she realised that the dice turned up fives and sixes more than other numbers. Then she did rather better. Even so, slowly but inexorably, her basket emptied until she came to the point of staking her last fish.

"Eleven."

But it was a one and a two. She stared in disbelief at the dice. How could that be? There had hardly been any ones or twos the whole time they had been playing, and now they came up together, and just at the point when she needed the exact opposite.

"Bad luck," Ernest said, with his usual smirk. "The dice are against you tonight, sister."

She was too upset to answer him, and only a tap on the shoulder recalled her to her surroundings.

"Hope?" Hugo said. "The game is over. Come and have a glass of wine. Or brandy perhaps."

His reassuring voice lifted her spirits. She had tried her best, but it was all in the fall of the dice and she had been unlucky, that was all there was to it. So she went with him docilely, and sipped the brandy he offered her and tried not to mind.

Lady Sara was the next to play, taking her place serenely opposite her son to play piquet. She lasted less time than Hope, or so it seemed.

Then Sir Matthew Graham said, "How about a game of whist, Allamont? We have three players here, if you are willing to join us."

"By all means."

Hope's spirits lifted, for Sir Matthew and Mr Bertram Graham were both excellent whist players, and they had contrived to partner Ernest with George Graham, and for a while it seemed as though the strategy was working, for the Graham brothers steadily won fish. But after a while, Ernest called for a break in proceedings, and then decided that he wanted a new pack of cards, and after that the tide turned and the Grahams began to lose ground.

"He is cheating, you know," Lady Sara whispered in Hope's ear.

"I wondered... but what can we do about it?"

"Nothing, I fear. Any challenge would lead to a duel and I make no doubt that Ernest is an excellent shot."

"Then all is lost and he will burn the Hall after all!"

"And he will be forty thousand pounds the richer, too. A very clever game indeed."

After the Grahams had withdrawn, defeated, and the other Allamont family members declined to take Ernest on alone, he threw the table open to all, with a game of faro. The table became a riot of waved hands, thrown fish, dealt cards and whoops of delight or groans of despair. Hope had never seen this kind of gambling going on before, so it was rather a shock. At first, the family held back, but one by one the lure of the table drew them in. Only the Grahams, Lady Sara and Hope were left on the side-lines, watching as the heaps of fish piled up. In the shadows, the servants came and went in silence.

Gradually players began to exhaust their supplies of fish.

"I can take your vowels," Ernest said, as one man rose to leave the table. "You there! Paper and ink!"

The servant scurried off to comply, and from then onwards, those who wished could play on, by writing an IOU.

Mr Ambleside soon withdrew, and Cousin Henry was not far behind. Mr Burford and Mr Merton lasted quite a while longer, but they too ran out of fish and were disinclined to write an IOU.

Hugo, however, managed to hang on for longer than any of them. Hope watched him, noting his high colour and glittering eyes, and his intense concentration. When he won, he could barely sit still for excitement, and when he lost he was cast into despondency.

And finally the moment came when he lost his last fish.

"I would be happy to take your vowels, cousin," Ernest said. "I know you are good for it."

"I do not think—"

"What, not afraid to play a little high, surely? I had thought your stomach stronger than that."

"I am not afraid, no."

"Well, then. Another thousand will not hurt, and look how many have dropped out already. Your luck is bound to turn at any moment, I have seen it happen over and over again. Just one more thousand."

Hugo hesitated. "Oh, very well." He laughed, suddenly, a high brittle laugh that made Hope's blood run cold. "I have had such a run of bad luck these last few plays. It must turn at any moment. Pass me paper and ink."

Hope was trembling so much it was a wonder she could stand straight. The night seemed endless as she watched Hugo consumed by a great fever, so deep in the game that nothing could withdraw him from it. She made no attempt to, for no lady could interfere in a gentleman's gaming. It was a matter of honour with them, and he would be mortified to have his wife remonstrate with him on such a subject.

She was forced to look on helplessly as he lost and lost and lost again, yet never saw what was happening. After the first IOU there had been another, and another, and yet another, and although she could scarcely bear to watch, she could not turn away, either.

"Will you sit?" said a kindly voice at her elbow. "There is a chair over there."

But she could not sit. If she sat down, she could not see Hugo, could not watch his face when he realised he had lost not merely a thousand pounds but her entire dowry.

"Thank you, Mr Burford, but I will stand."

"Then allow me to offer you my arm," he said, and gratefully she let him support her.

There were only a handful of players left at the table now, and apart from Hugo, she knew none of them. Ernest had great heaps of fish and IOUs in front of him, but one or two of the others had done well, too. Only Hugo was losing steadily and remorselessly.

228

He had exhausted his supply of fish again, and without asking Ernest had pushed the paper and ink in front of him. With shaking fingers, Hugo picked up the pen and dipped it in the ink. But then, some disruption further down the table — some wine was spilt, she thought — caused Hugo to look up. And in looking up, he saw Hope watching him.

His expression shifted, at first half-frowning, almost as if he did not recognise her, but then something else entirely. Perhaps a realisation came to him of what he had done, for, with infinite slowness, he laid down the pen.

"What is it, cousin? Not backing out now, surely?" Ernest said. "You have been doing splendidly so far. I never set you down for a coward."

Hugo rose to his feet, his eyes fixed on Hope. "Not a coward, just a fool."

"You are one of the last, Hugo," Ernest said. "You have a very good chance of taking the house."

"I do not want it," Hugo said with sudden force. "What is a house but stones and wood and glass? It is not a home. It has no beating heart, no soul. It offers no joy, no *love*. You can keep your house, cousin, for I have something infinitely more precious." As he gazed at Hope, his eyes lit up with passion. "I have a wife who cares for me, who keeps me warm at night and makes my heart sing during the day, a wife who is the gentlest, sweetest creature who ever lived. I do not need a house when I have a woman like that by my side, a woman I love with every fibre of my being. Good night, Ernest."

He walked towards Hope with a smile of the utmost joy on his face, and his eyes aflame with adoration. Tears blurred her view of him as she melted into his arms, and then he was holding her tight, rocking her gently, while she sobbed in bliss against his chest.

Somehow, she had no idea how, they escaped the room. The entrance hall was so brightly lit she was dazzled momentarily. Several players withdrawn from the game stood about deep in conversation, and servants passed here and there, but Hugo led her with certainty into a darkened room and half closed the door.

"Do not cry, little wife," he said softly.

Her pent-up emotions overwhelmed her, and she pressed him against the nearest wall, threw her arms around his neck and kissed him with such passion that her lips burned against his. He uttered a little groan, his fervour the equal of hers, his lips hot, his arms tight around her back, his body firm against hers. Her heart was so full of joy, she felt she would drown. It was a long, long time before they parted, she with a giggle, and he with a gentle finger running down her face.

"Well, little wife, this ardour is quite delightful."

And there it was again, that fire in his eyes that she had so longed for, but had never, ever expected to see in Hugo.

"Did you mean all that?" she said shyly.

"What I said? Every word. I love you so much, little wife, and never realised it until that moment. As long as I have you near me, the world will be a wonderful place. But... how foolish I was to let him draw me in. He wanted me to lose everything, you know, every last penny. How much did I lose, do you know?"

"I lost count. Maybe ten thousand."

He winced.

"We still have enough. You stopped in time," she said.

"But I have thrown away half your dowry tonight. Why are you not angry with me? You should be angry."

"Because we are still together. Because you look at me with fire in your eyes and I cannot resist you. Because I love everything about you."

He went very still. "Do you? I am not a very lovable person, Hope. I am weak and foolish and I get drawn in against all reason because I care too deeply. I cared too much about this house for far too long."

"You are a *good* person, Hugo. You have always been good to me."

"Who could not be, dearest, sweetest Hope? My adored little wife. Will you kiss me again?"

She was very happy to oblige.

23: Snow And Rain

It was some time later — and Hugo had not the least idea how much — when Hope said, "The sky is lightening. It is nearly dawn."

"Shall we go and see Ernest? We shall need to find out how much time we have before he reduces the place to ash. There are the servants to be thought about, and a few good paintings to save, even if he decides to turn the furniture into kindling."

Hand in hand they walked out of the winter parlour where they had been hiding and across the entrance hall, their footsteps echoing hollowly on the tiled floor. A housemaid scurrying into the book room with a bucket of coal was the only sign of life.

The dining room was dark, the few remaining candles guttering badly. Abandoned plates and glasses sat on every available surface. The room was still crowded, an intense silence hanging over it. Only two men remained seated at the table, Ernest and a man unknown to Hope. They were throwing dice and sliding fish and IOUs about with rapid hand movements, their faces rigid with concentration. Around them, a watchful, expectant audience had gathered.

At the far end of the room, Lady Sara dozed on Cousin Henry's shoulder, while Mr Ambleside and Mr Burford whispered together. Hope and Hugo tiptoed across to them.

"Is he the only one left?" Hope said quietly, gesturing at the table. "Who is he?"

"No one seems to know," Mr Burford answered. "Whoever he is, he is very, very good. He has been taking money from Ernest for an hour or more now. Soon there will be only the house to stake, and then it will be over."

"I know him," Hugo said in surprise. "His name is Kent. He helped me with Jacob after that business at the assembly."

"Hmm," Ambleside said. "I wonder, then, what his interest is here."

"The same as everyone's," Mr Burford said. "He wants to win the house."

"Yes, but *why?*" Hugo said.

A rumble of voices arose around the table.

"You cannot stop now, Allamont," someone said. "Bad sportsmanship to withdraw at the crucial moment."

"Aye, you offered the house," someone else said. "Have to play it now, dear boy."

"Until dawn, I said." Ernest's tone was petulant. "It is dawn, therefore I stop playing."

"Very bad form," a third voice said.

"Let me make it amusing for you," Mr Kent said, as calmly as if they were taking tea together. "Let us both put everything onto the table. One final throw of the dice, highest throw wins all. What do you say, Allamont?"

Ernest sat back in his chair, considering his opponent. Then, "Why not?"

The audience cheered. Mr Kent slid all his accumulated fish and papers into the centre of the table, and Ernest heaped his on top. Then, with a grin and a flourish, he carefully balanced the wooden house on the top.

"You may throw first," Mr Kent said languidly, leaning back in his chair, one arm over the back.

Ernest nodded. Picking up the two dice he rattled them together in his hands, shook and shook again. Then, with a sweeping gesture, he threw.

A five and a six. The crowd gasped.

"Your turn," he said with a smirk.

Mr Kent scooped up the dice. "Hmm. You have set me quite a challenge, Allamont. How about best of three?"

Ernest laughed. "No. You asked for a single throw, and that is what was agreed. So throw."

Mr Kent shook his head. "Maybe I should concede. What does everyone think?" He looked around at the waiting audience, and a buzz of excited chatter broke out. There were cries of "Play on!" and "You must try, sir!"

Ernest laughed, looking round at the crowd, before folding his arms and settling back in his chair with a smirk. "Get on with it."

Mr Kent nodded. He rattled the dice, lifted his hands to his lips and blew into them for luck, then rattled again. He exhaled with a rueful grin. "Ah well, here I go..."

He threw two sixes.

The crowd roared, Hope gasped in astonishment, Hugo yelled gleefully and even Mr Ambleside muttered, "Good God!" Mr Kent smiled, acknowledged the cheers, laughed, picked up the model house.

"No." The single word, quietly spoken, silenced the crowd. Ernest's eyes were cold. "No. You are a cheat, sir."

Mr Kent rose to his feet, still clutching the wooden house. When he replied, his voice was calm, his words very deliberate. "I am no more a cheat than you are."

With a roar and a lunge and a flash of steel, Ernest stretched across the table, and then, realising his reach was short, ran around the end of the table. Men scattered before him, glasses fell, a candelabra toppled over, its candles fizzling out. Hugo pushed Hope behind him.

But by the time Ernest had reached Mr Kent, Mr Burford was there. "I think not, sir." And with one economical movement, he grabbed the wrist holding the dagger and twisted the arm up behind Ernest's back. "Drop it. Now."

With a growl, Ernest did as he was bid, and George Graham snatched up the dagger and carried it out of reach.

Sir Matthew Graham looked around at the crowd. "Where are his friends? You, sir. And you two. Get him out of here, for God's sake, and see him safe to Liverpool. Get him and his wife onto a ship bound for the West Indies as soon as may be."

"My *wife?*" Ernest yelled. "My wife! Ha! You think I would marry a lightskirt like that? She's no wife of mine. Thought it would be fun to make her an English lady, and it *was* fun, until all you starchy people turned up their noses at her. You think you're so grand, looking down on her, and on me, too, but you're just snobs. All right, all right! I'm going!"

With no more than a few curses, Ernest was induced to leave the room in a small cluster of his friends.

"Thank you, gentlemen," Mr Kent said. "Your intervention was timely, and most welcome. I am obliged to you."

"Perhaps now we might know the identity of the new owner of Allamont Hall?" Sir Matthew said.

"I am Erasmus Kent of Shropshire," he said, with a little bow.

"Sir Matthew Graham. You will wish to discuss arrangements with Mr Hugo Allamont, I daresay."

Mr Kent smiled at Hugo. "Indeed. In fact, I should like to talk to all the Allamonts. As for the rest of you, since the spectacle is now over and it will soon be light enough for carriages to take to the road, might I propose that all those here who are not of the Allamont family take their leave? Yes, you, sir, and you. Not you, Sir Matthew. Or Mr Burford."

In this manner, most of the company departed, their voices in the hall calling for greatcoats and hats, and ordering carriages. Mr Kent likewise chased out the servants, and with the help of Hope and Daniel Merton, cleared away the detritus from the table, heaped all the fish into baskets and sorted the promissory notes and IOUs into neat piles.

"Please, will you all sit?" he said, settling himself at the table.

As they began to find seats, the sound of horses galloping up the drive could be heard, followed by shouts for grooms. Not long afterwards booted feet thundered across the entrance hall and the dining room door burst open.

"Are we in time? Damnation! We are too late!"

"Lord Carrbridge! And Lord Humphrey!" Hope cried, rushing across to them. "How splendid of you to come! Have you ridden through the night to get here?"

"My apologies for my language. I had no idea there were ladies present. Yes, we rode as hard as we could but it was all in vain, I see."

"Mr Kent is the new owner of the Hall."

"Mr Kent, eh?"

"This is a wonderful family," Mr Kent said. "I had not realised how marvellously you all rally round when there is a crisis. Please, my lords, do join us and sit down."

"If I might make so bold, sir." Mr Plumphett stood uncertainly, wringing his hands. "I need only your card, sir, so that I may begin drawing up the papers of transfer. I do not wish to intrude upon private family business."

"Quite right, Mr Plumphett," Mr Kent said. "The deeds must be transferred as soon as possible. But not to me. No, not to me."

"Not to you, sir? Then to whom? You have another beneficiary in mind?"

"I do. I wish the estate to be transferred to the man with the most right to it, to the man who should already be in possession of it. Pray make the estate over to Mr Hugo Allamont."

~~~~~

Hope could not believe it. Give the estate to Hugo? But why would anyone go to so much trouble to win it, and immediately give it away again? It made no sense.

Mr Kent smiled. "Here — this is yours now." He tossed the wooden model across to Hugo, who was so astonished that he made no attempt to catch it, and it sailed past his ear to land on the floor.

"But why?" Hugo said. "Why on earth would you do such a thing? Especially after all I have said this night."

"Because you have been wronged, and I came here with no other intent but to right that wrong. You were the one who wrote to me, imploring me for help, you might recall."

"I was desperate enough to pursue any avenue, but I did not expect you to come," Hugo said.

"But come I did, as did the many other members of your family that I see here now, even Lord Carrbridge who has ridden in great haste across the country to be here. We all came with but one purpose in mind, to rectify the damage caused by Mr Ernest Allamont. He had nothing but mischief in view from the start, you must know that. I am very sure he had no intention of settling here at all. His whole plan was to create havoc. Well, now he has been thwarted and I have the greatest pleasure in restoring your inheritance to you. Mr Plumphett, you have your instructions."

"I have, sir," Plumphett said. "Thank you, sir. I shall bid you all a good day."

With several low bows, and an especially deep observance to Lord Carrbridge, he departed, closing the door quietly behind him.

Lord Humphrey picked up the model house, and placed it on the table in front of Hugo. "Yours, my friend. I am afraid some of the chimneys are a little wobbly." Then he began rummaging among the discarded plates and glasses and chafing dishes and decanters on the sideboards until he had found food and drink for himself and his brother.

"You will forgive us, I am sure," he said, "but we are famished. We stopped only to change horses and the last few posting houses had no provisions, not even hot coffee."

"You are very good to have come at all," Hope said.

"I wanted to help if I could," Lord Carrbridge said. "Lady Carrbridge has been most distressed, and I cannot allow that, you know. I brought Humphrey because he is much better at this sort of thing than I am. Cards and dice and so forth. I thought he might have had a chance. If the weather had not been so bad, and Mrs Burford's letter had arrived but a day earlier, we should have been in time."

"It would have made no difference," Mr Kent said. "I am sure Lord Humphrey is an expert player, and up to all the usual tricks, but Ernest was cheating in a dozen different ways. Loaded dice, marked cards, stacked decks... a dozen ways or more. No regular gaming could have defeated him, although the Grahams came the closest. That was some fine playing, gentlemen. I should dearly like to try my luck against you some day."

"You would not be welcome," Sir Matthew said stiffly. "You were cheating too, sir."

"I do not deny it, Sir Matthew, for Ernest is a professional card sharp, and only another such could possibly best him. Would you rather have seen him keep the house, *and* all those extra thousands he wheedled out of his guests? Very sharp practice, that was. So, yes, I used every device to win, but I make no apology for that, since the house is now Hugo's, and all these promissory notes and IOUs will be returned to those who signed them."

"I still do not understand," Hugo said obstinately, fingering the loose chimneys on the wooden house absently. "It is one thing to offer assistance with an injured man, Mr Kent, but why would you voluntarily give away an estate worth two thousand eight hundred pounds a year? Who are you?"

He laughed. "Did I not say you would not recognise me? That even my own brother would not recognise me? Or my own mother? You did not know me, did you, Mama?" he said, turning to Lady Sara.

Her mouth opened in amazement. "I... No, I did not know you."

"Frank?" Hope whispered.

He smiled even more broadly. "Just so. With a little grey powder in my hair, and some padding about the waist, and an alteration to my voice..." His tone changed as he said, "This is my real voice. Do you recognise me now, little sister?"

She laughed. "That is astonishing! Even to fool Ernest!"

"Ah well, it helps that the lighting is so dim in here. And then, he thinks I am dead. One does not generally expect to see one's dead brother."

And then Frank had to explain his whole history to those in the room who were not aware of it, and the ladies cried and the gentlemen laughed and slapped Frank repeatedly on the back. Hugo sent for more food and champagne, if there were any to be found in the cellar, and the relief in the air turned the gathering into a joyous family party.

Lord Humphrey threw back the curtains, and pointed out of the window. "Look at that! It is snowing heavily, and appears settled in for the day. We shall never get away again today. You will just have to put us up for a while, Hugo. Perhaps we will be snowed up until Christmas or beyond. What jolly fun, eh?"

"The Allamonts reunited," Lord Carrbridge said, slapping Frank on the back. "What a pity the rest of the ladies could not be with us to enjoy this moment. It is always more fun with the ladies around. But how delightful to have another brother back in the family fold. Even as one is lost, another is restored to his proper place."

Hope watched them in silence, thinking of her two newly-found brothers. Two brothers, two cheats, two disreputable characters, and for all that Frank had generously given the estate to Hugo and returned all his IOUs, still she did not trust him.

~~~~~

Later that day, Hugo walked from room to room, Hope on his arm, assessing the damage. Here was a wine stain on a sofa, there a scorch mark on a rug where a burning log had fallen. The cellar had been the hardest hit, and Hugo looked at the empty racks in despair. The book room was thoroughly disordered, and the bedrooms that Ernest and Clarissa had used looked as if a whirlwind had whipped through.

"These rooms will take a lot of work to be made good," Hugo said. "Still, I should like to have them back. One night — that was all the time we had to enjoy the best bedrooms in the house. Can you ask Miller to begin on them today?"

"There is no rush," Hope said airily. "We are very cosy in our present accommodation, and... and I do not mind having only one bedroom, Hugo."

She blushed adorably, and Hugo was compelled to hold her tight and kiss her several times.

"I think, for the sake of appearances, we must have a bedroom each, my little wife, but it does not follow that we need use both of them, does it?"

She shook her head, looking up shyly at him.

"Besides," he went on, "I should like to have my book room back, for the gun room was *not* as convenient. So you can set Miller on to that, if you will."

"She will be busy for today organising rooms for all our unexpected guests," she said. "How we are to entertain them if this snow keeps on I cannot imagine. Even if Mama can walk back down to the Dower House, we will have twelve in the house."

"Three tables of whist," he said promptly. "That should keep them quiet. I am more concerned about the wine. Ernest and his friends made excessive depredations on supplies. And food! I daresay there is plenty of bread and cheese to be had, but what about meat and game, with the Garmins' farm so disrupted? Although at least what we have will not spoil in this cold weather."

Some of Ernest's destruction was more serious than wine stains or scorched rugs, and as soon as the snow had stopped that afternoon, Hugo went to the Dower House to inform Young that he might return to his role as butler at the Hall as soon as Lady Sara could spare him. Then he rode across to the Garmins' farm to tell them of the change in circumstances, and reassure them that they need not leave. He found them surrounded by boxes, on the point of departure, and had to endure being wept all over by Mrs and Miss Garmin, and receiving their effusive gratitude.

As he was leaving, Garmin came out into the yard to see him off.

"It's not just us, Mr Hugo," Garmin said. "Mr Ernest went all over throwing tenants off or trebling the rent overnight."

Hugo huffed in annoyance. "It was too bad of him! Naturally no one must leave their home, but I cannot get around all the farms and cottages in this weather. Will you spread the word where you can? Tell everyone that all will revert to the way it was before."

"Aye, I'll make sure everyone knows. I can ride the cob over to West Brafton tomorrow, if this break in the snow lasts, and they can pass the word on from there. And may I say, sir — we're right glad things have worked out as they have. We're very happy to have you and Mrs Hugo in the Hall."

"Thank you. As we are happy to be there," Hugo said.

He meant it, too, even though he was not quite so obsessed with the house as he had once been. He had become reconciled to the idea that the Hall was lost forever, and it was oddly jarring to have it returned to him in such a neat way. He need not now be an agent, or bow to a master, and he would be Mr Allamont of Allamont Hall, just as he had wanted. He could even have his cards printed and order the carriage, which he had never quite liked to do before. Everything was as he had always wanted, and yet everything had changed. *He* had changed. And he smiled then, as he rode home through the darkening winter's afternoon, thinking of Hope waiting for him at the Hall.

And there she was, almost the first creature he saw after settling his horse in the stable, standing in the entrance hall as if waiting for him, and perhaps she was.

"There you are!" she cried, her face lighting up as she saw Hugo approach. "I was beginning to wonder whether you would be home before dark."

Home. Such a small word, and yet full of meaning. He sighed with pleasure, and kissed her, not caring about the footman and housemaid passing by. A burst of laughter from the drawing room told him that the guests were well settled.

"Is all well?" Hugo said.

"Yes. Mama has gone back to the Dower House, and taken Cousin Henry with her, and... and Frank has gone."

"Oh, what a shame! I had hoped we might get to know him properly at last."

"I believe it to be better this way," she said quietly. "We have just been upset by one brother. I do not think we should instantly put our faith in his twin."

"You do not trust him? After what he did for us?"

"I am very grateful," she said firmly. "Nothing will take away from the unselfish goodness of Frank's actions last night, but..."

"But?"

"He told us that Ernest forced him onto a ship. And Ernest told almost the exact same tale of Frank. They cannot both be telling the truth."

"Well now, we have one brother who tried his hardest to destroy us, and one who restored everything with the utmost generosity, and at great personal risk. I know who I am inclined to believe."

"One good brother and one evil brother? Perhaps it may be so. But very few people are entirely good or entirely evil. Ernest may be more evil than not, but Frank is not so good as to be above cheating his way to a fortune. The fact that he gives it away afterwards does not absolve him of the crime, or avoid

243

the censure that *ought* to be heaped upon him. For myself, I wish him well but I should need to know him a little better before I would trust him completely. You remember all the IOUs and promissory notes he won from Ernest?"

"He returned them all."

"He returned the ones from the family. The rest are in his pocket still, and he made no attempt to find out the direction of those who signed them. So do not let your gratitude overwhelm your good sense, husband. Frank left here a good deal richer than he arrived."

"Do you know, Mrs Allamont, I believe you are turning into a very wise woman. Just one more reason for me to love you so much."

She blushed shyly. "As I love you, Hugo. Is it not wonderful how happily everything has turned out? We entered into this marriage with no expectations of ever being more to each other than friends and yet... here we are!"

"Here we are indeed," he said softly, cupping her face in his hands. "I only married you because of the house, and now I find that the house is nothing to me, except as a setting for your many perfections. You bring me such joy, my sweetest Hope."

"Oh, Hugo!" Her blushes deepened. "You pay me such lovely compliments. But the house is not nothing to *me*, for now you are Mr Allamont of Allamont Hall and that brings me immense pleasure."

"Ah, my little wife! And you are Mrs Allamont of Allamont Hall, and together we shall fill these rooms with love and laughter and vast numbers of charming children."

"Oh yes, and Hugo..." She lowered her head demurely. "I do believe that *that* part of your delightful vision may already be in progress. Oh Hugo, put me down! I shall be so dizzy! Hugo!"

He laughed, and set her gently back on her feet, and kissed her again and again. Then, with a sigh, he said, "I shall take very good care of you, my little wife. And now, shall we go and find our guests? For as master and mistress of Allamont Hall, we have a reputation for hospitality to maintain."

Taking her hand in his, he led her into the drawing room.

24: Epilogue

Henry Allamont sat at the breakfast table watching his wife spread butter on her bread. Such beautiful hands she had — so smooth and white, the skin still unblemished. She looked up at him, and rewarded him with that warm smile.

"So, my lady, how do you find Bath?"

"I find it very wet," she said, turning to the rain-lashed windows. "Does this rain ever stop? Shall I ever be able to poke my nose out of doors without becoming drenched instantly? It is fortunate that we are well supplied with amusements indoors."

That made him laugh. "True enough. We have not been bored, have we, my love? But what say you to moving on? Brighton, perhaps? Or London?"

"Not London," she said firmly. "That is my sister's territory, and it might be confusing to have two of us running around town."

"Well, what about your family? Hepplestone or Tambray? You are still welcome there, are you not?"

"They tolerate me, no better than that."

"How about Scotland, then? I should like to see Mark again, and you must want to find out how Dulcie is getting on. We could pay a visit to your sister Caroline, and have a little peek at our son."

"No, no, no! That would be a dreadful thing to do, when hardly anyone knows the truth of that little matter. It would be too awkward altogether."

"I suppose if we wanted to make nuisances of ourselves, we could invite ourselves to stay with Connie and the marquess," he went on. "Probably it is best to stay away from Brinshire for a while until we can be sure that Maud is quite forgotten about, but Drummoor is far enough away. Or we could find a place of our own — what do you say to a trim little cottage somewhere in the country, but not too far from a town?"

"That I should like to do, sometime, but not yet," she said. "For the moment, I am enjoying my freedom."

"I am sure you are," he said softly.

She must have caught something in his tone, for she set down her bread and looked at him quizzically. "I am, yes. I have been restricted for far too long."

"A restriction of your own making, though, eh, Tilly?"

There was a long silence, as she stared at him, her breathing rapid.

"How long have you known that I was not Sara?"

"Known? Not long. I suspected something odd was going on long ago, when you rushed to poor Vivienne's side when she was ill. That was something Sara would never have done. And then you were so unexpectedly friendly towards me. Sara had always been so cold, like one of those waterfalls that freeze solid in a cold winter — exquisitely beautiful but ice to her very core. Yet there she was, as it seemed, holding my hand, offering me kisses and more. That was not like the Sara I had known for so many years. And then sometimes the icy Sara was back, just as distant and elusive as ever. It was very confusing."

"I imagine it must have been," she said mildly. "I had no idea there was so much difference between us."

"But I did not *know* until that night of the gambling, when Frank turned up, and you did not recognise him."

"No one recognised him!"

"True enough, although his mother perhaps might have done. But then when he was telling us all about himself, you cried. When did Sara ever cry? She was closed up too tight for such a show of emotion. But you — you cried tears of real joy, and I knew for certain that you were not Sara. Then everything fell into place. Why you avoided meeting the first false Ernest, and kept away from the real one. You even said once that he was no son of yours, and that was no less than the truth!" He chuckled, thinking back on the moment. "You must have been changing places for a while."

"Yes, ever since she revealed... her little venture in Shropshire. She told you of it, recently, and your advice was the same as mine — it was too close to home, and sooner or later it would get her into trouble. But it was like an addiction with her, so I suggested she come to London and play about in *my* brothel, pretending to be me, for I had no reputation left to lose."

He shook his head sadly.

"Oh, you disapprove?" She gave a tinkling laugh. "I had to have some way to support myself after I was left alone. All terribly discreet, a safe place for a gentleman wishing to relax with a pretty young lady for a few hours, and I looked after those girls, Henry. I taught them elocution and deportment and proper manners, I dressed them nicely and several of them made good marriages as a result, and became respectable matrons in provincial towns. Is that not delicious? It was a very exclusive establishment, my little brothel, and the best of it was that I never needed to... participate myself, so to speak. But Sara... That was how Sara got into that game, you know, when she first stayed with me in London after William died. She wanted to try all that she had been missing. So, from time to time, she would go to London and be Tilly, and I would go to Brinshire and be the so-respectable Lady Sara Allamont. And I loved it! She found it tediously dull, but to me it was a novelty, and I adored those girls, and being part of a family." She sighed. "Such a delight."

"How on earth did you manage? So many people who knew you well, yet you had never met them. It must have been extraordinarily difficult, and no one suspected, I believe. Certainly your behaviour — well, in private, perhaps, there were noticeable differences, to me at least, but in company you did everything as she would have done."

"It was not so difficult. She had always written long, detailed letters to me, telling me about everyone. Not William — she never mentioned *him* — and very little about the children, but the neighbours, the people of Brinshire, those I knew all about. And when callers came, they were announced, so I always knew who they were. The assemblies were quite a challenge, but I enjoyed puzzling it out. The elderly lady who dressed like a debutante could only be the Baroness, for example. The military men were easy. One can get by in society, I found, by reading the degree of deference in a person's greeting and their style of dress, and saying as little as possible." She laughed, he face alight with mischief. "It was such fun, Henry! We became adept at switching over in Brinchester, to reduce the time away from the Hall. As for anyone suspecting, people see what they expect to see. I wore my sister's gowns, I looked like her and moved like her — I even had her voice. Why should anyone suspect? Except *you*. I rather wanted you to see through it and understand."

"That is obvious now. Yes, you were so different with me, quite unlike Sara. I was very obtuse, I believe, not to have guessed it a great deal earlier."

She laughed merrily. "Indeed you were obtuse, for I gave you every opportunity to work out what we were about, and was happy to wait until you did so. Then we could perhaps have sat down, all three of us, and worked out what was best to be done. But then life got rather too warm in Brinshire, and you were circling round talking about marriage, and we had to decide in a great hurry what we would do."

"You decided well."

"Is that truly your opinion? You were so angry when you believed you had been tricked all those years ago. Why are you not angry now?"

"I was a foolish young man, then. My pride was injured, such that I could not bear the thought that you two were laughing at me. The years have taught me humility... and patience, I hope. My dear, I cannot tell you how happy it makes me that you chose to marry me. I would have accepted any arrangement of your choosing, as you are aware, but this is perfect."

"Oh, I so much wanted to. She wanted my life and I badly wanted hers. It is understandable, is it not? She has been caged for years and now wants only to be free, to be herself and not be controlled by any man. Whereas I... I have had my fill of freedom, Henry. In this censorious society we live in, a woman may enjoy her freedom but only at a terrible cost. A man may do as he pleases, and be thought a fine fellow indeed, but heaven forbid that a woman should set one embroidered slipper over the line of propriety. As Grace almost discovered. Poor Grace! And Sara must accept some of the blame for that. Just as she was relishing her freedom from William's domination, so too were her daughters, and Sara would have done nothing about it if I had not forced her. Luckily, a cousin of Lord Carrbridge's is one of my... erm, acquaintance, shall we say, and I prevailed upon him to write and ensure that the marquess went to the assembly to rescue Grace from ignominy. After that, we agreed that it would be better for everyone if she had the freedom she craved and I became the respectably widowed Lady Sara Allamont. Oh, the pleasure of being part of society again! You can have no idea, Henry. And so... here we are."

He said nothing.

She reached across the table to take his hand. "Everything I have said to you, everything I have done has been from the heart, Henry, I want you to know that. I truly love you, and I will be the best wife I can to you. But I shall quite understand if you feel betrayed. I know I should have told you before we were married, but I was terrified that it was only *her* that you wanted, and you would not feel the same about ramshackle Tilly, the whore of London."

He smiled, and placed his other hand on hers. "I knew before we were married, so you did not deceive me. Once I knew, I was intrigued and... well, flattered, I suppose. Besides, you have always been so warm and generous. I would have had to be made of stone not to respond to that. When you first came to my bed at Willowbye, when poor Vivienne was so ill, I think I knew in my heart that you were not Sara, even then. With Sara, I loved her for so long because of the memory of the loving, free-spirited girl I knew all those years ago. She was lost to me, destroyed by a man who locked away all her spirit and beat the ability to love out of her. Yet here, by some miracle, I have her back again, unchanged, undamaged, as perfect as she ever was."

Her smile was all the reply he needed.

"There is something I must show you," she said softly, withdrawing her left hand from his and laying it, palm upwards, on the table. "Do you see this scar here?"

"This one?" He traced the jagged white line across her open hand. "It must have been a painful injury."

"It was. My last lover did that to me, in a drunken rage one night. That injury was what persuaded me to leave him, and not to put my trust in a man's protection again. For a while, life was… difficult. But I recovered, and now this knife-wound shall be the symbol of a new beginning, one of complete honesty, my love. For if ever you are in the slightest doubt about which of us you are with, you may look at this scar and know that you are with your Tilly. As I shall always be."

He lifted her hand to his lips and kissed it. "My dearest, dearest love. Thank you. You honour me beyond measure by entrusting yourself to me. But I shall continue to call you Sara, if you do not mind. Otherwise, I should be bound to slip sometime, and that would be fatal. We must never allow anyone to suspect."

"I think perhaps our overwhelming happiness might arouse suspicions amongst those who know my sister well."

"Then we shall avoid them," he said grandly. "We can go anywhere we like, now that we are rich. Or rather, *you* are rich. My eighty pound inheritance would not get us very far, I think. Where would you like to go, my love?"

"Bath will do very well for the present, especially if it should ever stop raining. Might we take a house here for a while? I shall get bored of it in time, for Bath is very tame, I think, but I should like to set up my own establishment for a while. My own *respectable* establishment. Lady Sara Allamont of Bath — that sounds very well, does it not, my dear?"

"It sounds perfect," Henry said.

Thanks for reading!

If you have enjoyed reading this book, please consider writing a short review on Amazon.

This is the end of *The Daughters of Allamont Hall*. The series is the culmination of an idea I had almost two years ago while I was a passenger on a long and very boring car journey. Once I had dreamt up the obsessively regular Mr William Allamont, I wondered what life would be like with such a man. I had one example in my own family: my father was called Ernest, and his siblings (Constance, Amy and Frank) were likewise named after desirable traits. It wasn't hard to add Belle, Dulcie, Grace and Hope to the list (where I stopped, quite unable to think of a suitable name beginning with an 'I' – or perhaps I took pity on poor Lady Sara!). Then I wanted to see what would happen if such a man died, because of course he wouldn't be able to resist controlling his family even from the grave.

So I set out to find out, and *The Daughters of Allamont Hall* is the result. But sometimes the characters in books take on a life of their own and surprise even the author. When Amy chose Mr Ambleside, and I discovered that Belle was falling in love with Mr Burford, I realised I had a pattern developing. So Connie fell for the Marquess of Carrbridge, Dulcie married Mr Drummond, Grace paired up with George Graham and Hope married Hugo Allamont. How perfect! And those of you who've read the free novella about *Mary* know who she will eventually end up with. But I had a problem. Henry Allamont was determined to marry Lady Sara, whose name has no matching 'H' (and having the same surname already was a bit of a cheat, it seemed to me). But then the sisters surprised me, and Henry married not Sara but – the Lady Matilda Heatherington. That's Heatherington with an 'H'. I can't tell you how pleased I was with this serendipitous solution.

All six Allamont sisters are now happily married, but not all members of their extended families are so satisfactorily situated, so there are lots more stories to come about some of the characters you've already met, as well as plenty of new faces. Coming later in 2017, watch out for a new series, *Sons of the Marquess*, in which Connie's husband, Lord Carrbridge, discovers that he's been living beyond his means for years. But Connie has a plan to save them: all her husband's expensive younger brothers must be married off to heiresses. She relishes the challenge of matchmaking, but not all of them are willing to be paired off, or to give up their idle lives to find employment. Book 1 of the series is *Lord Reginald* and you can read a sneak preview of chapter 1 after the acknowledgements. And yes, I suspect Reggie may well marry a lady whose name begins with an 'R'.

A note on historical accuracy: I have endeavoured to stay true to the spirit of Regency times, and have avoided taking too many liberties or imposing modern sensibilities on my characters. The book is not one of historical record, but I've tried to make it reasonably accurate. However, I'm not perfect! If you spot a historical error, I'd very much appreciate knowing about it so that I can correct it and learn from it. Thank you!

About the books

About *The Daughters of Allamont Hall:* a series of six traditional Regency romances, featuring the unmarried daughters of Mr William and Lady Sara Allamont. When their father dies unexpectedly, his will includes generous dowries for the sisters, but only on condition that they marry in the proper order, the eldest first.

Book 1: Amy
Book 2: Belle
Book 3: Connie
Book 4: Dulcie
Book 4.5: Mary (a novella, free for mailing list signups)
Book 5: Grace
Book 6: Hope

About the author

I write traditional Regency romances under the pen name Mary Kingswood, and epic fantasy as Pauline M Ross. I live in the beautiful Highlands of Scotland with my husband. I like chocolate, whisky, my Kindle, massed pipe bands, long leisurely lunches, chocolate, going places in my campervan, eating pizza in Italy, summer nights that never get dark, wood fires in winter, chocolate, the view from the study window looking out over the Moray Firth and the Black Isle to the mountains beyond. And chocolate. I dislike driving on motorways, cooking, shopping, hospitals.

Any questions or comments about the series? I'd love to hear from you! Email me at mary@marykingswood.co.uk.

Acknowledgements

Thanks go to:

My grandparents, Henry and Hannah Austin, who named their four children Amy, Constance, Ernest and Frank, and thereby inadvertently inspired these books

My good friends at AC (you know who you are!) who provided me with advice, support, encouragement and kicks up the backside, hand-holding and hugs, laughs and tears, woo chickens, tacos and tubesteak

My beta readers: Clara Benson, Mary Burnett, Marina Finlayson

Last, but definitely not least, my first reader: Amy Ross.

Sons of the Marquess Book 1: Lord Reginald: Chapter 1: A Family Meeting

Lord Reginald Marford was uncommonly nervous. The summons itself was out of the ordinary, but the serious demeanour of his oldest brother about the matter was enough to concern any man. The Marquess of Carrbridge was, as a rule, the most easy-going and affable of brothers, never letting any setback disturb his equanimity. If some extraordinary event should manage to ruffle his feathers, then the marchioness was sure to smooth everything out in the most delightful manner. Nothing was permitted to interfere with the regular round of pleasure which any well-born family expected to pursue. In such comfortable ways, life had gone on in the Marford family for generations.

But now, it appeared, all was gloom, the marquess was miserable and even his wife's good humour was replaced by anxious fluttering and an unusually short temper. It was not right that such a charming lady should have even the smallest worry to distract her, when her beauty and accomplishments entitled her to a life of unalloyed happiness. Such were Lord Reginald's thoughts as he made his way down the oak-panelled staircase at Drummoor.

Monty was there first, naturally. No matter how punctual one might be, Monty was always there first.

"Is it going to be bad, Reggie?" he said at once, raising those huge, innocent eyes to his older brother. Reggie was only six years older than Monty, but sometimes he felt very old, far older than his eight and twenty years.

"I think it might be," Reggie said.

"It is all my fault, I know it," Monty said, twisting his hands together. "I should never have bought that pair from Longman. I was completely taken in, for he told me they were such fine animals, and they certainly looked it. Such a bargain, as I thought at the time, but it was not so. I am sure we will have to retrench and it is all my fault."

"Nonsense, Monty, but you should remember to take Gus with you next time. He knows everything there is to know about horseflesh."

"Oh, I tried to! I told Longman I would wait until Gus was back from Devon, but he would not have it. He had another buyer, you see, and the deal could not wait even another day, so what could I do but close with him at once?"

"You could have called his bluff. He bamboozled you, and that is the size of it. But you need not despair, for your doings have been nothing to Gil's, and even Humphrey has been losing at the tables lately. If we are in the basket, it will not be because of that broken-winded pair Tom Longman managed to foist on you."

Monty tried a smile, managed only a lop-sided quirk of the lips and abandoned the attempt. "But it is going to be bad, I feel sure."

"Everything that Merton fellow has a hand in is bad, it seems to me. He has a face like a wet Sunday in Lincoln. There is no joy in him, and he delights in making everyone else's lives as joyless as his own."

"Oh no, Reggie, I am sure you are mistaken," Monty said. "He is a very good sort of man, I think."

Reggie sighed. "I am out of sorts today and not minded to be fair, but nevertheless I cannot dispute the point with you. He is indeed a most worthy sort of person, and was there ever anything more dispiriting than such a man?"

Monty managed a genuine smile. "You are just cross because he defeated you at chess."

Chess was the least of his worries, but Reggie managed a smile. "A perfectly valid reason to be cross with anyone, I should think. I would not mind so much if he would be so obliging as to lose occasionally. Not every time, for I am not unreasonable, but once a month or so would be enough to make me happy. Is it asking so much? Ah, here are Gus and Humphrey."

The third and fourth Marford brothers were laughing at some private joke, but seeing the long faces on Reggie and Monty, Humphrey said, "Cheer up, you two! How bad can it be, truly? If we are really in the basket, we must all marry heiresses to set ourselves straight. Ladies love a lord, you know."

"They love a peer," Reggie said, determined not to cheer up. "Being the mere brother of a marquess is less appealing."

"Nonsense!" Humphrey said. "They all want to be Lady Something-or-other. But if matrimony holds no attraction for you, Reggie, you might think about taking up a career."

Reggie shuddered. "Lord, no! Can you see me in the army, galloping about with a sword in my hand? Far too energetic for me. And as for the church, that is not nearly energetic enough. No, I should infinitely rather find myself an heiress."

"Heiresses are always bracket-faced," Gus said. "I prefer my horses, thank you all the same."

"Ah, but will we have any horses left us after Merton has done his work?" Monty said.

Gus's expression turned instantly to alarm. "No! Carrbridge would not — would he?"

"We must all make sacrifices," Humphrey said, his smile suggesting that he had no serious fears of such a thing. "Two or three hunters instead of six, perhaps, and you might have to give up one or two of your curricles, Gus."

"It is all very well for you," Gus said. "You do well enough at cards to keep you in style, but I seem to have done nothing but lose lately."

"You will not attend to the play," Humphrey said. "You get distracted too easily."

"Ah, here is Hattie," Reggie put in quickly, before the two could lapse into their familiar debate. "And Carrbridge and Connie. Excellent."

The marquess and marchioness made a handsome couple, but their usual smiles were absent today. Lady Harriet Marford, by contrast, wore an expression of determined cheerfulness.

"What a delightful family gathering," she asked. "Cheer up, everyone. No one has died, you know. Are we all here?"

"Still awaiting Gil," Reggie said.

"Perhaps we should wait," the marquess said, looking about the hall anxiously, as if he expected the youngest Marford brother to be lurking behind a pillar or hiding in the suit of armour at the foot of the stairs, ready to pop out at any moment to surprise them.

"Who knows when he might appear?" the marchioness said briskly. "Best get this over with, do you not agree, Lord Carrbridge?"

"Yes, indeed, my love, you are quite right. Let us go in."

The library at Drummoor was as large as a ballroom, and was indeed used for that purpose each winter when its three massive fireplaces almost kept the room warm enough for comfort. Now, in January, it was as cold as an ice house, and almost as cheerless, the endless shelves of books filling every wall and the dark-painted ceiling giving it the appearance of a cave. Reggie would not be surprised to spy bats hanging from the chandeliers. As a boy, he had always been terrified of the place, scene of the weekly summoning by his grandfather to be shown a new treasure — a stuffed peacock, perhaps, or a map of Persia, or a bone knife from some long-lost tribe — followed by a lecture on the ingratitude of the French peasantry, or the colonials, or whoever was in revolt at the time. The seventh marquess was long in his grave, but the familiar dread still settled in Reggie's stomach as he crossed the library floor.

The assembled Marfords filed past long lines of glass-topped display cases housing the collections of former marquesses — eggs, feathers, decorated snuff boxes, pocket watches, strange assortments of bones and numerous sets of miniatures chess pieces, enamelled or bejewelled or carved or gilded into a variety of fanciful shapes. At the far end of the room, the vast arched window depicted in stained glass the triumphant ride of the Earl of Deveron to the king's aid in the civil war, which resulted in the grateful monarch immediately raising him to the title of Marquess of Carrbridge.

Beneath the window, and painted in jewel colours by the glass, sat a desk large enough for a score of people to dine in tolerable comfort. Behind it, sombrely attired, Daniel Merton stood awaiting them, bowing. Reggie had no great liking for Merton, for he was sober to a fault, and what could be worse than a man who never gambled or drank to excess or even took a mistress? He was a decent rider, Reggie had to give him credit for that, but there was something unnatural about a man who enjoyed rummaging about with old documents and ledgers. And then there was his irritating skill at chess. No, Reggie could not like him.

Chairs were already arranged in front of the desk, and Merton waited politely while they disposed themselves,

Carrbridge and the two ladies in front, the rest behind, and one empty chair for Gil. Only then did Merton bow again and take his seat, and even his air of deference irritated Reggie that day.

"My lord?" Merton said politely.

"Yes, yes, do begin. We will not wait for Gil."

"As your lordship wishes. I have completed my initial assessment of the state of your estate, my lord. It has not been as complete or as detailed an investigation as I should have liked, for not all the relevant documents were readily to hand, and there are limits to what may be done in only one month, but I have done the best I could."

"You could have asked Sharp for help," Reggie said. "He knows everything. He has been here since grandfather's day."

"Indeed, and Mr Sharp has been most willing to offer every assistance," Merton said. "However, I felt it best to view the original papers wherever possible, and not depend upon Mr Sharp's memory."

"His memory is perfectly sound," Reggie said. "He is not quite in his dotage yet."

"By no means. Indeed, I can well believe that Mr Sharp's acumen in matters of business is every bit as acute as it ever was. However, when one has been managing the affairs of one estate for three generations, there is a tendency for events to blend together somewhat, or for dates to be confused. It is my habit to refer to written records only, to avoid any such lapses in memory."

The marquess shuffled impatiently in his chair, turning round to glare at his brother. "Reggie, I gave Merton a free hand to look into things, so there is no point quibbling about it now. Best to have a fresh perspective, you know. Take no notice of him, Merton. He is out of sorts because he thinks you will force me to sell off Marford House and all our hunters, but things are not so desperate as all that, surely? Are they?"

"No, no, but there are debts outstanding, and—"

"I am very sorry!" Monty burst out. "I will repay it all, I swear it! It was so foolish of me to buy those horses, and I shall find a way to—"

"Oh no, Lord Montague, none of the debts result from any action of yours," Merton said.

"Oh. Humphrey? Gil?"

Merton shook his head firmly. "I assure you, none of you are responsible."

"Then who is?" the marquess said sharply. "The fellow must be brought to account. If there has been any misappropriation, I want it set right immediately and the scoundrel made to answer for it. Who is it?"

"The eighth Marquess of Carrbridge," Merton said.

"Father?" the marquess said. "You mean that Father left debts when he died, and they have not been settled?"

"That is correct."

"Well, that is easy enough. They must be settled at once... oh. There is no money to do so, that is the nub of the matter, I collect?"

"Exactly so, my lord."

The marchioness adjusted her shawl. "What must we do, Mr Merton? Advise us, if you please."

"My lady, my advice is very simple — to reduce unnecessary expenditure and to increase income. A few very modest economies will bring immediate benefits. For example, his lordship maintains five separate residences in London for the convenience of his brothers, while Marford House sits empty for months on end."

"What, must we have no independence now?" Reggie said. "Are we to be rubbing shoulders with the aunts all the time, and enduring their disapprobation whenever a fellow might happen to have a glass or two of brandy? It is not to be borne."

"Then there are three hunting lodges, where one would suffice," Merton went on relentlessly. "As for stabling—"

"I'll not have my hunters moved," Gus said, his voice so low he was almost growling. "Under no circumstances, do you hear me, Merton? Tell him, Carrbridge."

"Well—"

"My lady's plans for the new orangery could be postponed," Merton continued.

"Now that is more sensible," Reggie said.

"Indeed, it is not as if one needs to grow one's own oranges," Gus said. "It is the easiest thing in the world to have them sent from... well, wherever one obtains oranges. They can be had by the sack, I daresay, at very little expense. You can manage without an orangery, I am sure, Connie."

"I shall not give up my orangery unless you give up keeping all those teams at post houses," the marchioness said. "It is not as if anyone needs to keep one's own horses for the journey to London, not these days."

"What, drive around behind hired hacks?" Gus said, scandalised. "As the brother of a marquess, I have a position to maintain."

"You are the brother of an *impoverished* marquess," Merton said crisply, "and if you do not retrench— Ah, Lord Gilbert."

"Gil! At last!" Reggie said in relief, for so much talk of economy was beginning to wear at his nerves.

The youngest Marford brother tap-tapped his way across the library floor in a brisk rhythm. He was a handsome fellow — all his brothers were handsome, Reggie reflected gloomily.

Carrbridge had more than once been likened to a Greek god, Humphrey was as big and golden as a bear, and the younger ones were fashionably dark and romantic, whereas Reggie had the face of a grocer. One of his Oxford friends had described him so, to his great mortification, and as he examined his uninteresting features in the glass later, he could not deny the truth of it.

"What is all this about, Merton?" Gil said. "I am missing an excellent mill on your account, and I have a monkey on the outcome, so I very much hope the matter is important."

"We are to give up two of the hunting lodges," Gus said. "We are not to stable our own teams at post houses."

"Ridiculous!" Gil said. "Impossible! How are we to manage?"

"There is worse," Reggie said. "We must give up our own lodgings and live in Marford House with the aunts."

"Insupportable!" Gil said. "I shall not listen to such nonsense."

He would have turned and left at once, but the marquess said, "Do not fly into the boughs, Gil. Something must be done, you know, for we have no money, it seems."

"How can that be?" Gil said. "We are one of the richest families in England."

"That is true, Carrbridge," Reggie said. "Grandfather was wont to boast that he had an income of twenty five thousand a year. Where has it gone to, that is what I should like to know. None of us is particularly extravagant. We do not gamble to excess or have—" He was about to mention mistresses before remembering the presence of two ladies. "We have no expensive interests," he finished lamely.

"It is a good point, Merton," the marquess said. "Where is all that money? We should be comfortably situated, heaven knows."

"Some of it is tied up in estates settled on various female relatives for their lifetime," Merton said. "The French holdings were lost a few years ago, so that accounts for a part of it, and the eighth marquess lost some profitable estates at the card tables. If you want my honest opinion, my lord, it is my belief that your income cannot sustain your present expenditure. I cannot be sure, because not all the relevant papers could be located, but I believe your current income does not exceed five thousand pounds a year."

They were all silent, contemplating this appalling state of poverty. Reggie had never thought much about money, for there had always seemed to be more than sufficient, but he knew that such a sum was inadequate to maintain them in their present style.

"What is to be done, Mr Merton?" the marchioness said. "You have mentioned some economies, but there must be more we can do."

"Indeed there is, my lady. There is a simple solution to the predicament. Lord Carrbridge's brothers might consider the options traditionally chosen by younger brothers of the nobility, and take up a respectable career. Or, if they prefer, they might wish to marry women of independent means."

"Heiresses, I suppose," Reggie said in disgust. "So it is the church, the army or government service, or else get ourselves leg-shackled to some fish-faced cit's daughter. Lord, what a dismal choice! I had rather become a pirate. Whatever are we to do?"

END OF SAMPLE CHAPTER OF *LORD REGINALD*

Made in the USA
Coppell, TX
21 June 2022